FINDING HER WAY BACK HOME

A Novel

CHAPTER 1

❖

I knew once I answered the phone, I'd be hearing something I did not want to hear. I was the least important thing on my parents mind. They were finally happy with the fact that their child is no longer in their care and are free from responsibility. Sonya and Jason, were back to their drugs and drinking ways. But they were also low on money.

The phone ringed three times. Do I let it ring? Maybe if I wait long enough it'll stop ringing. I didn't want to pick it up because I did not want to hear her raspy voice and her sniffling. I got tired of hearing it after the fourth ring. I answered. Wish I didn't. When I heard her voice, I hardly recognized her. If anything, I'm surprised that I still remember what she sounded like. It's like my brain instantly clicked at the sound of her voice. Her face popped up and I can somehow figure what she was wearing too.

She had this raspy, sick, disoriented, frog-stuck-in-the-throat sound of a voice. The earliest memory from when I was a child, was hearing my mothers smooth, butter like speaking voice. Even if you did not listen to word she said you could listen to her speak all day and never get tired of it. Now I don't even know who the hell I am talking to. I had chills going up and down my spine the whole time. One weird thing I noticed during this phone call was that she was very quiet, whispering actually. Like she didn't want anyone to hear her. It made me worry.

"You sure it was her?" I nod my head playing with my hands.

"What did she say?"

"She just wanted to say hi." I lied.

CHAPTER 2

❖

I was the only kid in the house who hasn't been adopted. All except for one person. His name was Lucky. He was my best friend in the entire world. We were inseparable, him and I. We made a promise to each other that once we turn eighteen we'll move to Beverly Hills and get married to our celebrity crushes.

"We'll be living in a big mansion in Beverly Hills by the beach and we'll both marry Chris Hemsworth and Megan Fox."

He said with a big smile.

The thought of us being rich and married to famous people made me forget that my best friend could possibly be gone by next week.

"Promise?" He nodded.

"Cross my heart. If you see a blue mini van coming up the drive way, it's me. But that is years from now. Let's enjoy what we have now."

We were little kids and we were talking about living together like we'll have the money to care for ourselves. I was naive. I know that living in the real world is not going to be easy. I didn't care about that. All I cared about was spending the rest of my life with the person who probably wasn't going to stick around very long. I knew that the real world is scary, I knew that I was not going to be ready, but Lucky didn't think about that. He didn't think about that in a few years from now he was going to be in debt, he didn't think about how he was going to pay taxes, bills, pay rent or get a mortgage on a house, instead I was the thing he thought was most important. I was on his mind instead of homework and dinner. Nothing mattered in his little world but me.

CHAPTER 3

❖

March 2010

The super, Mr. K, was outside doing his daily yard work. Mrs. K helps out too but today she had an emergency case and won't be home till later. She's a caseworker. So is Mr. K. The kids aren't as helpful around the house; they tend to hang on the porch and just eat ice cream watching cars drive by. Truth is, they are just lazy. Knowing Mr. K is getting old, they don't really help him when he's doing something that could potentially hurt himself.

"When I count my blessings, I count you twice."

He says with a smile.

"It's the human thing to do." I grunted dropping the tire on the grass.

"Why do we need this tire?" I pant.

"Oh you know, I thought that you kids should have your own little swing."

"Little?"

Mr. K laughed loudly. The swing was all set up and I decided to use it myself. Worked really well. As I swayed back and forth, it made me feel at peace. The way the cool air hit my skin, the sound of the trees moving with the breeze and leaves crunching beneath peoples feet as they walked on the sidewalks, it brought absolute comfort. It was like I was on a cloud; I was one with nature. Nothing mattered but this feeling right now.

"Boo!"

I was startled and fell off the tire, when I looked up I saw Lucky laughing on the ground holding his stomach.

I rolled my eyes dusting myself off.

"Oh I was only kidding."

He sat in the tire with me with an apologetic smile. I playfully rolled my eyes then smirked.

"So, birthday is next week. Any plans?"

I never really celebrated my birthdays. It wasn't as important to me. But it was to the super and his wife, Mr and Mrs. K. They'll probably make me a cake, give me presents even though I do not deserve them, and go out to eat. Whenever it was someone's birthday at the house, Mr and Mrs. K would take them to a special dinner that they pay for and just bless you for turning another year older. It was a tradition here in the house.

"They'll probably drag us to Olive Garden again."

I snorted.

"Yeah and then drink their 'grown up' juice they call it and pass out on the couch like last year."

I laughed shaking my head.

"Sounds like the perfect birthday."

Later that night, after dinner, Mr and Mrs. K were passed out on the couch just as we predicted. I scoffed shaking my head with a smile. I turn over to the clock. It read 11:40 PM. Only twenty more minutes till my birthday is over.

"Hey," Lucky whispered from the staircase. He had a big smile on his face.

"I gotta show you something."

I gave him a weird look, resisting to following him. He then threw me over his shoulder and carried me up the stairs and up to the roof. I shrieked and punched his back, playfully.

"Put me d-"

A roof that once reeked of dead mice and bird crap was now a dimmed light of beauty, absolutely breath taking. It was something you see out of a movie. A blanket with pillows, small lights hanging off the windows, and Mr. K's MacBook. I turn around and see Lucky with flowers, he didn't know what face to make so he just kept looking down. I laughed at his shyness.

I smiled.

I lifted up his chin so his brown eyes were looking into my blue eyes.

"You don't gotta be shy. It's me." He looked away, his face turning a bright shade of pink.

"I'm always going to be shy around you. You're the most beautiful rose in this house and I'm the dirt."

"Why would you say that?"

"Come on Charms. You could be friends with anyone in this house and we wouldn't even have to look at each other at the dinner table." He whispered the last part, his eyes searching for some kind of response. I've never seen this side of Lucky. I cleared my throat.

"I remember this boy coming to the house for the first time. He was the sweetest boy. He wasn't afraid to be himself, putting smiles on peoples face was what he loved to do. He certainly put one on mine. But, like I said, he wasn't afraid to be himself and that's what I loved about him. That, and his cubby cheeks and dimples."

A few tears came rolling down his cheeks but he quickly rubbed his eyes harshly. He never liked crying in front of people. I brought my hand to his face wiping his tears away.

"You're not dirt and I'm not a rose. Better yet, we're sunflowers because why not? Normal is boring. Sunflowers are bright and they stand out. Yeah most people don't usually pick sunflowers because it's not the most romantic type of flowers but they are still picked."

He chuckled wiping the remainder of his tears.

"We'll both be at our weddings. You'll be my maid of honor and I'll be your best man."

"You? In a dress?" He says with a laugh.

"Whose to say I'm going to wear a dress for my wedding?" He nod his head in agreement.

"That is true. You cannot stand dresses."

"And that is why you are my best friend!"

I exclaimed jumping on him, he laughed wrapping his arms around me.

We stayed on the roof till midnight. Birthday was officially over. Fireworks went off right as it hit midnight. People down the street don't usually do fireworks in March but I guess they were feeling festive tonight. Lucky wrapped an arm around me resting his head on top of mine. Lucky grinned at me.

"May have paid the neighbors to do that." I laughed shaking my head. It was a good night.

Mr and Mrs. K had massive hangovers the next morning. Guess they had a little more fun than we thought. The rest of us were eating breakfast at the table when they walked in all groggy holding their foreheads. The rest of the kids and I snickered.

"Did you enjoy your birthday, Charms?"

Mr. K said yawning then smiled. I took a glance at Lucky who was smirking, events of last night flooded my brain.

"It was great."

My eyes never left those brown eyes.

"You ever wonder what they could be doing right now?"

I said staring up at the stars. I mentally prepared myself on what he might say next. We never talked about our birth parents, frankly, I was too scared to mention it because I thought it was a sensitive subject.

Lucky shrugged.

"I am the least of their worries. They're probably having sex or getting high as we speak." Lucky said with a shrug. I looked at him with sadness, he looked at me and chuckled.

"What? You don't wonder that about your parents?" He was facing his whole body towards me.

"No."

I scoffed.

"Then what do you think they're doing? If anything they're celebrating with crack and rum."

"Stop it!" I screamed.

The entire neighborhood probably heard my scream. You could probably hear it from the rich part of town which is 50 miles from where we are. His face softened. I've never yelled at Lucky like that before.

"I'm sorry. That was out of line. But let's face it. I'm in the system because my parents didn't want me. I'm never getting adopted. No one wants a messed kid with psychological problems. Hell, not even a girl would want to date a kid with psychological problems."

I frowned at him.

"I'm gonna turn in."

CHAPTER 4

❖

May 2015

The natural reaction from getting a letter from the court is anxiety; *fear.* Your first thought is; oh my god what did I do? They know who I am?

Charmion Monica Smith is hereby removed from foster care. Since she is now 18 years old, she is old enough to live on her own and is no longer in the system.

The one thing that drove me crazy about court letters was that they used my full name.

"They can't be serious."

I said with a scoff.

"You are 18 now, Charms." Mrs. K sighed.

I knew this was going to happen. Eventually I was going to turn 18 and eventually would have to move out. I turned 18 two months ago and prayed they didn't know I was still living here. I can run but I can't hide. But I can't move out. This is my home. I don't know where else to go. This was the only house that I've grown attached to. A part of me isn't ready to let go just yet.

"Don't worry, Charms. We already found you an apartment which is down the street from here. I am friends with the owner of the building and he gave you a studio."

Mr. K reassured me. At least my heart can relax and stop beating so fast. But it came back when I started to think about how am I going to pay rent, or gas, or electric. Shit, shit, shit. "How will I pay rent and how much is it? I don't have a job or,"

"Relax. The rent isn't too crazy. We'll take care of your rent until you find a job."

They still didn't answer my question.

"How much?" I said uneasy.

Mr. K laughed.

"It's $800 a month. Everything is included in the rent, you're fine." Okay now my heart is beating normal again. I sighed in relief as plopped my body on the couch

"Thank you. For everything you've done for me."

Mrs. K smiled, her yellowish teeth showing.

"You're our daughter."

I've never been on my own for a very long time. And if I ever was on my own, I'd have Lucky by my side. There was a thunder storm happening and I'm deeply terrified of the flashes of lighting and the thunder clap. Lucky would come into my room in the middle of night, he wrap his arms around me and I would forget that there was a storm going on outside.

"How about we play I spy?"

He said.

"I spy with my little eye, something that is blue."

I looked down and see that he was wearing blue pajama pants. His favorite color.

"Your pajama pants."

I croaked, my voice raspy.

"I spy with my little eye, something that is pink."

I chuckled. He pointed out my hair.

"Hey I made you laugh!"

That he did.

"Stay here?"

I looked up even though the room was dark, but I could tell he was looking into my eyes as well.

"Of course."

He pressed his lips on my forehead and pulled the blanket over us, I completely forgot about the storm.

It was Sunday.

~

Every Sunday, when everyone would leave for the day, Lucky and I would stay home, make brownies and eat every single one while watching movies. It was kind of like a tradition whenever we were home alone. I mix while he looks for the pan. Over the years Lucky has turned into a really handsome guy. My feelings for him grew much bigger as we gotten older. His glimmering brown eyes, the messy brown hair, the dimples on his cheeks whenever he speaks or smile. Lucky decided to mix with me. His big strong arms wrapped around me, my heart was thumping faster now, butterflies in the pit of my stomach coming back.

"You want to stir like this. Otherwise they'll be lumps on them."

The way his hand caressed mine, it felt so nice. My hand may be small but it fit perfectly in his.

"Thanks."

14

I wish I hadn't looked into his eyes. The way he looked back at me made my heart thump harder, I could hear it through my ears. His hand made its way to my face. I was physically and mentally preparing myself for what was going to happen next; a kiss. A kiss I've been dying to have since the moment I knew I liked him, a kiss I wanted every Christmas whenever I see the mistletoe, every birthday wish when I blew out the candles.

I leaned up on my tippy toes and gently pressed my lips on his. I felt him kiss me back, wrapping his arms around my waist, closing the gap between us. The brownies were the least of our worries. My back was touching the edge of the counter and I didn't know the bowl was there till it fell to the ground, shattering in the process. Lucky quickly pulled away and practically ran out of the room. I still feel his lips. This tingling sensation filled my whole body; electricity. My lips wouldn't stop twitching due to the warmth of his lips colliding with mine. And it was then I realized that I didn't just like Lucky, no.

I loved him.

~

Like any other warm sunny day I spent being locked in my apartment, I was unpacking the last few boxes Mr and Mrs. K sent over when I heard a knock at the door. It made me wonder, who could that be? No one knew I lived here except Mr and Mrs. K, along with the rest of the kids at the house and the owner of the building. That, and the neighbors of course. I was eager to open the door. My heart was beating out of its chest, there was another knock and that made me even more nervous. At this point, I wanted to wait long enough for the person to realize that no one is home and

15

leave. I looked through the peep hole and couldn't believe who I was staring at. I quickly opened the door and there he stood, in a sweatshirt and blue jeans. He didn't change one bit. Though, he was way more handsome than ever.

"Lucky."

I forced a smile.

The expression on his face reminded me of the time I kissed him, it was regret.

"What are you doing here?"

I was so scared.

"May I come in?" I stepped aside and he walked in, looking around.

I took a long, hard look at Lucky. All the memories came flooding back. From the moment he stepped foot into the house, from when he stepped out. The times where him and I sneaked downstairs to play video games at two in the morning, when we woke up early on a snow day to make snow men and snow ladies in the backyard, the time I kissed him in the kitchen when we were making brownies on that Sunday afternoon. Lucky was staring out the window, lost in his own little world.

"I uh came by the house." He said that very quiet, almost like he didn't want me to hear it, but I did.

Anger rose up in me.

"After four years?"

Now he was facing me.

"You know, I believed you when you said you come back for me. That we would run off to Beverly Hills and marry celebrities, but that was more a fantasy than reality. Everything else was a lie."

"I'm sorry, Charmion."

Who is this Charmion? Never have I ever heard such a name. My name is Charms and always was Charms. It's the one thing I hate about myself.

"My name is not Charmion. It's Charms. And your name is Lucky, not Luke."

"Lucky was some psycho kid who had a helpless crush on a girl who was just as fucked up as him."

Did you hear that?

That was the sound of my heart breaking in two. All those years of wondering if he shared the same feelings as me, the nights where I cried myself to sleep when he went out on a date with a girl from school, the loneliness of him not being with me. I never knew he could say that. You would think after all these years I cry for every little thing, highly sensitive. The answer is no.

"That psycho kid was my best friend and that girl got more fucked up the minute he showed up."

Now whose heart is broken?

"You need to leave."

I grumbled opening the door, looking down at my feet.

"Charmion I-"

"Get the hell out!"

My voice startled him, hell it startled me. He took one last look at me then walked towards the door. Right as he was out of the door, he turned around.

"I'm sorry for not coming back. A lot was happening in Arizona with my family and I couldn't come back."

"Oh now look who is capable of telling the truth once." He frowned leaning in but I slammed the door in his face.

That is a slap in the face. We were his first family till he got adopted and left for Arizona. And I know I shouldn't be angry that he found the family he always wanted but I can't help but be angry. Angry at the fact that we meant nothing to him. Truth is, I was jealous. Jealous that my best friend got two parents who love him and wanted him. My parents, they didn't want me. They were drug addicts and thought that having a kid around the house being exposed to cocaine, marijuana, heroin, and alcohol, could rat them out. Even though I barely knew how to say a word.

The house was a mess and filled with empty bottles of liquor. The smell of weed covered the furniture as well as the atmosphere. You see trails, yes I said trails, of heroine on the floor and table where my toys were.

Or so I've been told by caseworkers and Mr. K.

After that, child services took me away and my parents did not give a rats ass. I was three years old. Barely able to walk right and speak properly. Every time I get reminded of them it makes me feel so sad. They got screwed up in their own way and I can't help but think that I was the cause of it. But I reassured myself that I wasn't.

So yeah, I was jealous of Lucky, I still am.

You're our daughter

I wonder if I am.

CHAPTER 5

I remember when I first met Kendall. She was the kind of girl everyone loved being around. The popular girl, people called her. It shocked me she didn't have any friends. Turns out, people from her past took advantage of her kindness and used her. She had long red hair that reached the middle of her back. Her eyes were brown but they told a story about her past. The girls would make rumors about her and the guys, well, they were worse. Some say she's crazy. But the only crazy thing about her is her insane obsession with Family Feud and pixie sticks. I bought a couple of shirts in a random store and a girl came rushing into the store and didn't realize how fast she was going, till her coffee spilled all over me.

"Oh god I am so sorry!"

She grabbed napkins and tried to rub off the coffee from my shirt but everyone knows that if you want to get rid of a coffee stain, you dab, not rub.

"Oh shoot it's not coming out."

She groaned.

"It's fine. I didn't like this shirt anyway." I actually did like this shirt. She was really focused on getting the stain out. She had this face of determination which alarmed me.

"Oh no I spilled it all over your bag!"

Was she about to cry?

"It's fine."

I said.

"No, it's not. We are going to buy you new shirts."

I was then dragged by the arm back into the store. Apparently there were more better looking shirts in the back.

"What's your size?"

She said rummaging through the racks. I didn't know my size. I just picked the ones I liked and didn't even bother looking at the size or price. She was looking at me now. I was starting to feel hot and sweaty.

"Size?"

My mouth was open, but no words came out. She rolled her eyes before spinning me around and ripped off my jacket.

"Whoa!"

I exclaimed.

"Medium."

I was given my jacket back which landed right on my face. She found so many shirts that looked way better than the ones I bought. I quickly followed her to the counter like a lost puppy. The lady at the counter looked discombobulated, so was I. It was because I already bought some stuff here and was wondering why I have some random person buying shirts for me. Not that I'm complaining. The total was $57.78. That was almost the amount money I spent on jeans. That, and a pair of combat boots.

"Here you go. I'm sorry about the coffee."

She handed me the bag of shirts and the change.

"That is very nice of you but I can't take it. You paid for it."

"I insist. Besides, it is the least I could do for the coffee."

I half smiled.

"Thank you."

"My name is Kendall by the way." She said with a smile.

"Charms."

"That's an interesting name." Kendall giggled.

"It's actually Charmion but I prefer Charms."

"I do too." She said with a smile.

I never had girlfriends growing up. I had Lucky and the other foster kids, who were mainly boys, but I was the only girl in the house. I was homeschooled my whole life. I didn't get along with others so Mr and Mrs. K pulled me out of school and homeschooled me. I never knew how to interact with people because I wasn't as social as a child. With Kendall, I barely said a word to her because why, a girl like her, who is popular and hot and is adored by others, wants to be friends with someone like me? I still wonder that today.

I invited Kendall to my apartment because well, why not? We were in the middle of a very strange conversation. Kendall has five older brothers who are very protective. And when she got her first boyfriend, they were all so outraged that they invited him over to have a "little chat". The boy was so traumatized that he had to move schools because every time he saw Kendall, he saw her five massive brothers.

"So you mean to tell me that your brothers just beat that poor kid up?"

"They just freaked him out to the point where he ran out of the house and screamed; it's over!"

I laughed covering my mouth and shook my head.

"Trust me, I wasn't allowed to have a boyfriend till I moved out."

"I never had a boyfriend."

That wasn't supposed to come out.

"You never had a boyfriend?"

She gasped.

"I was homeschooled. I was always quiet as a kid and never really met other people because I always locked myself in my house."

"Have you ever liked a boy?"

My heart stopped. My eyes shifted from her to the floor.

"Or girl, whatever you prefer."

She quickly said taking a sip of her latte.

"He was uh my best friend and also my foster brother. I knew it was wrong but I didn't care. One day I kissed him and everything changed. He got adopted and left. He made a promise to me that he'd come back for me. He didn't."

A knock on the door stopped Kendall in mid sentence. Lucky stood at the door. Kendall nearly spit her latte from one glance at him.

"That's the guy that left? Wow. He sure is hot."

I cleared my throat as I rubbed the back of my neck. That comment made me feel slightly uncomfortable. As it did for Lucky. He looked uncomfortable when entering.

"I uh thought we should talk."

He says staring at me, it's like he didn't even notice Kendall in the room, she couldn't keep her eyes off of him. He swallowed hard as he jerked his head at Kendall.

"I was gonna head out anyway. I'll see you later."

Later turned out to be never. There was this awkward silence. None of us knew what to say.

"Last time I was here I said something I didn't mean. I didn't mean for what I said, Charmion."

22

I exhaled sharply looking away. I am not use to hearing my real name out of his mouth or any other mouth. Just like I'm not use to saying his real name.

"We didn't part on the best terms. I..."

He stopped in mid sentence.

"I'm sorry, Charmion, for everything."

"Will you stop calling me that!"

I cried out.

"My name is Charms! It was always Charms!"

Many people are okay with change, some may even love change, but I don't. I just cannot accept the fact that Luke is something I have to start saying. Maybe I am in denial, or just being plain stubborn, but I absolutely cannot stand hearing my full name. Even when I was in foster care, no one called me Charmion because I would get angry very easily.

"Shouldn't you be heading home by now?" I groaned rubbing my temples to ease the pounding in my head.

"I wanted to see my best friend." He said with a pleading look.

His what?

"Best friend?"

He nod his head with a frown.

"Best friend." I repeated.

"The term best friend is associated with two people who have this special bond with one another."

I said with a scoff.

"We do. We do have that special bond with each other."

"Do we?"

He sighed deeply, his eyes drifting from time to time.

"You're still angry." Lucky breathed out.

"How can you tell?"

I rolled my eyes walking away but my arm was pulled back.

"Why you are acting like this?"

He snapped.

"Acting what?" I said so calmly.

"Acting like I meant for this to happen! A family finally wanted me and I wasn't going to give that up! Yes, Mr and Mrs. K provided me a home but I wanted a *real* family. One that actually loved me!"

"And we didn't love you?"

I said with eyebrows furrowed.

"You're saying as if we weren't family to you, like the last six years of living with us meant nothing to you. We were your family!" I exclaimed.

"Two old people and a bunch of fucked up kids weren't my family!"

Lucky practically screamed in my face. I got angry.

"Don't you dare come here and say that! I was one of those fucked up kids! Who was there for you when you had your first panic attack? Mrs. K. Or the time you got stood up by Bethany at the school dance? Also Mrs. K. Who did you turn to when things went bad? Mr. K, AND those fucked up kids."

Lucky ran his fingers through his hair with a sharp exhale.

"You were all I had in that house. Everyday I waited and everyday you didn't show up! Hell, you didn't even send anything for my birthday! Not even a stinking post card or phone call!"

"I was in Arizona, Charmion! You were in Delaware. I couldn't just hop on a plane and come get you! Truth is, I didn't want to come back for you. I didn't want to go back to that house knowing if I walked through those doors you would jump in my car and think we were going to start our lives together. I wanted to live my life out in Arizona and not worry about anything other than my family."

Emotions welled up within me. I could feel my heart breaking into tiny million pieces, I see the life I once saw in his eyes slowly fade away. The boy I once knew, who I grew up with, no longer exists. All this time, I thought he was going to come back for me.

I thought he was excited to come see me after all these years but the truth is, he never wanted to. He never wanted to come back and face me. He wanted to forget about me and all the good times we had. I can feel my heart breaking in two. I chuckled shaking my head.

"You should've stayed in Arizona, there's nothing for you here."

His stare that could've easily made me burst into tears. He paced the room, holding his jaw. He did this for 10 minutes then went to the kitchen and grabbed himself a glass of water.

"You know what? Clearly I made a mistake showing up here. Have a nice life, Charmion,"

I watched him grab his jacket and was heading towards the door. My heart jumped. Don't let him leave, I thought. I had to say it, I needed to say how I feel before he leaves, before it's too late. I won't make that same mistake again. And finally, after years of bottling it inside, I finally said it. I said the words that I've been dying to say the moment I kissed him.

"I fucking love you!"

It just burst out of me. Everything I've been dying to say ever since I kissed him that Sunday afternoon, poured out of me like word vomit. I couldn't stop.

"There, I said it. God, you don't know how long I've kept that. I am in love with you. I still am. And I don't think I'll ever stop loving you, even if you tell me not to."

All of a sudden, he grabbed my face and I was given something I've longed for years. I felt that same feeling the first time I kissed him in that kitchen; sparks. As corny as that sounds, I felt sparks. I immediately wrapped my arms around his torso and held onto him for dear life. We ended up making out in the middle of my living room, sorta. Suddenly, it turned into something more. The kiss became to get heated and rough. He pushed me against the wall. My hands immediately went to his belt. We proceeded to remove each other's clothes off. I was lifted up and was carried to the bedroom.

I moaned against his lips as he placed me gently on the bed. His lips went to my neck and I moaned. I wanted him so bad. I gasped loudly as he proceeded to enter in me. Grunts escaped his lips as he moved his hips. I never had sex, ever. The first couple minutes hurt but after a while it turned into sweet pleasure. I dreamed of losing my virginity to Lucky but thought it would be impossible with us being foster siblings. But it is actually happening. I didn't think it would. I always wanted this.

Our eyes locked for a moment. He bit his lip and held one side of my face. He moaned still looking into my eyes which made me more excited. I held him in my arms. I gripped his back as I panted in his shoulder. It's only me and him.

I grabbed his face and made him look at me. His hips were moving much faster till he came to a stop. I watched his face

26

the whole time. I was in love with this moment. His mouth turned into an O shape. I knew he came as he screamed out my name, my real name and I was okay with it this time.

Lucky rolled off of me with his hands running through his hair. I had sex with Lucky. I couldn't help but smile. Lucky saw me and smiled back at me. It's like he read my mind and knew what I was thinking.

"I thought of doing this too."

Why was I being awkward about this? I started to get shy and hide myself with the blankets. Lucky scooted closer to me and slowly pulled the blanket off so my whole body was exposed. I started to get nervous. I gasped as he traced his fingers down my thigh.

"You don't have to be shy around me." He says pushing my hair behind my ear. I am thinking, is this a dream? Will I wake up and feel disappointed? I almost didn't want to believe this was happening.

"I've always loved you, Charmion. From the moment I saw you. You were the most perfect girl in that house but I thought you were too good of a sunflower to be with me. We were foster siblings and we would've been caught up in some legal agreement and we'd probably get sent to different foster homes. Knowing what I know now, I don't want to miss my opportunity."

I was still processing what just happened. I just had sex with the guy I'm madly in love with and he admitted that he too loves me. I was lost in his eyes, not paying attention to what he is saying.

"Opportunity for what?" I mumbled, still lost in his eyes, his beautiful brown eyes. He smiled.

"To give us a shot."

He was leaning in for another kiss but he pulled away to grab the phone that was ringing on the counter. I didn't even hear it because my mind was just screaming. The phone had to be placed on my ear so I could hear it. Once I spoke, I heard the panic in Mrs. K's voice.

"You need to come home."

CHAPTER 6

I didn't know how to react. It's been years since I last heard from my mother. The day I found out why she didn't want me anymore, I wanted no part of her. Mr and Mrs. K made sure that I was off the grid, made sure to lose all contact with them and told me not stay outside for too long for all I know they could be watching me. Why is she reaching out to me now? After all these years? I don't know if I should feel angry or happy.

"I can't believe this." I muttered.

"Charmion calm down."

Mr. K cooed.

"Calm down? My mother is finally reaching out to me after all these years and you want me to calm down?"

Mr. K frowned. I sighed in my hands.

"I'm sorry, really. But this is crazy. Why all of a sudden does she want to talk?"

"Maybe to catch up."

Lucky chimed in.

"Don't patronize me she probably just wants money for drugs or for god knows what."

I scoffed.

"How did she figure out where we live?"

I've been asking myself that the whole time I paced. It just blows my mind that this is actually happening right now. I should've expected it but at the same time I never thought it happen so soon. It's unlikely that I would get a phone call from my birth mother years after I've been taken away from her, then when I'm eighteen, she is now begging to see me? I am at a loss for words.

"I haven't seen her in fifteen years."

"There's something else too."

"Haven't I suffered enough?" I exclaimed.

"Yes, wait no, anyway she sent you this."

Mrs. K pulled out a box from behind the couch. I instantly turned away when it was placed in front of me. I had to fight back the tears.

"Charmion-"

"No! I don't want to look at it! That picture is a lie!"

"You look so happy." Mr. K couldn't look at the picture either but his response was sincere. It's not the picture that made me crazy, it's how it got here. My parents know my address, zip code, they are living in the same area as me and I don't feel safe anymore.

"I was a baby! I didn't know that my mother was a crack whore!"

"Where's your dad?"

You would think I'd say he wasn't around. He was. My father spent his days in the basement getting high and having sex with women he finds in the streets. Yet, he had a wife that was just as fucked up as him and could get what he wanted from her.

"Hello?"

I didn't realize Mr K was out of the room. I can tell from the look on his face, something was wrong. The phone was handed to me, my hand trembling as I placed it on my ear.

"Charmion?"

CHAPTER 7

❖

Insomnia plagued me and sapped my strength. I miss the feeling of my warm bed but the couch seemed more comforting. The TV on all night, the rain outside brought peace to me. The dark circles under my eyes, my empty stomach, the pounding headache, all of it was part of it. The sun began to rise as well as Lucky. He walked in yawning and rubbing his eyes.

"Come to bed, Charmion." He sighed.

My body was screaming yes but all my mind was saying was no.

"Why?"

My throat was screaming for water.

"Because everybody needs sleep." He says sitting next to me holding my hand.

Lucky sighed.

"Charmion, this isn't healthy."

I kept a poker face. I was good at that.

"Well, I'm going to gym. I'll be back in an hour."

I gave him a thumbs up and pulled the blanket over my body. I heard him sigh and walk into another room.

I began to sob.

~

I walked past Lucky's room and saw him packing his suitcase. I can tell he was so happy because he was humming to I'm Yours by Jason Mraz, his favorite song.

"So this is it." I said walking into the room.

"Can you believe it?"

He couldn't stop smiling. I was sad that he was leaving but I was also happy that he finally got a family to adopt him. It's good to see him happy. Makes my heart flutter.

"I'm really gonna miss you, Lucky."

He half smiled bringing me into his arms. I can feel my palms getting sweaty and the butterflies in my stomach.

"I'll miss you too, Charms. But don't worry, we'll see each other again. And if we see each other in the streets or anywhere, I know it'll be one hell of a reunion."

There was a car horn coming from outside. It was time to go. Mr. K helped Lucky with his bags and stuffed it in the trunk. I stood in the doorway. He looked up and saw me.

He dropped everything and ran at me. Tears welling up in my eyes as he hugged me tightly.

"See you later, alligator."

He chuckled wiping my face.

The car drove down the street and it made my chest hurt. He was already out of view and I still stood at the front door. I already miss him. I wanted to run after the car and tell him something that could have changed everything. Having some kind of relationship with Lucky is an aspiration. If I told him how I felt, would he had stayed?

~

I've been having flashbacks lately. Most of them about Lucky, me as a child, my mother and father. It makes me angry that I'm thinking about them. Why now? Wondering where they are and how they're doing? I couldn't sit on the couch and torture myself with what ifs. I had to get my day going. I stepped out of the bathroom and stumbled when my stomach started to almost stab me.

Crap.

I ate the food that Lucky left me on the counter. He always was the chef of the house. I sat in the kitchen eating in silence till the phone rang. My head snapped towards it. I almost didn't want to swallow my food. I looked at the caller ID and of course it was a blocked number. I knew once I answered the phone I'd be hearing something I did not want to hear. I sucked in a shaky breath and placed the phone to my ear.

"Hello?"

My voice cracked.

"Charmion?"

My eyes went shut. The voice I once knew was now unrecognizable. And I bet her face wasn't as well.

"How are you?" I sighed deeply.

"Fine." There was a brief silence.

"I hear you have your own place." I nod my head even though she couldn't see it, but she took my silence as a yes. I'm not surprised that she knows about my apartment.

"I'd love to come see it one day." She said.

"I'm sure you do." That came out harsher than I thought.

"Charmion, I'm calling because I need-"

All of a sudden, there was a loud crash in the background, then I heard, "Sonya! Where's my beer!"

My heart stopped. It was him.

"Who are you on the phone with? Better not be that Jeff guy! Who is this?"

I was almost paralyzed with fear, my mouth was open but no words came out.

"Jason hand me back the phone!"

Sonya cried in the background.

"Or what?"

That's when I heard a slap and shriek. Something inside of my snapped; my body reacted when I heard the slap.

"Leave her alone!"

I screamed with hot tears streaming down my face.

"Wait. Charmion? Is that you?"

I gasped throwing the phone to the wall, breaking it in the process. He remembers me. For all I know he could be tracking me down and plan on paying me visit and probably take me to wherever he lives. I quickly ran into the bedroom and packed all my stuff. I don't feel safe anymore. I know Lucky and I are together but it's better if we don't see each other anymore. I don't want him to get hurt. I couldn't risk staying here. I ran to the door but Lucky stood there. My eyes got big. He looked confused then noticed the bag in my hands then his eyes landed on the broken phone behind me. He sighed folding his arms.

"Going somewhere?"

"You sure it was her?"

Lucky didn't believe me when I said my mother called me. If I was him I wouldn't believe me either.

"What did she say?"

He said as he handed me a cup of coffee.

"She just wanted to say hi."

I lied.

"Really?"

He says raising his eyebrows, taking a sip from his cup. It's like he didn't want to believe me, I tried to just act natural but it's so damn hard. She did call to say hi but she also wanted a favor of some sort. I left that part out. It was only a three minute conversation but all I heard was screaming and slapping. Something snapped in me when I heard him slap her. She may be a drug abuser but at the same time she is still my mother. She doesn't deserve that. When I heard his voice and I panicked. I know what kind of person he is. I was 15 years old when Mr. K had a talk with me about my birth parents and how they were drug addicts. When I found out why I was in foster care I lost it. How can two people do that to a baby? Why have a baby in the first place? It sounds crazy. Am I going crazy?

"So you have no idea how the phone broke?" He raised his eyebrows at me, he was leaning over the counter.

I shook my head quickly chugging my coffee.

Another lie, when will I ever learn?

I laid flat on my back, staring up at the ceiling. Lucky was fast asleep, his back turned to me. I sighed putting my face in my hands. I turn to the clock and it read 2AM.

Dammit.

The conversation that transpired earlier in the day was still in my head. I have spoken to both my parents in one day. That is too much for me. The sound of the phone was still haunting me. I heard it ringing right next to my ear. Oh wait, it was my cell phone. Who is calling me at this time of night? It was a number I didn't recognized. Should we answer it? Or go back to bed? I was having an argument with myself and answered for the heck of it.

"Hello?"

I said groggy.

"Hello, Charmion."

No.

CHAPTER 8

❖

It was him. Dear god it was him. He is calling my cell phone.
My heart was racing, my hands were shaky and I felt my
body getting warm. The amount of anxiety I have right now
and he's not even saying anything. I don't remember much of
him growing up. All I know he was worse than my mother
and had serious anger issues. And I know how loud he can
yell even if he is a mile away from the phone.

"How's it going?" He said that way too cheerful, it's two
in the morning and he has so much energy. Then again, he's
very impulsive.

"Are you sleeping?"

No, I have insomnia.

"I was already up before you called."

I lied.

"I've missed you honey."

"You didn't even know I was alive till Sonya called me."

Notice how I didn't call her mom.

"That is not true baby. I've been looking for you since you
got taken away from us."

"Are you kidding me?"

I guess I said that too loud.

"You were in the basement getting stoned when child services showed up. You did not cry, you were not angry, nothing. You did not give a damn about me."

"Is that what your foster parents told you?"

He scoffed.

"If the only reason why you called was ask to come see me the answer is no."

There was a long pause in between my words.

"We'll see about that."

The last thing I heard before the line went dead. What the hell did he mean by that? I turn over to Lucky who was still asleep. It amazed me how he is such a deep sleeper. I sighed wrapping my arms around him. I felt him roll over and warm lips touched my forehead. My anxiety instantly vanished.

Mr. K seemed to be out doing yard work with the kids when I came by. Weird. He only does yard work when there needs to be work done, and that's usually on Saturday's, it's Tuesday. Yard work was something that calms Mr. K, makes him feel at peace with not only with himself, but the world. I worry sometimes that he might hurt himself from bending his back so much. He always did have back problems. Ever since he was younger.

"Should he be working out there?" I said looking out the window into the yard.

Mrs. K sighed.

"I can't get him to come inside. He's been very distance lately. Ever since that phone call he hasn't been the same."

"But why does it bother him so much? If anything, I'm the one who hasn't been the same since."

Mrs. K shrugged going back to doing the dishes. I carefully watched her body movements. She was moving extra slow today, her muscles seemed tense and probably full of nots. She tends to hunch over once in a while. I even saw her limp a little to the fridge.

"Are you all right?" I ask.

"Just had a rough workout this morning that's all."

"You never go to gym."

"Wanted to change up my routine."

Why was she lying?

"So how's Lucky, Charmion?"

She said changing subjects. I chose to answer the question than ask her way she is acting so weird later. I didn't want to dwell on it any longer. Maybe she did have a workout, I don't know. Maybe she wanted to try something new.

"Lucky's doing all right. He's been working none stop. I barely get to see him."

Mr. K came back into the house out of breath and sweat dripping down his forehead. Mrs. K sees this and gives one of her lectures. Some of the lectures consist of, "You need to quit the yard work before you pass out," or, "one day your body is going to quit on you," and, "i've been through so much in my lifetime and losing my husband will not be one of them." Mr. K usual responses to all of those, is nothing. He knows that he'll probably pass out due to heat stroke, he knows he is pushing himself too hard, he knows he'll eventually die doing yard work but at least he'll die happy. Doing yard works keeps him busy, what he says.

My thoughts were disturbed when I heard two or three or more plates crashing onto the floor. I rushed in the room seeing Mrs. K passed out the floor. The kids and Mr. K came running in surrounding her, I stood not knowing what to do. Should I call 911 or start crying hysterically? It was like she received the worst possible news. That one phone call that could ruin your life, that could break your heart in half.

I heard the sirens.

Paramedics came rushing in, kids were huddling around Mr. K as they put Mrs. K on the stretcher, stained tears were on all their faces. As the paramedics wheeled her out of the kitchen, I felt a hand grab my arm. I looked up and saw Mrs. K staring up at me with teary eyes, she slowly removed the oxygen mask from her face and whispered something in my ear that nearly made me pass out. My knees buckled as they took her out of the house and rushed her to the hospital. Her words replayed over and over in my head.

I sat in the empty hallway, my head in my knees. The doctor's voice played in my head over and over again. I stopped crying after the third hour of sitting here. I just ran dry. I was numb, my entire body in pure shock. I just assumed that she would live longer till I get married or have kids of my own. Mrs. K was forty-five of age but looked thirty. Young and beautiful, is what people said when they saw her walking down the street. How can we move on from this? How can Mr. K move on from this? I heard faint footsteps coming down from the hall. They'll pass, I thought. I felt the presence of someone. The person slid down the wall and wrapped an arm around me. I instantly knew who it was but I refused to lift my head up from my knees. I felt a gentle kiss on my head. I heard another set of footsteps that were getting closer and closer and stopped in front of me.

"What did she say to you?"

The voice said.

"Does it matter?"

I finally spoke.

"Yes, it does! I want to know what my wife said to you before she died!" I never liked Mr. K when he yells. His voiced bounced back from the walls and it ringed in my ears.

I began to sob. I felt pair of hands lift my head and my blue bloodshot eyes were now looking at brown bloodshot eyes. Tears began pouring out of my eyes.

"Dammit what did she say!"

The pain and fear in his eyes as he screamed, it'll just break him even more if I say it. The person responsible for the whole thing is the person who called me at two in the morning, just to say that he misses me. That same person who when I said I never want to meet up, said we'll see about that. His hands gripped my head tighter as he stared down at me, he was getting impatient.

"Tell me right now, Charmion. I need to know who killed my wife."

That's the thing, he's not human nor has a soul, he never has and never will. He's a monster.

I can still hear the doctor's voice in my head.

"Time of death, 12:15 PM."

CHAPTER 9

❖

Everyone mourns in their own ways. Some eat tons of food, some cry for hours, or stay locked in their bedrooms and hide from the world. I do none of the above. Instead I sat at the table feeling sorry for myself. The house was dead silent. No one came out of their rooms. I shoved my food away from me and sighed, placing my hands on my face. The sound of the phone ringing bothered the headache that was starting to form from the crying I've done earlier. I answered it not even bothering to say hello.

"I told you."

Suddenly my headache was the least of my worries. All my sadness quickly turned into anger. I should've broken the phone with my hand clenching it as hard as I can.

"I'm sorry for your loss. Must be hard on all of you." The sincerity in his voice sounded more fake than his teeth.

"How would you know?"

I spat.

"Why I too lost my mother. But you already knew that." Jason said.

"I know you're responsible for her death."

I heard Jason snicker on the other end.

"You are blaming me for your mother dying? Oh, honey," He scoffed.

"Where are you?" I said completely ignoring what he said.

There was a long pause. Why make me more nervous than I already am?

"75th Street."

"You're not seriously thinking about going over there, are you?"

Lucky exclaimed.

"You wanna come then?" His face dropped.

"Tell me now before I leave." Lucky stammered throwing his hands up in the air, very dramatically if I say so.

"Fine. But I'm only going because I believe that Jason is the reason for Mom's death."

"So it is Mom now?" Lucky said.

I sighed.

I never called her that. But she knew that she was my mother and didn't mind I called her Mrs. K. As long as she thought that I saw her as my mother, she was happy. I guess I never appreciated her as much.

"You're insane."

He scoffed under his breath. I chuckle.

"Insane, no."

Appearances are everything. How else are you supposed to get a job without dressing professionally? Or clean up the house a little when you have guests coming over? All things people should do, even if the person isn't a cleaner nor knows how to act professional. Still you should at least have some respect. Just looking at the lawn and the busted mail box, I knew the inside was a pig stall.

The smell of urine and feces was intimidating. How can anyone live in this dump let alone maintain the smell? The wood on the porch was slowly breaking away, the windows cracked from throwing rocks or smashing them, the house that was once white started to turn moldy. The kind of mold you see on bread. The condition of this house is just plain awful. It never occurred to him to move? My hand was given a tight squeeze. Lucky gave me a reassuring smile. If only that made the sharp feeling in my gut go away.

When I said the house was in terrible condition, I meant everything and everyone in it. I knocked on the door only for it to come crashing down, the screen door with it. Some house. I heard yelling coming from the upstairs.

"Goddamn it! For the last time ring the-"

There he stood. At the top of the stairs, staring at me horrified. The feeling is very mutual. His smile is more intimidating than the smell.

"And you brought your boyfriend? Oh my little girl has found love!"

He clapped like a little kid with joy and then snickered. That made me very uncomfortable. Same goes for Lucky. He was starting to regret coming with me. Frankly, I'm starting to regret coming here as well.

"Where's Sonya?"

Jason tried to hold in his laughter, that just made me more angry. The fact that he just hurts the woman who was stupid enough to marry him is unreal. Though, you can't really blame her. She must've saw him as a gentlemen and instantly fell in love with his good looks and charms, before the drugs

45

and alcohol of course. He went from opening doors for her to opening her legs without consent.

Why do we live in a world where men think it's okay to hit women, to use them, to make them their slaves? It makes me so angry that this how most men think women are. They treat us like dogs, like we don't matter to anything. Women need to be cherished and be treated with respect. Not just respect but love. But the idea of love in Jason's eyes is the opposite. He feels as if women should please the man and do everything in their power to keep pleasing them or they'll be consequences. It is men like Jason that should not be allowed to walk this earth with the intension of brutally terrorizing women for his own amusement. That's more sick, and disgusting than this house.

"Who?" He says completely clueless.

"Sonya!" I exclaimed.

"Oh, her, she's working."

"Least a good job I hope." I mumbled.

"You think being a prostitute is a good job?" He snorted.

"The hell is wrong with you?"

Lucky snapped, finally after standing there for ten minutes he speaks.

"Oh he speaks." Jason grinned.

I prayed that nothing will happen to me or Lucky while being in this house. I pray we walk out of this house unharmed. I can't take another funeral.

"First of all, she was the one that wanted to do this."

"Did you have a gun on her?" I said.

Jason laughed hysterically nudging Lucky's shoulder, Lucky let out an 'oof' holding his shoulder. He did always punch hard, so I've been told.

"Where would I keep a gun?"

My eyes landed on the pistol that was not very hidden in his pocket. Lucky followed my gaze and stepped back slowly.

"All right you caught me. I only pulled it out to scare her that's all. You honestly think I would shoot my own wife? The woman I love?"

Jason pouted.

"Are you even capable of loving someone?"

I noticed his eyes swelled up with rage and the gun was pointed at my face. Lucky's eyes went wide and tried to take a step forward but that angered Jason even more.

"Take one more step or I'll shoot her!"

I swallowed thickly keeping a brave face when all I wanted to do was cry. Cry that my father is holding a gun on me, that he wouldn't care if his only child could be dead at his feet, that I will never see the light of day ever again. I never thought I'd be standing in front of a man who is holding my life in his hands. I was then grabbed, with his arm firmly holding me by the neck, he pointed the gun at Lucky. My heart jumped.

"Now, you're going to walk out of this house and never come back."

"Put the gun down. There's no need for that." Lucky quickly said with his hands up.

"You leave him be!"

I said with my jaw clenched. Jason smirked pulling the trigger and shooting him in the leg. Lucky screamed in agony.

"No!"

I tried to run towards him but I was shoved to the wall, gun buried in my neck. My breathing was now labored as he cocked the gun so it was ready to fire.

"You son of a bitch!"

He laughed bringing me into his arms and hugged me. I tried to push him away but he placed the gun to my temple. I swallowed hard. Lucky cried out in pain holding his leg. Jason laughed pointing at him. Lucky glared at him then groaned. I cried feeling useless. I wanted to run over to him and help him but Jason had a strong grip on me.

"Now, if you excuse us, I'm sorry I didn't get your name?"

"Let her go." Lucky gritted finally back on his feet. He managed to use his flannel and wrap around his leg. Jason scoffed shooting him in the leg again and Lucky went down again.

"Stop!" I cried. "Please, just leave him alone! He needs help!" Jason sighed shoving to the ground. I quickly grabbed my sweater and wrapped it around his leg. He groaned loudly then grabbed my hand. I quickly pulled out my phone about to dial 911 but the phone was snatched out of my hands. Jason pulled the trigger and the bullet went through the phone. My eyes widened. Lucky gripped my hand tight. He turned his attention to me. The pistol was pointed at me.

"Get up." He gritted. I held onto Lucky which only made Jason more angry.

"Get the hell up or I'll shoot him in the head." I did what I was told and stood up, my hands were up. I gasped when his arm went to my throat again. My eyes never left Lucky. He was too scared to move because he thought Jason would shoot him again.

"Now, he's going to stay here while we go on a little ride."

I shook my head running towards Lucky but a bullet hit the wall above Lucky's head.

"Wow, you really don't get it? You want me to kill your boyfriend?"

I hate myself for coming here. I put myself and Lucky in danger. I should've just listened to him and stayed home. Why is this happening? Why did I agree to come here? It's all my fault Lucky got shot and I can't do anything about it. My life could be gone in minutes.

"Charmion, it's okay. I'll be okay. Don't worry about me." Lucky breathed out gripping his leg. I cried. It kills me that I can't do anything. I feel so helpless. Jason pouted resting his chin my shoulder. I shivered.

"Sure about that?" My eyes widened. My instinct kicked in and pushed myself away from him and tried to shield Lucky. Next thing I knew, Jason whacked Lucky in the head and knocked him out. I ran to him but I was shoved to the wall. I couldn't breath with his hand around my neck.

"Let's go for that ride." His smirk was the last thing I saw before blacking out.

CHAPTER 10

The white lights burned my eyes. I could feel the pain in my leg, I bled out. I immediately looked to see if Charmion is okay and then that's when I realized I was in the hospital. The way he pointed the gun at her, it gave me this feeling in my chest. That feeling was fear. I still feel it. I failed her. I failed her years ago, I failed her again when I said I would always protect her. The pain I caused her was far more painful than the wound in my leg. My head was pounding. The last thing I remembered was being hit in the head by that pistol.

"Son of a bitch!" Gabriel furiously yelled.

"Gabriel, please," I explained what happened to Gabriel and I tried to calm him down but nothing worked. I watched him pace the room.

"No! You mean to tell me that that motherfucker is responsible for my wife's death?"

"We don't know that."

"I don't think my wife would ever cheat on me with a rapist!"

"We don't know if he even is a rapist, Gabriel."

"Who are you trying to convince, me or yourself? For all we know he could be doing what he did to my wife to Charmion."

"Don't say that." I gritted.

Gabriel sighed with his face in my hands. I cannot imagine the stress on this man right now. He lost wife 24 hours ago and now his daughter was taken by her biological father. Honestly, it makes me so angry that I let this happen. How could I let this happen?

"We have to find her." I said sitting up on the bed.

"There's no where to look! He could be in Mexico or China right about now!"

He was right. We had no clue where to find Charmion or Jason. I should not be sitting in a hospital bed right now, I should be finding her. The promise I made her six years ago, the pain I caused her by leaving and not coming back for her, when I said I will always protect her turned out to be lies. Finding her, putting her father in jail, is what needs to be done. I could redeem myself and prove to not only myself but to her too.

I know what I have to do.

CHAPTER 11

❖

I remember stepping out of the car, with fear as my guide, walking up to the house and knocking on the door. I remember seeing the look on his face when he saw me after so long. The way he looked at me was something I will never forget. It's like seeing the one person who you met as a child and wondering what happened to them, if they somehow remember you in any way. They cross your mind from time to time, by seeing little things that remind you of them, but you never *really* thought of them. Until you meet again after so long. You get lost in your own little world where everything around you doesn't matter.

All those thoughts of wondering what happened, wondering if they remember you or spoken of you, is now standing in front of you. It was everything you dreamed of. The adorable child with short sandy blonde hair suddenly turned long and black, the smile that use to light up a room was now hidden between a straight line they call their mouth. The eyes that were once brown and full of life was now lifeless and colorless. And yet, it was everything you dreamed of. My mind seemed to be in a different place. I didn't realize the gun was still pointed at my head as we drove to god knows where. I just kept staring at Jason. But he wasn't staring at me like I thought he would.

"I've got to say J, you got balls."

I almost wanted to puke when the driver spoke. You can tell he was a smoker due to his raspy voice and constant cough. Though, you couldn't at the same time because of his appearance. I would have to say he is in his mid thirties, young of course, he had the same hair color as Jason, brown, different eyes but I couldn't tell what color they were. He seemed to be the same height as Jason. And he doesn't have the same intimidation that Jason has. My guess, they are brothers.

"The hell is that supposed to mean?" Jason gritted now turning the gun on him.

"Whoa J! I'm just saying you aren't capable of pulling something like this."

"And whys that, Cooper?" So his name is Cooper.

"Well, you never really talked about her until now. You didn't even know she existed until Sonya called her a few weeks ago."

Out of no where, Jason climbed up to the front of the car, his foot kicking me in the process, he pointed the gun at the side of the Cooper's head. I notice little things about this. His finger was never on the trigger to begin with, and he likes to scare people thinking he is going to shoot when really he isn't.

I was right.

Talks shit but is too much of a coward to do anything.

"Yeah? Well, maybe I did want to talk about her. Maybe shooting that kid in the leg was part of my plan to have her here right now. Maybe, just maybe, I was planning on raping her mom that way she would have no choice but to come see me."

53

My heart felt like it was going to explode. I could only imagine how Mrs. K was feeling that day. My mind went to a dark place; it was playing tricks on me and made me in vision what Jason did to Mrs. K. I see her, she's too scared to scream or breathe, tears streaming down her face. The gun was laying in front of her that way if she tries something he could grab it and kill her on the spot. Her mind is trying to distract her by thinking about her husband and the children. He's laughing at her weeping. She was begging for mercy. It made me cry. He kept going and going.

It was a coincidence to see a revolver laying under the seat. And I thought they searched the car before we took off. I took a glance at Jason who's eyes were firmly looking out the window holding firmly onto the gun, Cooper focused on the road. I carefully moved my foot to grab it, my eyes looking up from time to time. I am risking my life for this, I thought to myself. I took a deep breath before quickly grabbing it and pointed it behind Jason's head. Cooper looked back at me and back at the road with his eyes about pop out of his skull. He had the same eyes as me. I also noticed we had the same features as well.

"Give me the gun." Jason didn't move, I pushed the gun forward, adding more pressure to the back of his head.

"Give me the damn gun!" I yelled.

"Give her the gun J!" Cooper exclaimed.

"Better listen to him, J." I mocked.

"Or what? You'll shoot? You won't." Jason snorted.

"You sure about that?" I glared.

Jason began to laugh hysterically. Cooper and I looked at him with the same puzzled expression. Just hearing him laugh like that makes me scared.

"You think you're gonna walk out of here alive?"

He says in-between laughs. I shifted uncomfortably as he kept on laughing like a maniac.

"The only way you'll be getting out of this car is in a body bag." He says winking at me through the side mirror. I growled.

"Need I remind you it is you being held at gunpoint not me. So hand me the gun or I'll shoot you in a place that almost every man needs to have intercourse. That goes for him too."

I heard him sigh and slowly raise his hands from his lap. I snatched it and pointed it at Cooper. His body stiffed. I looked out the window to find some empty parking lot or something. I found an abandoned building coming up on the left. I pointed to the building.

"Pull over there."

Cooper swallowed thickly putting the car to a gentle halt.

"Step out of the car with your hands on your heads. Now!"

"You heard the girl." Jason said turning to his brother. They both stepped out of the car with their hands on their heads. Their backs were up against the car.

"Turn around."

Both men turned around and I began to search them for any weapons. I noticed something poking out of Jason's ankle. He had one those pocket knifes that has that strap you wrap around your leg. Clever man.

"Gotta hand it to you, you almost had me." I roughly turned him around putting the pistol in his neck. He stared down at me blankly.

"You never thought your daughter would do this, huh?"

"You're not my daughter." He says coldly.

"Finally something we can agree on."

I moved to Cooper till Jason spoke again.

"You should've seen the way she begged for mercy, how she would do anything to live. She took it like a champ."

I saw him grin in the corner of my eye. His plan to get me riled up was working. Even though my back was facing him, I can see that smug smile of his face whenever he gets his way. I wanted to wipe that smile off his face with the end of the revolver and shove it up his ass.

"J."

Cooper said eyeing my hand that was trembling.

"You're no better than your mother. Oh, I'm sorry I mean mothers."

I know Cooper will grab me or one of the guns out of my hands and shoot me but I didn't care. All this was getting my adrenaline pumped up. In my mind, a voice was screaming at me to pull the trigger, do it. You could end this right now. You could go home and live your life. Live your life with Lucky, Mr. K, the kids. Not worry about whether or not being targeted or constantly sleep with one eye open. Now I'm the one holding his life in my hands.

"Did I struck a nerve?"

Something in me snapped. A body was already on the ground. Though, it wasn't Jason or Cooper's. I screamed in agony as Jason stood grinning, lowering the pistol he snatched out of my hands. Cooper looking shamefully at his brother. Or making some other face, my vision was off.

"Now this is getting fun. Get her patched up. Gotta hit the road. We got a long ride ahead of us."

Somehow Cooper knew what that meant because his face dropped, his hand on his arm. He'd look back at me from time to time.

"J." Cooper begged.

Jason kept walking tucking the gun in his pants. Cooper growled before yelling, "What would mom think if she knew you were like this!"

Weakness; the state or condition of lacking strength.

Everyone on this earth has at least one weakness. Either it's a strength of some sort or an everyday skill. A weakness can also be a person. Key term; *mother.* Jason ran back over and slapped Cooper in the face, he stumbled back holding his face. His head hung low as Jason pressed his body against him, he was glaring down at him. I carefully watched this. I gasped at the pain in my shoulder.

"She would be afraid of me. If I was like this from the start she would be alive today."

The last thing I remember was being thrown into the car and hearing the sound of an ice cream truck driving by, and a voice that yelled,

"You can't do this to my daughter!"

CHAPTER 12

❖

*I was playing on the swings as the rest of kids were on
the jungle gym. Lucky decided to join me and started
to spin the both of us. We laughed hanging our heads
back till we fell off. We were still laughing. Lucky's
laughter started to die down when he saw something
that made him nervous.*

*I turned around and saw a man was sitting at the bench
across from the house. He was just sitting there, watching. I
tilted my head as I walked over to the fence.*

"Hey!" I called out which made the man stand up.

"Quit stalking us!"

*Then he walked away. I turn to Lucky who was hiding
behind the tree. I turned back to the bench to see if the
man was still there but the only thing I saw was his face
that was three inches from mine. He wore sunglasses
that were so black that you couldn't see his eyes. I
gasped jumping down on the ground. Lucky quickly
came over and helped me up, he held me in his arms.
The man just stared at me. His stare, it was telling me
something. I pushed the fence open and started running
down the street.*

"Charms!"

I heard my name being called but it was faint.

Why didn't he say anything?
I found the man getting into his car.
"Hey!"
But he already drove off. I coughed as the smoke smacked me in the face.
Why didn't he say anything?

~

I watched Jason constantly walking in and out of the room. He was bringing stuff in and stuff out. I whimpered when I saw a torch on the table. My shoulder was patched up, barely, but it still hurt. I was sitting in a rusty old chair in an empty room, not even tied up or handcuffed to the chair. Guess he kinda has a heart. He knew I wouldn't dare move a muscle because I'm too banged up, and he's right.

"It was you that day, wasn't it?" He chuckled.

"The day you came to see me at my house. I was in the yard playing with the kids and you sat there watching me."

"Yup, that was me. I kept tabs on you since they took you away. I knew what school you went to, medical records and dental, I tracked your every move." He nod his head pulling the rope out of the bag.

"They'll come looking for me." I said with a glare.

"You mean that boyfriend of yours or the cops?" He snorted.

"I want your boyfriend to come looking for you, just him. I want him to come barging in the room, so happy to see that you're alive and breathing, and then get shot for a third time."

He grinned waving the gun in my face. The same gun he used on Lucky. My chin was lifted up with the gun, now I'm looking into his bitter eyes.

"You look just like your old man." He said with devilish grin.

I was given a sucker punched by the end of his pistol, knocking the wind out of me. I felt a warm, sticky liquid dripping down my face.

"Where's Sonya?" Bits of blood came out of my mouth as I spoke.

"She's fine. Though, she doesn't look very good from here."

From here?

I gasped turning around and seeing the sight of her. She was covered in purple and black marks, her clothes were torn off, and her face was badly bruised as well as her eye. Head to toe, all bruises. It didn't look like she was breathing from here. I cried trying to run towards her. Yes, I knew she was a drug abuser, an alcoholic, had meaningless sex with strangers just to get some extra cash, but she was still my mother. She groaned slowly and carefully tried moving her body, as if her bones were glass. Jason kicked her in the ribs making her cry out in pain. Blood came out of her mouth.

"Stop it she's in the pain!"

"Oh I'm just getting started."

The scene I witnessed next was something that will haunt me for a lifetime. I quickly turned my head away from it. Her shrieks and cries was all you could hear over the harsh skin slapping. Dear god make it stop. I couldn't bare to hear it.

"Cooper! Hold her down!"

Two hands held my head into place, I sobbed watching Jason be all over defenseless Sonya. The pain she must be feeling when he roughly shoved himself inside of her. But he wasn't done. Anger welled up in me as he rolled her on her back, I tried to charge at him but a gun was pointed to my head. Jason chuckled seeing this.

"Now, if you even blink or try to look away, I will burn a lit cigarette on her flesh." I cried, I couldn't stop crying. My head was held tightly and even if I tried to move it, I was kicked in the leg and Jason lit a cigarette. What made it worse, she was looking right at me. Her eyes were pleading, begging me to do something. There was nothing I could do to save her. Her loud screams made it impossible for me to stay still. He groaned and that only added more fuel to the fire. When I heard her sobs, I lost it.

"Fucking stop!" I screamed at the top of my lungs.

"Stop?" He says grunting.

His eyes were full of lust when he looked up at me.

I felt so helpless. All I wanted to do is run to her, hold her in my arms, cry with her, thinking how and why my father is such a cruel man. Once it was finished, Jason pulled up his pants and grinned. My body was numb. I can still see him on her, grunting and moaning, Sonya was crying hysterically. I saw Mrs. K the whole time. Sonya slowly turned into Mrs. K. The fact that he did the exact same thing to her, the majority of me wanted to black out. I can't lose another mother. Cooper didn't put much of a fight, I threw my head back and I heard a thud. Before Jason got the chance to grab me, I grabbed his gun and shot him in the leg. He screamed. Cooper slowly stood up with his eyes widened.

"Do what she says." Jason groaned in pain.

"Don't shoot." Cooper begged with his hands up in the air.

"Give me one good reason why I shouldn't." I gritted.

He stumbled on his words.

"Because I'm your father."

CHAPTER 13

❖

Gabriel and I have filed a police report on Charmion. We gave a very detailed description on Jason but so far they found nothing.

"We're doing all we can."

Somehow that wasn't very comforting at the moment.

"Can't you use face recognition or something on the guy? The man shot my son in the leg for gods sake!"

"Sir we need you to calm down. We are doing all we can. For now, go home and we'll call you if we find anything."

"No!"

Charmion was given a kick to the stomach, making blood come out of her mouth. She whimpered clenching her ribs. She was defenseless. She didn't have the strength to fight back.

"You know, that boyfriend of yours, what's his name? Liam? Logan? Whatever his name is, he's really gonna need a new girlfriend after I'm finished with you. I mean the kid won't even be able to look at you and then he'll leave you because your face is so fucked up. I mean you guys aren't intimate right? Because that would suck if you were."

I woke up in a cold sweat, my chest heaving. My mind started to become a dark place. It was jumping from one thought to another; playing tricks on me. I forced myself not to give in but they just kept coming. Sleep didn't interest me anymore. My bedroom door burst opened and anxiety came rolling in along with his buddies; fear and doubt. The anxiety of the bully coming over to steal my lunch money, the fear of not having enough that will please him, the doubt if I should stand down or stand up. All three crowd around me, belittling me. Ears covered, eyes closed. Voices coming from left and right and all I could think about is the anxiety, the fear, the doubt having such a huge toll on me.

The anxiety of making me overthinking every possibility, the fear of having Charmion in so much pain, wishing for all of it to be over and done with, doubting whether or not I should come to my senses that she is dead. I don't want to believe that all of this is happening. I don't want to believe that the girl I love is suffering somewhere in the country and I'm not there to save her. I already lost her once I can't lose her again.

I don't want to believe.

"You look awful."
I rolled my eyes taking a long sip of my coffee.
"I'm guessing you didn't get any sleep last night."
Gabriel sighed sitting in front of me with the paper.
I always wondered why he still reads the paper. These days people use their phones to look at the news. This generation is all about Instagram, Snapchat, Facebook,

causing everyone to forget their humanity and hide behind screens when everything goes wrong. But it is people like Gabriel who isn't attached to his cell phone, and hasn't lost his humanity due to the advance technology we now have.

"Have the police found anything about Charms?"

Lily said with a frown. I smiled to myself for a moment. I remember the day I gave her that nickname. The day a friendship was born.

~

She watched me as I grabbed a bowl from the cabinet and sat happily down in front of her. Her eyes never leaving the bowl placed in front of me. I smiled at her. She was wearing a pink flower shirt and khakis, her shoes were adorable(Dora the explorer light up shoes), her hair were in small pigtails that went down to the middle of her back. She was very cute.

"I like your shoes." She looked down at her feet that were kicking back and forth.

"You like my Dora shoes?" She said shyly.

I nod my head.

She smiled softly then looked down. She was blushing.

"You wanna go play outside?" She asked still looking down.

"Yeah!"

I didn't even ask her name.

"What is your name?" She looked up at with those blue eyes and smiled.

"My name is Charmion." I scrunched up my face.

"I don't like that name. How about I call you," My eyes
landed on the box of lucky charms on the table. Then it came
to me.

*"I'll call you Charms, it goes with your name. And you
call me Lucky since my name is Luke."*

*She smiled again and we both ran outside, and played tag
till the sun went down.*

~

It wasn't just my first day at the house, it was also the day
I met the one person who changed my life. I think about that
moment everyday. Lily sighed walking out of the kitchen.

"We have to tell them." I said.

"You know we can't." Gabriel said with a look.

"Why not?"

"Okay then you tell them that Charmion was taken by her
birth father who, by the way, raped and killed their foster
mother, and is somewhere in the country doing god knows
what to Charmion. Yeah like they haven't been through
enough."

Gabriel scoffed storming out of the house. I sighed putting
my face in my hands when the door slammed shut and heard
the engine of a car. Of course he goes on a drive at a time like
this. I don't blame him for getting away from a bit. I would
too but I won't. I can't. Not when Charmion is still out there.

Oh Charms, where are you?

Gabriel barged into my room the next morning sweating
like crazy. The man looked as if he ran a marathon. He shook
my body till I fell off the bed.

66

"What!" I exclaimed.

"They found something."

"Okay so we know where they were last. They were at this abandoned parking lot just off of route 13. Someone was walking past that area and saw blood mixed into the dirt. The blood was a match, it was Charmion's."

My face went pale, my knees felt like it was going to give out. They found her blood. The thoughts from a few nights ago came flooding back.

"We also believe there was someone else there." The officer said leaning back his seat.

"What do you mean? Like an accomplice?" Gabriel said.

"We found another trace of blood just five feet away from where Charmion's blood was. We believe that he is holding two people hostage."

"Did you trace the other set of blood?" I stammered my words.

"We did. His name is Cooper Bennett. He is the brother of Jason Bennett."

I looked over at Gabriel who was staring back at the officer with a sour face.

"That can't be right. Charmion's last name is Smith. Her father is Jason Smith."

The officer turned back to his computer and started typing.

"Her mother's maiden name is, Mendez."

This isn't adding up. Charmion's last name is Smith, it always has been. This wasn't making sense to either of us.

"Originally, her name was Charmion Monica Andrews Mendez but on her record she had a name change a few years ago."

Gabriel and I looked at each other, then back at the officer who didn't look as surprised as we were.

"Where did the Andrews come from? No one in her family had the last name Andrews. When was this name change?"

The officer looked at his screen again and raised his eyebrows.

"Says here she was about two years old when the name change occurred."

What?

"Who the hell would change her name? My wife and I were well certain that her full name was Charmion Monica Smith."

"Date, February the 5th, of 2000, you signed the consent form."

"That's impossible!"

Gabriel exclaimed shooting up from his seat. The form looked real and it had Gabriels exact signature and everything.

"So, you mean to tell us that Jason is not Charmion's real father and had a name change at the age of two and that I was the one who signed off the consent form to change her name?"

I can see how frustrated Gabriel is, I am too. None of this is adding up. I know I wasn't brought into the house till Charmion was at least eight but theres no way Gabriel would pull something like this. I know him.

"We are 100% certain Jason is not Charmion's father. We ran Charmion's blood in the DNA system and Jason did not come up. Her real father supposedly died last year."

"You didn't find a body?" I said. The officer shook his head, looking defeated.

"Then how do you know he died?"

"Someone sent us a video of his death. He was walking home when four men came out of no where and jumped him. He was beaten to death. His body was gone at the scene, there wasn't even a blood trail. We also checked if he had a record of any kind but he didn't. He had decent job, had a girlfriend who was a year younger than him, he didn't commit any crimes, not even one parking ticket."

I put my face in my hands. I don't know what to think at this point. This whole time I thought of something different. I was wrong. So wrong. This is all new to me and Gabriel. We couldn't process anything at this point.

"Well, how do you know it was him? For all you know it could be some random guy who just so happen to be walking home from work. Do you have a name?"

"He matched the description." Was all he said, his face was stone cold, completely disregarding the last question. We couldn't get a name out of the officer. Gabriel clearly had it with the officers attitude. So did I.

"You say her real father died and yet you can't even provide a name? How do we know you're not lying?"

The officer rolled his eyes and leaned over his seat. He turns and face the computer towards us and the name of Charmion's father was Fred Dunlap. Gabriel and I looked at each other and then the video. He had the same nose as Charmion and cheekbone structure.

69

"So who is Jason?" I said changing the subject.

The officer pulled out a file from his desk and placed it in front of us. Jason's name was on it. And it was a pretty big file.

"Jason Bennett, he was released from prison three years ago for assault and battery on his wife. He has four gun charges, seven arrests on drugs and selling drugs illegally, and just last year he was charged for attempted rape."

"Attempted rape?" I swallowed a lump in my throat.

Why the hell is Jason claiming to be Charmion's father when he isn't? Is he even related to her? It just doesn't make any sense. I wanted to ask more questions but Gabriel practically drag both of us out of the station and raced home. He quickly ran to the spare bedroom and started rummaging through the closet. He then pulled out a safe from the closet that had copies of birth certificates of every foster kid that ever stepped foot in this house.

"Here."

My eyes scanned the page till they reached the bottom right corner of the paper. There was Charmion's mother, Sonya Mendez, and her father, Cooper Richard Bennett. Wait a minute. Gabriel gasped.

"There's no way in hell Jason's brother is Charmion's father. Wasn't her real father name Fred Dunlap?"

I was in disbelief. How can this be real? We saw actual proof that Charmion's real father died in some alley. Read a full description of the guy and everything, photo ID. I can't even begin to wrap my head around this.

Gabriel pulled out a folder with Charmion's name and case number on the side of it. I never saw this until now. I didn't dig into Charmion's family nor wanted to because it

70

wasn't my business. I assumed she would tell me when she was ready to tell me. Even as a child I never said anything because it be rude of me. I watched Gabriel roughly go through packets after packets until he found the exact same birth certificate but with Jason's name. Instead of saying, Jason Bennett, it read as Jason Smith. The birth certificates were side by side and they both looked identical.

"This can't be." Gabriel whispered nearly dropping to his knees. I held the two pieces of paper and stared at the names. I can't tell which one is the real one or not. They look the same. Like really, really the same.

"This is what they gave us when we adopted Charmion. I was sure that this was her actual birth certificate. The one which says Jason's name on it. I have no idea where that one came from."

Gabriel said winded and had to lean against the wall so he wouldn't lose his balance again.

"How'd you know this was here?" I asked turning to him.

"Mrs. K was the one who organized all the children's birth certificates when they were adopted. She put them in that safe. One day Mrs. K and I had to go to the hospital to receive Charmion's medical records because they forgot to give it to us when we adopted her. I guess that birth certificate with the name Cooper was in there. We assumed the hospital made a copy of the original, the one in her case file, and we put it in the safe."

My eyes were still glued to the two certificates. I'm looking at it like a math equation and I'm trying to get the best possibly answer. But there is no answer. It's all too much. The overwhelming feeling was killing me. Two men claim to be one little girl's father and that little girl doesn't know. Why did this have to happen to Charmion? What makes her so special? That's when everything started to click in Gabriel's mind. Gabriel quickly stood on his two feet and looked me at with his eyes widened.

"Jason changed her name. It all makes sense. He was furious when child services took her away from him or Cooper or whoever. He must've figured out it was me who sent child services, found out where I worked, stole one of my files with my signature attached. From there, he changed her name signing the form with my name to make it seem like I did it."

Gabriel gasped.

"If that is true, why wasn't Cooper in the picture? If he is Charmion's real father, where was he and why did he lie about being Charmion's father? You think Jason had something against Cooper?"

My heart was racing as I paced the room. Gabriel sighed.

"It is a possibility. Knowing Jason, I'd believe that. My question is, how the hell did he trick everyone thinking he died, use someone else's identity and manage to keep himself in the dark after all these years?"

Gabriel scoffed slamming the closet door. Then it hit me.

"They said Jason has another hostage and they traced the extra sample of blood they found at the scene. It is very clear that government doesn't know who Charmion's real father is nor know he is alive. You could be right he probably changed his name and skipped town. Maybe this Fred guy helped Cooper go off the grid. But he is on Charmion's birth certificate! Jason most likely has some vendetta against Cooper. But he could be more aggressive and dysfunctional."

I exclaimed. Gabriel was on the verge of having a panic attack. I caught him before his body could hit the ground.

"I don't want to take that chance, Lucky. The police aren't doing anything so we have to take matters into our own hands."

I narrowed my eyebrows at him. He gave me a look that I instantly knew what it meant. The look that will get us both in trouble with the law, and almost jeopardizing his role as a parent, but if it meant getting back his daughter then so be it.

"We are not going to do anything, Gabriel. We have to wait this one out and let the police do their jobs."

He scoffed pushing himself away from me.

"So we sit on our asses and do nothing?"

"Yes."

CHAPTER 14

❖

I stared at Cooper in utter confusion, still pointing the gun at him. I was holding Sonya close to my chest.

"You're not my father." I breathed out.

"I am." He says slowly.

He slowly got off his knees. My instincts turned on and I panicked, I cocked the gun so it is ready to fire. I felt a lot safer having a gun. If someone tries something, I have this to stop them. He raised his hands up and walked towards me.

"You were born on March the 9th, 1997. You weighted 6 pounds, and 11 ounces. You were born with light brown hair and blue eyes. People said you looked exactly like your mother when she was a baby but you looked more like me and a little bit of Jason."

I wanted to cry. Not about him knowing my birthdate and weight, or the fact that he is my father, but that I looked like Jason when I was a baby. Gross. Just being compared to that freak gives me this awful feeling in the pit of my stomach. I heard coughing and I turned my head and saw Sonya slowly opening her eyes. I sighed in relief and hugged her but she groaned loudly in pain.

"Sorry!" I exclaimed.

"It's okay." She coughed.

Even with her bashed face, she still smiled, weakly of course.

"This isn't how I wanted us to meet." She mumbled then coughed. Seeing the blood stain her teeth made my heart ache. I take a look at Sonya and is amazed she is still breathing. She's been through hell and back and I am determined to make sure we all leave here alive.

"I'm so sorry." Cooper stood next to me, tears staining his face.

"I never wanted this to happen. I wanted us to be a family but I messed everything up."

"You didn't, Cooper. I'm just to blame for this than you." Sonya said with her raspy voice.

Cooper carefully ran to Sonya's side and gentle held her head in his chest.

"We're going to get out here and bring you to a hospital. You're going to be all right."

All of a sudden we heard a loud crash that made us jump. Cooper held Sonya tight, I hid behind Cooper.

"Well, look at this." Jason snickered, barely getting on his feet.

"Cats out of the bag. Finally, mommy and daddy reunited with their daughter."

I felt a hand touch mine. I looked up and see Cooper nudging me to hand him the gun. I slow nod my head, carefully handing it to him. Cooper shot his hand up and pointed the pistol at his brother, with a glare. Jason smiled, arms out and laughing.

"It's even more perfect than I imagined! I knew something like this was going to happen. Sonya half dead, Charmion in the middle, and, the two brothers fighting for what they want."

"I will not let you hurt my family again."

"Shoot him!" I screamed.

Jason raised his eyebrows, then chuckled. All of a sudden, my body hit the floor and I was screaming in pain. The hole on my shoulder was reopened again and my vision was on and off.

"No!" Cooper screamed.

"Face it, Cooper. You and your family aren't walking out of here alive."

Cooper's eyes began to water. Both his girls were badly hurt and he couldn't think what to do next. His mind is racing. Next thing I knew, I heard; freeze! Police officers came barging in and tackled Jason to the ground. Three of them ripped Cooper off Sonya and handcuffed him.

"Wait! Sonya!" It was like my voice was gone. I tried to say stop it, he's my father. I heard; Charmion!

Then, I blacked out.

CHAPTER 15

I woke to the sound of beeping and bright lights. I look over by my bed and saw Cooper asleep in the chair. I sat up but groaned in pain which made Cooper shot up and ran over to the bed.

"Are you okay? Are you hurt? Of course you are, what is wrong with me?"

It's like Cooper didn't know what say or do. He was afraid that he would make things worse with his words. I studied his face as he paced the room. We really do have similar features.

"I'm fine, Cooper."

The room got very quiet all of a sudden.

"Were you there when I was born?" I said breaking the silence.

"Your mother didn't want me there." Cooper said with a sigh.

"What do you mean? You're my father of course she wanted you there."

"No, she didn't. As time went on, her and I got into fights. She suspected I was cheating on her with another woman because I come home late. I got extra hours at my job. One day I told Jason about our fights and he flipped out." I didn't think Jason be the type to lash out whenever he sees his brother hurt. Most siblings wouldn't care, let alone get involved.

"But it still doesn't make sense to me. You left and made me believe that Jason was my father but you were. Did you at least try to get me back?"

"I tried and believe me, I tried but no matter what I did it never worked. Somehow Jason convinced your mother that I was the bad guy and made her believe that I wanted to take you away and sell you. Jason knew my plan to get custody over you and used it as leverage to get me to do his dirty work. He said if I did everything he told me to do that I would be able to see you at least once a week. He forced me to do illegal things that I never knew that were illegal. He wanted me kill people, sell drugs like cocaine and meth and marijuana, he wanted me to become a pimp that way the money I get goes to him and your mother. I said no to all of them because I am not like him."

Cooper said.

"I lost hope on trying to get you back and left. I made sure to lose all contact with Jason, your mother, the government, everyone. The state knew I was your father but didn't know Jason and I were brothers. I didn't want anyone tracking me down so I got a buddy of mine to throw me off the grid. He had a plan to make it happen. He agreed to hack into the police data base and put himself as your father that way they can't trace it back to me. We tricked Jason to believe that we told the police about you, his business and he panicked. Fred, the guy who was helping me, made himself bait. Jason and a couple of his 'friends,' found Fred in an alley by Fred's workshop and beat him up to the point where he couldn't move, making it seem like they beaten him to death. Next day, he sent the video to the police over from there, we lived our lives somewhere else."

I was speechless. I didn't know how to react to all of this. It's all coming at me all at once and it's hard to keep up. This whole time, Cooper was my real father. I don't know whether to be angry or relieved. I mean at the same time I don't blame him for what he did. Jason is a complete psychopath. But he could've done something else or at least gotten some help from the higher ups. I didn't think too much of it but it stayed in the back of my mind. Aside from that, our features were very similar. We have the same eyes, same nose, hair is bit off but I've seen pictures of me when I was a baby and had brown hair. He does that little grin whenever you try to make him laugh and smile.

"I finally found you."

He smiled with a hand on my hand.

"So how old are you? Fifty? Oh how about sixty?" Cooper laughed.

"For your information, little girl, I am thirty-nine."

"Really?" I scrunched up my face. He nod his head with a hearty laugh. It amazes me how much Cooper and I are alike. We kinda act the same; silly. The laughter has died down and the room got quiet again. I didn't mind it this time.

"I'm sorry I forced you to watch your mother get raped, I held a gun on you, I caused this." Cooper says with teary eyes.

"Hey, I held a gun on you and you were forced to watch too."

"I was crying the whole time. I should've done something instead of standing there, I loved her!"

He screamed knocking the vase to the floor.

I wasn't as scared as I thought I'd be when he screamed. That, and I knew he wasn't going to slap me like Jason does. I felt safe. I watched Cooper pace the room, bitting his nails he sighed. I reached out my hand to him and he quickly ran over asking me what's wrong with his eyes. I carefully wrapped my arms around him. He relaxed at the warm embrace.

"You're fine. I'm fine, we're both fine. We got out of that place and we finally have a chance to be happy together; as a family."

"When did you become this amazing?" He chuckled then sniffled. I pulled away wiping his tears with my thumbs.

"When I found out you were my father."

Sonya was in the ICU. She was stable but she was badly hurt. Cooper and I went to go see her. She looked much better than before. The bruised eye is still there but it'll fade over time. Two of her ribs were bruised as well, thankfully not broken. I was very relieved that she was up and moving. She was eating her pudding in bed and looked up and she smiled when she saw us.

Cooper walked over and gently kissed her. I half smiled watching this. They stayed like that for a good five minutes. He slowly pulled away and rested his forehead on hers.

"I thought I lost you." He whispered.

"You'll never lose me." She smiled.

I think that was the sweetest thing I've heard since this happened. After all the shit Sonya and Cooper gone through, they still love each other no matter what. It almost made me emotional.

"Don't think we should do this in front of our daughter."
Sonya giggled.

"I don't care." Cooper smirked.

"Hey!"

Cooper and Sonya laughed as I sat down in the chairs next to the bed. Regardless of what happened, we still managed to smile. Even share stories. Stories that blew me away. This was nice. This is how my life should've been. Full of smiles and laughter and happiness. But every family is crazy in someway.

"So, Charmion, you have a boyfriend?"

That's an odd question a father asks his daughter. Well, not really. But he wasn't angry when he asked that like most dads are. Sonya's eyes lit up. It frightened me to see that much excitement in her face.

"Do you?"

Frankly, I don't know if Lucky and I are together. We proclaimed our love for each other and slept with each other the day Sonya called the house and from there never talked about us. Everything kinda all happened at once.

"I don't know, actually."

The door burst open and Mr. K and Lucky barged in. Lucky smiled big and ran over to me and hugged me. Our lips touched and I was shocked that he had the guts to kiss me in front of everyone. Cooper raised his eyebrows at the huge gesture, I felt embarrassed. Mr. K sighed in relief and joined in the hug. I was in pain but that didn't matter to me. Cooper cleared his throat and stood up and eyed the two men embracing me in their arms.

"So you're Charmion's dad? Is it Cooper or Fred?" Mr. K studied Cooper's face. Mr. K wanted to punch him, I saw him clench and unclench his fist. It made me nervous. Cooper chuckled looking at his feet.

"I can explain that." Cooper said.

"Can you? You sure as hell owe us more than an explanation. Lying about being Charmion's father and somehow flying off the face of the earth? I'm surprised you're not in jail."

Ouch!

Mr. K came packing. He clearly wasn't too happy with Cooper, I'm assuming Lucky too because he looked ticked off just as much as Mr. K. This tension was making me nervous and I wanted to leave the room. Cooper's expression changed very quickly. The two men glared at each other. The tension was so sharp you can cut it with a knife.

"We just want some answers." Lucky said pulling Mr. K back.

"And I'll be happy to answer them." Cooper said nodding his head. Mr. K gave him a suspicious look, Lucky nudged him in the arm which made Mr. K groan. I watched these three grown men scowled each down in silence. I looked over at Sonya who was just as confused as me.

"Can't we all just get along?" I said breaking the silence. But that didn't make things better. Mr. K sighed.

"Okay. Let's talk."

I groaned falling on the couch. Never thought I'd be so happy to be reunited with this couch, this soft yet lumpy couch. I really needed a glass of water, my throat was really dry I started to cough a little. Both Cooper and Lucky ran to the kitchen and grabbed water bottles. They looked at each other weirdly.

"Uh Cooper? Can we have a moment alone?"

"What do you mean? We are alone." It took him a while to catch on that I meant that I wanted him out of the room. His face dropped. I chuckled.

"Right. I should go."

Lucky cleared his throat before taking a seat next to me. I blushed when he kissed my cheek. I missed being in his arms. I didn't think I'd ever feel them anymore.

"How you feeling?" He asks me.

"Better. I feel safe again." He smiled.

"I'm so happy you're home where it's safe, I will never let anything bad happen to you for as long as I live." And I believe him, I know he will live up to that promise.

"I really missed you." His hand trailed up and down my thigh, I chuckled.

His lips gently pressed mine, one of his free hands rubbed my thigh making me shiver. I was lifted off the tiny couch and carried down the hall into the room, the door was slammed shut. His body pressed gently against me, moaning with delight. I missed this feeling, I missed feeling loved and wanted. Nothing mattered at this moment, the pain in my shoulder, the events that's happened in the last few days, the pain I have endured suddenly vanished. The way my body was held in his, made me feel safe. We laid in silence. It was comforting being in his arms, hearing the sound of his heart beat. I was already falling asleep until he broke the silence. I was not ready to talk about what happened and he knew that but he still asked anyway.

"I don't want to talk about it." I grumbled. Lucky sighed and sat up on the bed.

"Look at how you're reacting right now. You're home, nothing will happen to you when you're with me or at home. We have to talk about it, Charmion."

He said with a calming voice. Somehow it wasn't calming at all to me. What's there to say? How do you begin to explain a traumatic experience? How I feel, what I saw, it changed something inside of me. I started crying. Every time I close my eyes I see Jason on top of Sonya. That will forever haunt me. Just sitting here and reliving those horrible moments makes me angry at Lucky. I am not ready nor want to discuss this with him. That's what therapy is for.

"I'm not forcing you. I just don't want you to bottle it up inside. I'm going to make dinner." Right as he got out of bed, my mouth opened and everything spilled out.

"I thought I was going to die. The whole time, I was waiting for it. And when I saw…"

It's like I was reliving that moment all over again. I hated that I am talking about it. I don't want to talk about it, it is too painful. My body was reacting badly and I couldn't stop shaking. The room was spinning and I couldn't catch my breath, I felt like I was dying. After what seemed like hours of trembling and not being able to breathe, I managed to come back into my body. Lucky laid over me with concern eyes. I got angry.

"Leave me alone." I grumbled. He stammered.

"Get out!"

I raised my voice which made him jump. He looked sad and defeated.

"I'm sorry…"

I sobbed as he shut the door. I hate that I talked about it. I hate that it made me have a panic attack and I pushed him away. I don't want to but he made me. I am not ready to talk about it. It is too traumatic and painful. The smell of food made my stomach growl. I have to eat but I can't stand to look at Lucky.

I wished he never asked me.

I upset her. I never should've opened my mouth. She had a panic attack. I feel awful. I should've let her come to me, I basically forced it out of her and I hate myself for that. I shouldn't force her to do anything. God I am so stupid. She can barely look at me. After what she went through I should be gentle and patient with her. If roles were reversed I would've reacted the same. I sat at the table alone, I sighed looking at the empty seat in front of me. I feel so upset about this, I don't ever want her to think I'm just some pushy boyfriend. I turned to the clock and saw it was almost 10PM.

Poor thing is probably starving and is too scared to come near me. I opened the door and still see her curled up in a ball under the sheets. I sighed. I placed the plate on the night stand. She didn't even move. Say something to her, I thought. I didn't know what to say. I don't want to upset her even more. All I want to do is hug her close to my chest but she'll just push me away again. I sighed. I left the food and proceeded to the couch. I know she wouldn't want me sleeping next to her. I wasn't tired so I watched TV. The bedroom door opened and Charmion walked towards the kitchen with her plate. Well, at least she ate. I jumped when she slammed the bedroom door. I sighed laying down on the couch and soon fell asleep.

Around 3AM I heard feet shuffling. My instincts kicked in and grabbed the baseball bat by the wall. Charmion jumped. I sighed setting the bat down. She held her arms behind her back, looking down at her feet. I lifted her chin up so she's looking up at me. I smiled softly. I pulled her into a hug and this time she didn't pull away. I pulled us to the couch and she wrapped her arms and legs around me. I didn't say a word, I let her sob in my chest.

"I love you." Was the last thing she said before drifting off to sleep.

CHAPTER 16

For past couple days I felt the urge to vomit. Though, it could be that I haven't eaten much since I got back from the hospital. It was mostly small things. Last time I had a full meal was the day after Mrs. K was pronounced dead. It had to be the hunger doing this to me, it has to be. I didn't make it to the kitchen. I groaned flushing the toilet and let myself sit on the bathroom floor for a bit. It kept coming back and I was locked in the bathroom for two hours. My phone was ringing non stop and I realized I was supposed to meet up with Cooper and Sonya. Shit.

"Son of a bitch got me pregnant!"

I exclaimed, with fingers in my hair, Cooper sat on the couch awkwardly, while Sonya watched confused. A terrible habit of mine when I feel overwhelmed is bitting my nails. I shouldn't do that but it's instinct.

"I'd always wanted to be a grandmother." Sonya half smiled.

Stood up, Cooper pulled me into a warm embrace but I denied it.

"This can't be happening." I whispered.

"It's not the end of the world. Think of it as a gift from God." Cooper reassuring me. I sighed.

"Cooper, I can't bring a child into this world with what is happening around me. Knowing what we both went through, there is going to be a trial and that's just going to add more stress. Plus I'm only eighteen."

It terrifies me that this happens in the thick of everything. Being a mother is a huge responsibility and the cost of having a child is insanely expensive. My worst fear is having my child go through what I am going through right now. It would crush me.

"I know it's scary. I was terrified when I was pregnant with you. I was so scared that Cooper would leave me because I was still in my 20s, I barely made enough money as it."

Sonya said holding my hands.

"But I made the decision to have you and I never regretted it."

I was very conflicted. It couldn't be at the worst possible time. I don't even have a job to support a child. How can I provide for this baby if I can't even provide for myself? I sighed deeply as I paced the room.

"What do I tell Lucky? We're both too young to be parents and…"

"Hey, listen to me, you are going to be a wonderful mother and Lucky will be a great father. Do I still call him Lucky or Luke?"

Sonya gave him a look and shook her head which meant not the time.

"I think he'll be excited sweetheart."

I'm not so sure.

I sat on the toilet, the pills were on the counter. The pills that could kill this baby inside me in just 72 hours. I held the pills in my hand, a water bottle in the other. I tossed them into my mouth and drank the water till it was empty. I sat there for a while, thinking over what I just did. It was a mistake, tears stained my face, I started sob. I stuck my fingers to the back of my throat and out came my breakfast from this morning and the four pills. They still look the same as they were before I put them in my mouth. I dropped my body on the ground panting deeply then flushed the toilet.

What would have happen if I didn't puke the pills out? I be committing the most dangerous crime ever known; murder. I would be murdering a human being. What kind of person does that make me? I can only imagine what Mrs. K is thinking right now. She's probably looking down right now with disappointment on her face. Her death stare could kill you from a mile away. And that famous line of hers; don't make me knock some sense in you with the book. "Book" meaning the bible. But in this case, it's different. The look isn't the playful, annoyed look you get when you've been caught stealing another cookie from the cookie jar, even though you just had three that night. This look had sadness, anger, and embarrassment. Her arms folded across her chest. You would think it'll pass. It doesn't. I knew if she was here, she would knock some sense in me with the book, drag me by the ear and force me to do the right thing.

I thought of Cooper. A future grandfather. He's been through more hell than me. I didn't see much excitement in him but he wasn't angry either. His life was full of chaos, rage, and violence. Finally, the smokes clear and he saw the light. I was the light he's been searching through that black thick smoke, his last hope of survival.

I thought of Gabriel, Mr. K, another soon to be grandfather. A man who has provided for me when no one else could, guided me through this miserable world we call life, loved me at my worst and as well my best. I feel as if no words can describe how strong this man truly is. I never told him how much he meant to me. Of course he knew that but I never said it to his face. Guess I never came around to it, I suppose.

Next person, is Lucky. Dear god he is the father. All kinds of different scenarios are playing in my head at this moment. One scenario is him all excited and happy about having a child of his own. The other scenario is confusion on why and how this happened but he's still happy. The last one, he is angry. He is yelling and screaming at me, how could I do this to him, why would this happen, we are so young to be having a child. Which scenario is most likely happen? My money is on the last one.

I thought of Sonya. The women who was beaten, victimized, and was mentally abused by a no good scumbag. The one person who can really relate to this. She must have at least thought about this, right? With all the crazy things she has done, she still decided to have a baby, regardless of her living conditions and I turned out good.

The last person I shouldn't be thinking about is Jason. The man that put me and my mothers and Cooper through hell. If I was Jason I would not hesitate for one-second. He would do anything in his power to get rid of this baby and he would not lose a bit of sleep because of it. I felt sick to my stomach. How dare I compare myself to a rapist? How can I sit here and think about all my loved ones and how they feel about me having this child, and all of a sudden, think of the one person who doesn't deserve a crumb of food nor the satisfaction of anything?

I am not Jason.

I waited for Lucky to get home from work to tell him. A phone call or text isn't the right approach when you find out you're pregnant. Can't believe I'm old enough to use pregnant in a sentence. I heard the sound of a car door and the alarm. I took a deep breath standing up from my chair and waited. My heart felt like it was about explode out of my chest. Breathe, Charms. Breathe.

"Jesus!" Lucky exclaimed placing a hand on his chest.

"How long have you been standing there?" I shrug.

"So what do you want for dinner? I'm thinking chicken and pasta tonight, your favorite." He sang with a smile. I followed him into the kitchen. I watched him put the groceries away as he hummed to himself. God I was so nervous. Do I just come out and say it? How do I approach this?

"So how was Cooper and Sonya's today?"

"It was good. We just talked and had lunch." I nod my head looking slightly awkward. Lucky saw this and looked at me confused.

"Are you okay? You seem a little nervous. Wait, I know what's going on."

My heart dropped.

"You do?" My voice cracked. Damnit, I suck.

"You still feel a little weird about the other night."

Just go along with it Charms. I faked a laugh.

"Right! Yeah, just a tad bit." Then there was a knock on the door. Please don't let it be Cooper, please don't let it be Cooper.

"Surprise!" Cooper yelled. Son of a bitch, I thought. Can he come at the worst possible time? Before he even got the chance to step foot in the apartment, I shoved Cooper out in the hallway.

"What are you doing here?" I loud whispered.

"I came to see the soon to be parents of my grand child." Cooper said beaming.

"I haven't told him yet, Cooper. I'm scared."

"You shouldn't, he loves you, I can see it. And I am sure he'd be thrilled to be a dad. Let's head back inside and have some dinner because I am starving."

I opened door and saw Lucky eyed wide. Shit he heard us. I stammered, I was frozen in fear. Cooper stood there rubbing the back of his neck whistling awkwardly.

"You're pregnant?"

I closed my eyes, mentally and physically preparing myself for what happens next. All of a sudden, I was lifted in the air and was given a soft kiss on my lips. Well, this is surprising to me. His eyes lit up with excitement as I opened my eyes. Cooper smiled.

"You're not mad?" I said.

"Mad? Why on earth would I be mad? This is fantastic news! I'm going to be a father!"

He laughed with joy, spinning me around yet again. This time, I smiled.

"I gotta go tell Gabriel! Call everyone! I'm going to be a dad!"

I was paranoid for nothing. All those scenarios were nothing but my mind playing a dirty game on me. The look on his face made my heart flutter and I got the biggest smile on my face. Maybe this could be a good thing. I can see Mrs.

K looking down at me with a smile. I turned to Cooper was leaning against the wall with a smirk.

"Told ya."

CHAPTER 17

❖

I hate lawyers. They are nothing but liars and evil people, hiding behind their suits or pants suit, if you are a female lawyer. I hate courtrooms as well as the people in it, such as the jury. They watch as the lawyers eat you alive, make you feel weak and helpless and you can't do anything to stop it. You can't run, no one can come to your rescue because you are sitting in the most dangerous chair ever created.

I hate courtrooms.

We had to look presentable which I found completely ridiculous. Why should I look like a corporate sellout when the jury can wear jeans and a flannel? I would rather wear a skirt than this disgusting pantsuit. I squirmed as Lucky fixed my tie.

"Hold still, Charmion." He sighed.

"Wait, why are you wearing a suit?"

Cooper comes into the room adjusting his tie as well.

"It is a pantsuit. Women wore these in a courtroom. Most of them, at least,"

"Yeah if you're a scum of the earth. I am referring to the lawyers, just so you know."

I rolled my eyes.

"I know you were referring to the lawyers."

He nod his head stepping to the door.

Lucky gave me a warm smile, pressing his lips on my forehead.

"Is Sonya coming?" Lucky asked.

"She didn't want to come. And I don't blame her." Cooper muttered the last part.

"But they need her testimony."

"And they will. She's going to send a video from Cooper's apartment with her lawyer present."

Lucky nod his head.

"You remember what I told you?"

"Stick it in the man and give nothing back?"

"No, I told you that." Cooper snickered.

"Right. Then I don't know." I chuckled.

"Don't be afraid to share a little more information about what happened. Now let's get going."

We pulled up to the courthouse and I felt a shiver going down my spine, then it went through my entire body. The doors were bigger than I last remember.

~

I didn't want to let go of her, I was too scared to look up at the tall doors. Mrs. K held me in her arms, my face in her chest the whole time. I screamed when I was pulled out of her arms. People watched with sadness in their eyes. They never seen a five year old girl get ripped out their parents hands.

"Hi sweetie!"

I stared at the young boy who was smiling at me. I gulped.

"Can you tell us your name?" The tall man said.

I shook my head. The man frowned.

95

"Why not?"

"Because you're mean."

"I'm not mean. Why would you think that?"

"You're going to put that man in jail." I pointed my little finger to the sad man on the table, he was holding a woman's hand.

"He did something bad."

"No, he didn't. You did."

I jumped off the stand and walked over to the man. No one stopped me, no one didn't try to grab me, they didn't do anything. I hugged the sobbing man and his wife.

"No need to cry. You're going to be okay."

~

My eyes never left his figure, he hasn't aged a bit. He was sitting at his table reading something that looked like a folder. My heart stopped when I saw my name on it. Cooper and I were escorted to our table which was on the left side of the courtroom. I looked over to the other table and saw him staring back at me. I yelped when the loud doors slammed and in came Jason. Our lawyer, Mr. Samson, gave us a little pep talk which somewhat calmed me down.

"Mr. Gallows please call your first witness."

His eyes landed to me. Cooper gave my hand a squeeze and I took what I thought was the longest walk of my life.

"Please state your name to the court."

I shook my head.

"Miss Smith you are eighteen of age, correct?"

I nod my head.

"Then act like one and state your name to everyone in this courtroom."

I'm wondering, where is all this stubbornness coming from? I'm thinking it's 2002 and I'm a little girl again. The grown adult in my head screaming stop it and answer the stupid question, my inner child is hiding behind the wall.

"Charmion Monica Smith." I sighed.

"Just Charmion Smith, thanks."

I scoffed. Asshole.

"Now Charmion," he opened the folder which made me tense up, "I understand you are pregnant, is this true?"

"Objection, how does this relate to the case?"

Samson scoffed.

"I'll allow it. Answer the question, Miss Smith." The judge said.

I scoffed.

"What does that have to do with this?"

Mr. Gallows shrugged his shoulders and leaned back against the table. I sighed.

"Yes, I am pregnant."

"Who's the father?" My eyebrows rose. Should a lawyer even ask that question? Over stepped in my opinion.

"Objection! Relevance?" Samson snapped.

"Watch yourself, Mr. Gallows." The judge said sternly.

Gallows grinned then turned his back to me. I stared down Jason, he was looking up Gallows but I knew he could feel me staring at him. If looks can kill, he would be on the floor.

"Is it true your mother is Sonya Mendez?"

He left out Mrs. K in that statement. That got me angry.

"No," I said

"Says right here that your biological mother is Sonya Mendez." His eyes scanning the page. You really need to read the page if you already know the answer?

"You said biological. But my real mother, is Katherine Klein."

"You had two mothers?" He questioned.

"Yes, I did. One of them is dead because of that man right there."

"You think my client killed your mother?"

"My mother's last words to me was your clients name. My biological mother was sexually assaulted right in front of me and I was forced to watch, as well as my father. He is sitting right there."

All sixty heads and sixty pairs of eyes turned to Cooper, he shifted uncomfortably in his seat. You can see the sweat starting to form on his forehead. I need to watch how I use the word father. Jason's glare could kill from a mile away. I couldn't figure out if he was glaring at me or Cooper. Most of the jurors were whispering amongst themselves. I wish I could make out what they were saying. I saw Jason still giving Cooper daggers. Did I make this case a lot more complicated? Yes, I did. And I am not upset about it.

"You may step down, Miss Smith."

"So Mr. Bennett, you reconnected with your daughter." Samson said with a smile. Cooper nod his head.

"Why didn't come forward before?"

"Jason wouldn't let me. He knew Charmion was mine and knew my plan to get her back, he used it as leverage to make me do things for him that were illegal."

"What kind of illegal things did he make you do?" Samson said leaning next to Cooper.

"Sell drugs, kill people, basically become a pimp."

"Did you do those things, Mr. Bennett?"

"No, I did not want to do something that could possibly jeopardized my chances to be with my daughter."

Samson nod his head walking back to our table. I was impressed how well Cooper is handling this. I'm still a nervous wreck and it's only been 10 minutes since the trial started. Gallows stood up.

"You said you would do anything to get your daughter back but you gave up all of a sudden. Why is that?"

It took Cooper fairly 5 minutes to answer that question. I didn't want to dwell on it for too long but I can't help but wonder why.

"I knew Jason wasn't going to let me see her."

"You needed your brother's permission to see your child?" Gallows chuckled looking at the jury, they weren't pleased with Cooper's answer.

"Yes, because he was a dangerous man!"

Cooper exclaimed.

"Dangerous how? Why didn't go to the authorities?"

"I tried, but no one was going to believe that she was my daughter."

"And so you decide to give up? Instead of fighting for what's yours, you ran away, and with that, started your life over without your daughter. You even lied about being her real father. Why is that? Did you even care about her?"

"Of course I still cared about her! She was still my daughter! And I didn't have much of a choice!"

"Tell me, Cooper, if you are Charmion's biological father, then why is my clients name on her birth certificate?"

"He changed it that way no one knew that I was really her father. The original copy was hidden until it was given to Charmion's foster parents. It was tossed in with her medical records."

"What is your relation with the defendant?" Mr. Gallows said walking back over to his table.

Cooper and Jason had this stare down from across the room. Like two cowboys having a showdown in the middle of town, all you could do is watch intently, wondering who is going to fire the first shot. Jason, the bad guy, loves to make people suffer and take their belongings. Cooper, the sheriff, the good guy, fights for justice and keeps everyone safe from danger. Then there's me, in between them.

"He's my big brother."

"Did you two fight a lot growing up?"

"All siblings fight." Cooper shrugged.

"Would you say that he's protective of you?" Gallows said.

"No," Cooper snorted.

"Are you sure?"

Gallows turns to Jason who was grinning from ear to ear. My eyes went big when he turned his attention to me. Cooper sighed.

"Okay, yes. He was sometimes protective of me but that quickly faded away once I met Sonya. He grew jealous that I had a good life with a woman I was crazy about. He knew he wasn't going to have that so he wanted to hurt me. And by doing that, he took away the two people I love most in this world."

"Wasn't it the other way around?"

"Excuse me?" Cooper raised his eyebrow. Gallows scoffed.

"Nothing further."

Now it was Samson turn to speak. He adjusted his tie before giving Cooper a sincere look.

"Mr. Bennett, my apologies for what happened to you, your wife, and your daughter."

Cooper nod his head with a small smile.

"What was your first thought when you saw Charmion after all these years?"

He looked at me with the biggest smile on his face, I smiled looking down. I knew I was going to cry today. But I was still smiling.

"I thought she was beautiful. She looked exactly like me which was unreal to me."

"When did you tell her that you were her father?"

The more farther Samson went with the questions, the more it made Cooper uncomfortable. I paid close attention his face and body language. I could tell he didn't want to answer them but he was under oath. We both were.

"I was held at gunpoint. I knew in that moment, I needed to confess before things get more out of hand. Her mother was already suffering I didn't want her to as well. But, in my eyes, it was already too late."

It was really hard to be sympathetic with Cooper. I feel like it's excuse after excuse. I get that Jason blackmailed him but I assumed he would've come up with something. He's not that dumb. By the sound of it, he basically let Jason walk all over him.

"At that moment, leaving was my only option. But when I found out Jason kidnapped Charmion, I came home. I didn't care if I lived or died. I just wanted to be with my daughter."

"And you are. Nothing further."

"You may step down, Mr. Bennett."

"Were you aware that your brother was the biological father to Charmion?"

"Yes."

Jason was natural on the stand. After all, he is an ex convict and has been to court so many times. I hate that this is how I have to spend my Saturday. I have to sit in a courtroom and listen to this piece of trash speak, and Jason.

"Why didn't you say anything to anyone?" Sure, Gallows, just casually sit on the furniture, blocking my entire view. Better yet, hope he stays there so I don't have to look at the criminal.

"Because I thought he wasn't fit to raise a child on his own. I was there the day she was born. Cooper came for a second then took off. I raised her. I'm more a father than he will ever be."

He said proudly. I scrunched up my face.

"You were a better father than your brother?" Samson raised a brow.

"Yes," Jason nodded.

"So by doing drugs and drinking with an infant in the house, somehow makes you qualified to be a good father?"

"Okay maybe I had a few drinks in the house and smoked a little weed. But I gave her all my attention. Her mother was out working, I stayed home and took care of her."

"You mean her mother was working as a prostitute that you forced her to do?"

Jason let out a long sigh, too long for my liking.

"Yes."

"Did you ever touch Charmion?" That triggered Jason. He lashed out at Samson.

"No! She was a baby. Who in their right minds would molest a child?"

"Who in their right minds would rape two women for their own amusement?"

Jason scoffed shaking his head and leaned back on the chair.

"Okay I raped her, so what? I raped her mother in front of her, so what?"

Dear god he just confessed. Is that even allowed? Can a person really confess on the stand without discussing anything to their attorney? And the fucked up part, he doesn't care that he confessed. Samson chuckled throwing his arms up in the air. He was looking around the courtroom as if we won. Did we?

"You just confessed to raping two women."

"No, I confessed to raping Sonya. I did not confess to raping her foster mother."

Jason smirked.

"Then how did the police find your DNA all over her and bite marks on her hips and thighs? Her last words to Charmion was your name. You raped her and then she died due to the amount of trauma she was given. You raped Katherine Klein."

"Did I?" Jason smirked with his bottom lip chewed.

"Did I go to her house while everyone was out, threaten her with my gun, force her into the bedroom and take off her clothes? Did I force her to go on her knees? Did I, come undone in her? Did I beat her to the point where she couldn't move or speak because she was so traumatized and consumed in fear? Did I watch her struggle?"

I sobbed making every head turned to me. I didn't dare leave Cooper's side, he rocked me back and forth staring at his brother with tears in his eyes. The look on Samson's face, the panic and fear in his eyes when Jason stared at him creepy like. This wasn't some kind of sicko you see in the park, this man is a psychopath. In his mind he feels he did nothing wrong. The rape, killing an innocent human being, kidnapping, he thinks he deserve a medal for his achievement. Even if he is found guilty, he will think that what he did was right. I thought of what he could've done to her. I had nightmares of me seeing it all happen and I couldn't do anything about it. The image would play in my head over and over again. But I never thought this is how it would come out. The way he detailed every thing killed me. Every fucking detail killed me so fucking hard.

"Tell me, counselor, is that rape?"

I mentioned a folder with my name on it, a folder that contained every bit of my life story. Everyone in the courtroom is gone and it was just me and the folder. My fears and insecurities glued me down to a chair. They're laughing as a figure appeared opening the folder and began reading it. The figure was Jason. I'm screaming at the top of my lungs, screaming stop but no sound came out. I couldn't hear my own voice. The next thing I saw was horrific. He was on top of Mrs. K, his hands roaming her body and she liked it. She was actually smiling and enjoying every moment of it.

Then I woke up.

My forehead was sweating and my heart rate was through the roof. The feeling of discomfort consumed me. I didn't bother going back to sleep. I'd see them. I managed to make it to the kitchen with my wobbly legs. The burning sensation of coffee made me feel alive. Events from yesterday played over and over again in my head. How can they ask for more time? There is enough proof to throw that sick bastard behind bars. Then again, they might say not guilty for reasons of insanity. But he knew what he was doing, this was premeditated from the start. The day he found out about me, this was his plan to get back at me for reasons unknown. Although, the reasons are starting to look very clear from where we are. All this stress and it's only been a day.

Dear lord I'm pregnant.

I cannot have this huge weight on my shoulders if I am going to have a child. Stress is a huge factor when pregnant. You must not be stressed or tensed or it will increase your chances of having a premature baby. It's almost like he knew I would get pregnant too and wants to kill my baby too. I'm making myself paranoid. My getting pregnant was just a coincidence and has nothing to do with Jason.

Or does it?

CHAPTER 18

"Miss Smith," the stand is my least favorite piece of furniture.

"You've been through nineteen different homes and had 237 adoption interviews. And through all of that, you were three years old."

Mr. Samson finished dropping his glasses on the table.

"Yes," I said.

"It's not uncommon for a baby to speak late. You didn't even learn how to walk till you were five because Mr. Bennett never showed you or took you outside, correct?"

I nod my head.

"Thank you."

Samson nods his head sitting back to his seat. He turned to Cooper and whispered in his ear. Mr. Gallows cleared his throat adjusting his suit.

"You didn't learn how to walk till you were five years old?" He said uneasy.

I nod my head.

"I'm sorry but why do I suspect that you're lying?"

"Excuse me?" I raised my eyebrows.

"My client did everything in his power to help you and somehow you believe that you didn't speak till you were four and then a year later, take your first steps?"

"I am not lying."

I gritted.

He chuckled.

"Miss Smith I have a hard time believing that. With you being under oath, what do you have to hide?"

"This is a trial, not an interrogation, Your honor."

Samson barked.

"Sustained. The jury will disregard that last comment. Get to the point, Mr. Gallows." The judge said nodding his head at me.

That folder became his best friend. What I would love more is to rip that folder out of his hands and burn it in a nearby trash can. There's not another piece of paper on that table but that folder. There's no folder with Cooper's name, or Jason's, or Sonya, or Mrs. K. Those three pages of pain and sadness is his excuse to ruin my life and crush my spirit. That folder is the lion and I'm the sheep. Damn you folder for tearing me down, for making me vulnerable and doubt every thing in my life. Damn you for creating this hole in my heart that will take years for me to fill it.

Damn you.

"I would like to show the court exhibits A through F."

Pictures were placed in front of the jury, the judge, and one in front of me. It was a picture of me as a baby. I'm walking towards Jason and I was smiling and so was he. I wanted to cry when I saw Sonya sitting on the couch smiling with a cup of coffee in her hands. She looked so happy. We all did. The other two were me in Jason's arms and him kissing my cheek and me laughing into the camera.

"Miss Smith what do you see in this picture?"

This picture is a lie. His white teeth, nicely cut hair and well dressed self. Her dark brown hair and crop top with high waisted shorts, all bullshit. People must've thought we were this perfect family. Perfect meaning, an ex con as my father, a drug addict as my mother and me. Compare this photo to what it looks like now, one of them is dead.

"Me, Jason, and Sonya." I muttered.

"And what are you doing in this picture?"

I almost didn't want to say that distasteful word. We all know what I am doing in this picture. Why make me state the obvious?

"Walking towards Jason," I said, my breath was shaky the whole time.

"What age do you think you were in this picture?"

"11 months."

I kept my head down. I couldn't bare to look into the eyes of my father who I knew damn well was staring back at me with total sadness. I wanted to run and hide.

"Please take look at exhibit F on the screen."

"Come on, Charmion. Walk to daddy."

No.

A baby was on the floor sucking on a toy. She was waving her little hand at the camera then laughed. She then began to stand up and wobble her way towards the man behind the camera. That adorable baby was me. The man behind the camera was Cooper. Jason laughed.

"Dada."

I said poking his nose with a laugh.

This is the first time I've ever seen a video of me when I was a baby, that picture too. I started to cry. Not because of being antagonized on the stand, but the fact that I did have a father figure in my life and I had a normal childhood. This whole time I thought he didn't care about me. I was wrong.

So wrong. Jason actually treated me like a daughter and a human being. Is this how I find out the truth? Everything they told me was one big a lie. My entire life was one big lie.

This whole time Jason never went to the basement to get high or have sex, he never left me alone in the house, he never let me go hungry. An ex con, was my father and my real father was my uncle. My real father was in my life the whole time but never stepped up to the plate. I turned over to Mr. K who'd look like he seen a ghost. His eyes landed on me and all of a sudden I felt this rage inside of me.

Liars.

CHAPTER 19

A single lie destroys a whole reputation of integrity.

Seems about right. A lie can destroy a person's spirit and the broken trust with it, cannot be fixed. The spirit within me, is gone. Everything was spiraling out of control including my mind and my heart. I sat in the empty conference room, my foot tapping rapidly. A terrible habit I have, bitting my nails in situations like this. The door opened.

"Charmion, please, let me explain." Cooper said.

"Don't you dare and try to make up an excuse why you lied to me. You let me sit there and get antagonized by that video!" I stood up.

"I know you're angry but-"

"Angry doesn't even come close, Cooper!"

He frowned at me. Mr. K stood in the corner fidgeting his fingers. I kicked the chair to the wall causing both men to jump. I wanted to break everything in sight, I wanted to cry till I couldn't breathe and black out. I wanted this day to be over. I wanted the lies to be over.

"Everything you two said to me, every word, all lies."

"We didn't lie to you, Charmion. If anything, Gabriel did and pussy out."

Mr. K raised his eyebrows, taking a step forward.

"You never ran off and started your life over! You were around her this whole time and you didn't say anything. You're a bigger pussy!"

Mr. K exclaimed.

"Fuck you, you both lied and you're both pussy's!"

I exclaimed and pushed them apart and both stumbled against the wall.

"Where's Lucky?" Cooper said uneasy.

"Don't worry about where the fuck Lucky is!"

"Charms let us explain."

Mr. K said quickly then nod his head at Cooper. Cooper sighed rubbing the back of his neck, he stepped closer towards me but I stepped back. My body refused to be anywhere close to these men.

"I was around you when you were a baby. You, Sonya, Jason and I, we were one big happy family. I was still your dad. I was still there when you were born, I saw you take your first step, when you said your first words."

"You mean when I said my first words to your brother." I scoffed.

"You liked the idea of having two dads." He tried to make it sound like; but on the bright side! That doesn't make it better, Cooper, it makes it worse.

"But you were my dad!"

Cooper sighed nodding his head.

"I was. But I did not lie about the other stuff."

"What? That he forced you to do illegal business? You know at this point, nothing you say will make up the fact that you lied to me."

"Cooper, can we have the room?" Mr. K said. I let out a bitter laugh.

111

"No whatever you have to say, you can say it in front of him."

"Fine. I heard about Jason in the streets, how he was sometimes violent and has serious anger issues. He had a kid and I got scared. I was afraid he was going to hurt you so I told child services but they didn't believe me. They needed a reason why you should be pulled out of that house. I made up a rumor that he was using drugs in the house and sure enough, they searched the house and found a case of meth in the basement. You weren't three when you were taken from them. You were two."

It's like my whole world came crashing down on me and for what? Because a man thought a beautiful child being raised by two people who didn't "look" the part of a parent? This lie nearly ruined my chances to have a good life. A stupid, fucking lie that nearly cost everything. A heart can only take so much.

I turned to Cooper.

"So what you told me at the hospital, you lied about that too?"

"After child services took you away, Jason found the family you were staying with and took you back. You were in the park. It was my fault for not saying anything in the first place. I wanted to say something but Jason threatened me and that's when he became violent, that's when things started to get bad."

"But the thing is, Cooper, you could've done something! You could've said, hey, I'm her real father, don't take her. Instead you just watched it all happen."

"Everything we did was to protect you."

Mr. K chimed in.

112

"That's bullshit and you know it!" I exclaimed.

Both men stared down at the floor in shame. They aren't men. They are sad excuses of men. Better yet, they are both children.

"If you have never taken me away from them then none of this would've happened. Jason would have never raped Mrs. K and she be alive today. He would have never raped Sonya, I would have never gotten kidnapped and gotten shot, and I would still be with my father!"

"Yes, but you would have never met me, Mrs. K, Lucky, and the kids. You'd have a better life with us."

"That was not your choice to make, Gabriel! I was happy with a family and you took that away from me! What did you actually erase my memory of them?"

The look on his face said it all. My jaw dropped to the floor. Cooper was in complete shock and angry.

"Gabriel, you didn't." I gasped.

"You need to understand that we did it for you!"

"You drugged me? And Mrs. K knew about it?" I exclaimed.

"How could you do that to a baby?" Cooper was seething in anger, that makes two of us.

"That house wasn't safe for a baby!" He exclaimed.

"Dear god, you're not just a pussy. You are fucking crazy, too."

I breathed out hunching over as if I was going to vomit. Am I here? Is this what I am hearing right now? My mind was mush at the age of two. That is wrong, that is cruel. Who would do that to a child? What killed me the most, my dead mother knew this whole time that my real family was sane and normal. Gabriel saw that and took all of that away from me because he thought that it wasn't okay for a baby to live in a somewhat trashed house. He drugged me so my memory of them were gone and told lies about them, which gave me the image I saw of them today. The image they blinded me with. They looked into my two year old self in the eye said it to my face. Did I even have a normal childhood? Hell, did I even go to an actual school, with actual kids and teachers? I have to question everything about myself now.

"Has the jury reached a verdict?"

"We have, Your Honor."

"What's say you?"

The judged folded his hands as one of the jurors stood. They were holding a small piece of paper.

"On the charges of rape in the first degree, we find the defendant, not guilty by reasons of insanity."

"On the charges of kidnapping in the first degree, we find the defendant, not guilty by reasons of insanity."

My knees buckled, both men next to me pulled me up. I felt like I was going to faint from dehydration.

"On the charges of murder in the first degree, we find the defendant,"

Time stopped.

I can hear my own heart beating through my ears. I see everything go slow. That feeling when I saw Sonya being brutalized, the feeling of numbness, consumed every part of me. I'm back in that dark, scary place where no one can hear me scream. The hole in my chest was absorbing all that pain and numbness.

I heard a bell tolling in my head. It was counting down. It kept going until finally, the middle aged man with a small piece of paper, said two words that changed everyone in that courtroom.

I cried hysterically.

CHAPTER 20

❖

Everything happens for a reason.

Bullshit.

What would be the reason for this? What reason could possibly justify what took place yesterday? I had a chance to be happy and it was ripped away from me. Aside from everything that happened, life was good. I was a happy baby living with my mother, father, and uncle, till one man decided to ruin it. But I am not saying that what Jason did was justifiable. I am simply saying what might've been.

The story I was told years ago, both my parents, Sonya and Jason, were drug addicts and alcoholics and they did not want me. All they did was drink, get high, and have meaningless sex in their basement. No one took care of me, no one gave me any attention, and I was barely fed and bathed. The story that corrupted my mind.

But the *true* story, my birth mother, my birth father, and uncle were all living in a regular neighborhood here in Delaware. We were your average American family. Even though, my uncle was acting more like a father. My real father was still around. He just never did his part. But we were still your average perfect family. Of course we had our fair share of fights but hey, that's every family in America, right?

As ridiculous as that sounds.

"I'm sure there's better places. You just have to keep looking."

I reassured Lucky. He sighed putting his face in his hands. Since we are expecting a baby, Lucky's job isn't paying him as much. Though, before he didn't mind but now it matters a lot. Minimum wage doesn't cut it in this life.

"Have you tried that country club downtown?" I asked.

"I've checked. They're not hiring."

I reached across the table and held his hand with a sincere smile.

"Don't worry about a thing, I'll get a job."

"You working?" He snorted then covered his mouth to hide his laughter.

"I can get a job!" I exclaimed.

"Charmion you cannot stand people let alone fake being nice to people. Remember that time when we went to the mall and someone asked you the time? You literally screamed; time for you to get a motherfucking watch ass hat!"

Ah that day was fun. I was high off of Mountain Dew and airheads. My tongue was mixture of every color and my eyes dilated from the amount sugar.

"Oh you make it sound like I'm not a people person."

He playfully rolled his eyes.

"What job could you possibly get?"

"Undertaker."

Lucky broke out in a fit of laughter. I always loved his laugh. It wasn't too deep nor too high. His laugh is very contagious, even as a little kid it still was.

"You know, I think you be perfect for that job. 'Cause you don't have a heart." He joked with a grin.

He leaned over to the table and cupped my face and pressed his lips on mine.

"I was about to jump into the shower. Care to join me?" He smirked.

"I'm disinclined to acquiesce your request, Mr. Mitchell." I grinned.

"When have we ever taken a shower together?"

I thought for a moment.

"That one time when we went skinny dipping in the pool."

"That was so 2009!"

I chuckled.

"Still counts in my books."

He playfully glared at me and stormed out of the kitchen like a little girl who doesn't get her way. I laughed shaking my head. There was a knock on the door. I opened the door and sighed. Cooper was the last person I wanted to see.

"What do you want, Cooper?"

"Can we talk?" He said nervously.

"No, I don't want to." Of course he puts his foot in the door. I sighed again.

"I'm sorry, Charms. I really am."

"So it's Charms now?" I scoffed.

"Please?"

Cooper begged putting his two hands together like he was saying a prayer. I sighed in defeat and stepped aside. Lucky came into the room in basketball shorts and a tank top, his hair was still wet from the shower.

"Cooper? I didn't know you were dropping by today." He chuckled.

"Neither did I." I muttered.

"I just came to talk to Charms."

There he goes again with that name, why is he all of a sudden calling me Charms? The day he told me he was my father he always called me Charmion. He probably wants something.

"Whatever you came to say, you can say it to the both of us." Cooper took a glance at Lucky then at me.

"See ya." Lucky gave me a peck on the cheek and practically ran out of the room, damnit, Lucky.

"I uh thought I should come see you after, what happened yesterday."

There was an awkward silence. The ticking of the clock made me twitch. I hated the silence. But at the same time what can I say? Nothing, I can't say anything. Cooper was standing awkwardly by the door. He was avoiding eye contact with me. So was I.

"You know how you got your name?" He says with a smile. I shook my head.

"We waited till the day you were born and the name just came to us. The first thing I saw was those amazing crystal blue eyes that made your mother burst into tears. She knew you would get my eyes. Jason cried, your mother. The words I used to describe you was beautiful and charming. So we went with Charmion because you were like a lucky charm to us, pun intended."

I chuckled. That story made me smile. I haven't done that in a while. I didn't know whether or not that story is true or if he's lying again. I still haven't forgotten.

"And I'm not lying. You can confirm it with Sonya."

"I will." I said. I lost all trust with Cooper so anything he tells me, I won't believe a word. The only person I can trust now is Lucky.

Cooper nervously laughed rubbing the back of his neck.

"I'm glad we're talking instead of yelling. It's progress."

Cooper half smiled.

Believe me, I want to yell at him but it isn't worth my time and energy. I'm this close to losing all respect for him, and talking to Cooper, it is gone. I feel like I still need more answers. And I wasn't going to get any from Cooper. I needed answers from the horse's mouth. The person who started all of this.

My body cringes at the sound of his name.

CHAPTER 21

My foot was tapping the floor as I sat in one of the couches in the waiting room. You have to wait in these uncomfortable, dirty chairs for 30 minutes to see a patient. I've been here for 10 minutes. Men and women in white clothing were everywhere. There were people screaming and loud crashes. I guess that's what you see in a mental asylum. The buzzing of the door startled me and in came Jason with two officers behind him. He gasped when he saw me.

"It's my daughter!" He exclaimed with joy.

He jumped up and down like a kid and grabbed the nurse's shoulder, the look on the nurse's face was screaming; get off of me. This place doesn't live up to their expectations. The slogan here is; *You are not the root of your insanity.* I beg to defer.

"It's my daughter." He winked and walked over to the table, his sorta white teeth showing. I assume they're turning him into a new man.

"I see you have new teeth." Why did I say that?

"You noticed." He blushed. I mentally rolled my eyes. There's like a little boy trapped inside of him. He doesn't even act like an adult.

"They thought it be the first step in my recovery. Well, so they say."

I nod my head looking around. Jason was watching my face the entire time.

"You look upset. It hurts my feelings to see you upset." He pouted.

I scoffed.

"Like you have feelings." I rolled my eyes.

"You're right, I don't. But hey, I'm still your dad." Jason said with a wink. My body quivered.

"You are not my father." I spat.

"No, but I actually am. If you really think about it, I took care of you, I raised you. Whether you choose to believe that or not, I am your father. Cooper was just there, he didn't even bother helping out. It was me."

I sighed deeply. As much as I want to argue with that, I kept it to myself. Jason snickered taking a sip of his water and then placed a hand on his cheek, staring lovingly at me. I cringed inside.

"I must say, I am curious why you showed up. The trial wasn't enough?"

Jason exclaimed loudly throwing his head back, some of the nurses rolled their eyes at his childish behavior. Probably not the first time he acted like this.

"Were you like this before?" Jason laughed.

"I was just like Cooper. Course I wasn't that boring, I did smoke and a few nights have a drink at the bar. When you came along, everything changed. I was happy, actually happy. Yeah you weren't mine but it was nice to see Cooper smiling for once. The day you were born, it was the happiest day of his life, as well as mine. But as time went on, Cooper was so busy, working from early in the morning to getting out late at night, he didn't have time for you. Same goes for your mother. She was a nurse and always did night shifts. Neither of them had time for you. I don't mean that in a rude way but it's the truth. Then you know what happened after that."

I stared at him.

"That's the story?"

I scoffed.

"I've never given you a reason to lie." Jason shook his had, folding his arms.

"I find that hard to believe." I muttered.

"I may be an ex convict, a drug addict, and an alcoholic but I have never lied to you. Cooper did, your boyfriend did at some point, Mrs. K, and Gabriel. They all lied to you and the one person who never did, the one person everybody hates and is the total bad guy, was completely honest from the very beginning. Yours truly, moi,"

Every fiber of my body wanted lash out at him and defend Cooper and Gabriel. But I couldn't do it. As much as I would love to, I couldn't. Everything he was saying was killing me, his words stabbing me in the chest, the room is spinning again. Maybe I was going in a state of shock. Maybe it's because I am hearing the truth from the man who killed both my mothers physically and emotionally and never thought was capable of telling the truth.

"Cooper said you took me back. How?" Jason shrugged his shoulders.

"You were in the park, you saw me and screamed, dada. You ran towards me and we went home."

"Just like that?"

He nod his head.

"And that's when you forced Cooper do all those things?"

123

"Maybe I did, maybe I didn't. You were a baby, you didn't care."

"A simple yes would have sufficed." I mumbled. He sighed.

"All right fine. Yes, you were with us for about a year. Happy?"

No.

I sighed.

"Well, it was nice talking to you." As I got up, my arm was grabbed. The hairs on the back of my neck stood up. I was expecting dry skin touching me but it was soft. My body went into shock.

"Stay for a couple minutes." There was something in his eyes that scared me. It was sadness and pleading. It's unusual for me to see that in him. I sat back down.

"Look, I know what I did was slightly wrong."

"You raped and killed my mother! You shot me and my boyfriend twice, and kidnapped me! And raped Sonya right in front of me!" I exclaimed.

"Okay yeah but at least I didn't kill them!"

"And that is supposed to make me feel better?"

I exhaled sharply.

"All the nurses here won't tell you the truth, but I will. You are nothing. You are the scum of the earth and I wish you never see the light of day ever again."

His hands brushed against mine which made me yank my hand back with a glare. Jason saw this and frowned.

"I understand why you are angry, you have every right to be. I caused so much pain on you and your family. But seeing I'm not getting out any time soon, I want us to be okay. Maybe you can come visit me once in a while."

"Why on earth would I do that?" I sighed.

"Because unlike Cooper and Gabriel, I am the only who you can trust at this point."

CHAPTER 22

❖

The minute I woke up, my phone was ringing like crazy. I groaned in anger thinking who the hell would be calling me at 7 in the morning. I exclaimed when I saw a blocked number. I already knew who it was. I didn't even say hello, I yawned as my response.

"Charmion?" Jason said.

"What do you want?" The line was quiet for a good 7 minutes. I don't have the time nor the energy to play telephone. Right as I was going to hang up the phone, he spoke. Son of a bitch, why?

"I want to get better. I really do, Charmion." Jason whispered.

I looked back from down the hall and saw the bathroom door still closed. I sighed.

"Please, Charmion. I need a favor."

"And what is that? Steal you a phone?" Again, the silence answered my question. I was joking! I exclaimed.

"I could possibly get sent to prison if I did that!"

"It's not that hard." He whispered.

I threw my arms in the air dramatically, as if he could see them but he knew I did it anyway.

"I'm using someone else's phone I found in the bathroom."

I heard the toilet flush and the door opening and panicked, I heard footsteps coming from down the hall.

"Fine."

I quickly hanged up and turned to Lucky entering the room fully clothed. He was wearing blue jeans with his red flannel, and his free runs. His hair was pulled back in a white beanie to finish off the look.

"I'm heading to the house later to do some yard work. You want to come with?"

That's when an idea struck my mind. I couldn't make out words so I nod my head.

"I thought you'd say no."

"Why would I?"

I finally spoke.

"With everything that happened, I didn't think you want anything to do with Gabriel let alone be near him."

"Things change." I lied.

Gabriel has a whole bunch of burner phones locked up somewhere in the house and all I need is a working one. One that no one ever uses and has enough minutes to last a month. The car ride wasn't as great as I thought it would be. Lucky kept rambling on and on and on about where I was yesterday and that phone call from this morning. If I even so call say the first letter of his name, I will never hear the end of it. I just said it was one of those phone scammers and I was doing a few errands with Sonya. Thankfully he didn't ask specific questions. Did I actually agree to do this? What is driving me to do this? Something inside of me is telling me to do it just for the heck of it. Maybe it's because I feel sorry, or just to get back at Gabriel for what he did. Or, maybe, I still have love for the man. And I hate myself that I do.

"The serpent finally decides to leave her hole." Gabriel scoffed.

When you are told something insulting or offensive in anyway, you try not to show a reaction. To hide your anger or annoyance just give a big fake smile. We have a word for that, it's called being *passive aggressive.*

"I believe the term you are referring is that the serpent is no longer in sleeping mode. The serpent is now stalking her prey."

Prey meaning Gabriel.

"I see you managed to speak to me without screaming." Gabriel said, his eyes never leaving the newspaper in hand.

"Doesn't mean I want to." I said, staring at him with a cold expression.

He looked up for a moment, then back down at the paper.

"I see. And why did you come? To lash out at me?"

"Like I said, I want to but I won't. I do have some self control."

Gabriel scoffed.

"When have you ever had any self control?"

Keep it together, Charms. I knew he was trying to get a rise out of me, make me lose my temper. I will not sink to his level. Even though he has no level the waist down.

"I am here because I want to be here. After all, this is the house I grew up in. There are so many memories."

Kill them with kindness and a dashing smile!

"Right. I'll get you set up, Lucky."

The minute they left the room, I sprinted down the hall to the spare bedroom. This spare room is like Gabriel's man cave or a hideaway. A man cave is usually filled with a recliners, pool table, a flat screen TV or a mini bar. This, this

128

was far from a man cave. Hell, it's far from a bedroom. There was clothes, shoe boxes, papers, the mattress was on the floor. I huffed falling on the busted recliner in the middle of the room. The hell did he do with those phones? Just as I was about to get up, a shadow was under the door. I panicked and climbed out the window and landed on a rose bush in the lawn.

Shit.

CHAPTER 23

❖

I laid on the grass, catching my breath. I looked down at the medium size cut on my leg as well on my arm. Blood was staining my jeans. I sighed letting my head fall back down. My mind wondered, and soon enough, I was thinking about what might've been. The pain in my leg no longer had an affect on me because I was thinking about something far more painful than a stab wound. This type of pain cannot compare to any others. It is more of an agonizing, brutal pain.

Heartbreak.

The ultimate pain, the number one cause of death worldwide. I felt it when I was in that courtroom, when my life came crashing down on me as I sat in the deadliest seat known to man. It was the same feeling I felt when I saw the only man who raised and is now a mental patient. And now, this mental patient, wants me to steal them a phone. A phone is very vital to the human race, we'd do anything to have one. We'd risk it all. Am I willing to risk my entire family's trust? I didn't bother moving. I was able to get back up but I chose not to. I chose to lay in the grass and stare at the clouds passing by.

"Dear god! Are you okay?"

And sometimes, the person who caused that heartbreak, can heal the wound they created. Even if it is a cut on the arm and leg.

"Oh hush it isn't that bad."

Gabriel said with an eye roll. I returned one back.

"Let me see your arm."

I almost hesitated to show him. He gave me a look that he use to give me every time when I was a kid. Whenever I hid something from him, he'd have this look that was deadly, you could sense a mile away. I thought it was his superpower. I finally give in and lifted my sleeve up. It still has an affect on me.

"All set." He says.

"What were you doing climbing out the window?"

I sighed.

"I was looking for one of your burner phones."

He gave me a confused look.

"Why do you need one?"

I gulped.

A part of me wanted to tell him but the other part of me was reminding myself what he done and all the lies he told me. Yet, despite what he did, I don't feel the need to lie to him. I won't.

"I just do."

I jumped off the table and followed him down the hall to the backyard where Lucky was working.

"Whoa! What the hell happened?" Lucky exclaimed.

"She climbed out of a window and landed on the rose bush."

Lucky's eyes widened.

"What the fuck, Charmion!"

"It was only the first floor." I rolled my eyes.

"You're pregnant and you could've seriously hurt the baby!"

"I am not even showing yet and I am fine!"

"Okay enough!"

Gabriel yelled. Lucky and I glared at each other like we use to as kids whenever we had a disagreement. Gabriel groaned in annoyance.

"God it feels like 2010 all over again. She did not land on her stomach nor her back. She landed on her ass and thats just about it. Now what we really need to be concerned about is why the hell was she looking for a burner phone."

Lucky's face scrunched up.

"You still have those? I thought they were extinct."

"That is not the issue here! The real issue is why the hell are you stealing from my house and why do you need a burner phone so bad!"

"I just need it!" I exclaimed.

"Whose it for?" Lucky said, he had his arms folded across his chest, looking very bleak.

"Does it matter who?" I said with a nervous look.

I was stuck. I couldn't just blurt it out the truth without causing more pain to this family. I already did enough damage for one day.

"Charmion, we want the truth. You owe us that."

You owe them, Charmion. God damnit, I dug myself a hole with this one. I am starting to regret doing this. I didn't even have to say it, Gabriel already figured it out.

I slowly crawled my way to the kitchen, constantly looking back at the dimmed lit staircase and the man passed out on the couch. The clock read 2AM but all I saw it was still nighttime. The sound of my stomach made me stop dead in my tracks for what I thought I woke up the sleeping man. I sighed in relief then stood on my two feet, about to reach for the rainbow colored jar, until the lights turned on and the man stood there. His arms folded across his chest and he was giving me a look that you could sense a mile away. I laughed nervously.

"Hi Mr. K."

~

I sat down in one of the pool chairs as Gabriel raised his voice. Out of all the angry outbursts I encountered, this is on top of the list of the worse ones. Lucky mumbled with a hand on his forehead.

"Have you lost your fucking mind?" Lucky screams out in anger. I take it back. Lucky wins.

"No, I have not." I kept my voice fairly low and quiet.

The shovel that was once in Lucky's hands, is thrown across the yard, shattering the window on the shed. Surprised me.

"You are giving the most dangerous man a valuable asset! For all we know he is just using you to get things out here to bring in there for him! I mean look at you, you are already under his control."

"That is not fair!" Stood up, and I glared at him.

"What's not fair? The fact that you are willing to risk your freedom for a convict or that you are so sure he wants to change? He is never going to change! He's a criminal and rapist and a murderer!"

"And a good man!" Did that just come out of my mouth?

Gabriel scoffed putting his hands on his head, an angry smile on his face. Somehow that is more terrifying than what I witnessed in the last few weeks.

"He killed the love of my life! He raped your birth mother and almost killed you and Luke!"

"He wouldn't have if you just left me and my family alone!"

"The hell is going on?"

Cooper came running towards us, still in his work clothes that were covered in dirt. Gabriel turned around, he covered his mouth, for what he was hiding were the sobs that muffled through his hand. The sobs were contagious. The sobs were making me nervous.

"Tell him. Tell him that you were going to steal a phone for a man that raped your mothers. Tell your father that his precious daughter is gonna go to jail if she continued to pull this crap! Tell him." Gabriel gritted.

My eyes went to Lucky who couldn't even look at me, he just kept shaking his head looking at the trees. I am not going to stand here and be intimidated by this man. I will not let this shell of a man tear me down by the sound of his loud voice unlike the rest of people here. I stepped closer towards Gabriel and glared at him, he did the same. I didn't care if Lucky was doing the same or Cooper. This tension, what I am feeling right now, is between me and Gabriel. No one else, I feel as if it is only me and him right now and no one is around us.

"He has not given me a reason to lie. You had yours."

In that moment, I realized, I was offended by that whole conversation.

CHAPTER 24

The alarm blared throughout the hallway, waking everybody up. I jolted up causing me to fall off the bed. I still get stares whenever that happens.

"Bennett! Get dressed, you got a visitor."

My heart jumped.

Charmion.

I had the biggest smile on my face as I walked down the hall to the visitors center. I expected a pink haired girl but it wasn't. Instead, a brown and gray headed man. The man who ripped her away from me sat in the chair. I was told Charmion was coming, not that bastard.

I don't like change.

I hate change.

"I was expecting my daughter, not a corporate asshole who can't seem to keep his nose out of everyones business."

"Her visiting you is my business, Jason." He said cold.

"So you found out about the favor." I snickered.

"Yeah, I did. And you can forget about it. I will not let my daughter give you something that will just cause world war 3."

"She's not yours!" I yelled causing everyone look at our table, nurses stood up and watched us intently. I saw the needles, I sank down in my seat a little more.

"You can't keep the training wheels on forever, Gabriel." I scowled.

"That may be true, but she is still my daughter and I am her father."

"Cut the shit and tell me the real reason why you're here!"

Gabriel sighed deeply, I stared at him with hate in my eyes.

"I'm only going to say this once; even if you somehow get out of here and make parole, knowing what you did, you are not going anywhere near her."

"That's big talk for someone who you just lost a daughter and a wife."

I smirked.

It only made him more angry, his knuckles were turning white from clenching his fist really hard. It made me laugh; how cute.

"I knew it was you who called child services. I saw the looks you were giving me when I was in the park with her. And I knew that all of this would rain back down on you. You didn't know when, where, or how, but eventually it will happen. So I did a little research myself. I found out where you worked and got access to all your stuff. Home address, your financials, credit cards and my favorite, your social security. Maybe next time you should think twice before taking a child away from a family just because you could not have a child of your own."

I found out that dear old Gabriel could not have a child of his own due to infertility that was passed down in his family. It skipped his father so when Gabriel and Mrs. K tried to get down to business, he couldn't reproduce. I mean it's no wonder he and his wife adopted so many children. He was lonely, he longed for a child he can call his own. So what does he do? Sees a child that was so beautiful and decides to kidnap that child and take it home like a cheap dollar bill you find on the sidewalk. But that wasn't the case. He already adopted a bunch of children that he could call his own. Why did he have to take Charmion?

"How do you know that?" He gritted.

His hands gripping the table tightly, I feel like his hands will fall off and I'll start laughing.

"I know everything about you. I own your bitch ass. Now, why don't you shut up and listen for once in your life because you see my lips moving, but you are not hearing me. I will do whatever it takes to get out of here and have some kind of life with my daughter whether you like it or not. I don't care if Cooper is her biological father, she is *my* daughter. I raised her!"

I am not going to sit here and let this man spit lies to my face. He did not raise that little girl, I did. From the day she was born, to the day she got taken away from me. I cared about her more than anyone else on this damn planet. He was just lucky that she wasn't ten years old when she was already fully grown and knows what 2+2 equals.

"So tell me, Gabriel, was the only reason why you took Charmion away was because you thought I didn't look like you, a man with a good paying job who only associates with the same people? Or did you just not like how a guy like me could possibly be a father to a beautiful little girl and actually turn out okay?"

The man in front of me refuses to look me in the eye because he knows the man sitting opposite of him is right. He doesn't want to believe that I raised her right, nor admit it to

138

himself. Matter of fact, no one wants to admit that I was Charmion's father, not even the princess herself. That's going to change. It has to change.

"You take a look at a guy like me and you can't stand the fact that a beautiful baby was walking down the street in the arms of a man who didn't look like you. You judged me before knowing me. And you couldn't stand it. She was smiling in my arms, she was fucking happy with me and you took her away from me!"

I panted deeply. I am so angry, I couldn't control myself. The day Charmion was taken from me, it changed something in me. A part of me was missing. And I knew exactly who ordered child services to invade my home. I knew one day I was going to be face to face with this poor excuse of a man and I was going to extract my revenge. Now that time has come.

"And you know something? I enjoyed what I did to your wife. She knew who I was the minute she opened that door. Believe it or not, she kissed me."

I laughed and then I was sucker punched in the face. Game on baby. I tackled Gabriel to the ground. Patients and their visitors started to freak out and ran out of the room. Gabriel gasped for air as I tightly wrapped my arms around his neck.

"I hope our little chat shed some light on you, Mr. Klein. And for that you can go to hell."

He tried to push himself off but I kept my grip on him. I chuckled watching him struggle. I let go and Gabriel fell to the ground. He was coughing uncontrollably. I grabbed him again and put him in another choke hold.

"I expect the next time you come here, you will have what I asked for. Consider *that* your business."

I roughly threw him to the ground and was escorted out of visitation. My grin never left my face as they shoved me back into my room.

I win.

Gabriel sure can punch. The shiner on my face was pretty big. That same day I had another visitor. My expectations were very low because, well, it wasn't my daughter. But this visitor was far more better, I was shocked to see him sitting on the couch. Cooper. I haven't seen him since the trial. Why is he here? I slowly sat down in front of him, eyeing him. With what happened earlier, there was officers in every corner of the room.

"Hello, little brother."

I grin.

Cooper chuckled then looked closer to my face.

"The hell happened to your face?" He said.

"Oh, this? It was a gift."

I'm sure he'll figure it out when he leaves and goes back home. I left a little something on Gabriel too.

"I can't help but wonder why you randomly decide to come see me after all that has happened."

Cooper frowned.

"I wanted to see you."

"See me?" I said as I cocked an eyebrow, then scoffed.

"You were always the liar in this relationship."

"Why would I lie?" Cooper scoffed.

"I don't know, why would you?"

He sighed, I stared blankly at him.

"Just answer me this, why did you do it?"

"Cooper," I sighed putting a hand on my face.

"Look me in the eye and tell me why you raped and killed Mrs. Klein and raped my wife in front of Charmion."

I don't know why it was so hard to look at him in the eye, I couldn't do it. He may be a pain in my ass but he was still my brother, my family. I can feel the tears well up in my eyes as I slowly lifted my head up.

"What happened to us, Jason? We use to be best friends. The minute Charmion got taken away from us, you changed. She wasn't yours, she was mine."

"I couldn't have kids!" I exclaimed. All heads turned to us. There, cats out of the bag.

"Why do you think I never brought home a girl? Or even spoke to a girl? I couldn't reproduce. I found out when I was 25 years old. I couldn't have a child to call my own and when you had Charmion, I was so happy to be an uncle. That meant she was mine too."

Truth is, Gabriel and I are very much alike. Makes me sick to my stomach.

"Why didn't you tell me?" Cooper whispered.

"You and Sonya would have pitied me and I hate that. If there's anything I hate most in this world is being pitied by others. You of all people should know that."

"You still didn't answer my question." I looked at my arm and dropped it on the table. Tears stained my cheeks as I wiped my mouth.

"You were finally happy. You had a wife, a kid. I knew I was never going to get that so I got jealous and resented you for it. I didn't think I did anything wrong. The day they took her I did change. I turned dark and cold and that is why I made you do all of those things. I took it harder than you and Sonya because I loved that little girl so damn much. You don't know what it's like to come home everyday seeing your brother in love and have a beautiful baby and not be able to have that."

All of a sudden, I was wrapped into a tight hug. You cannot hug the patients here, but that didn't bother me, the nurses saw and did nothing. When he touched me, everything that I held in me came out. Every emotion, every thought and every insecure, poured out of me in one hug.

"I'm sorry, Cooper."

I kept a poker face and forced myself not to cry on his shoulder, but I couldn't fight it. I lost it in my little brother's arms. It's been years since I hugged Cooper and cried to him.

"I forgive you."

He held my red and puffy face in his sweaty hands. His reddish blue eyes piercing through mine.

"Do you hear me, Jason? I forgive you."

I sobbed and hugged him. My knees buckled and we both fell to the ground, still wrapped in our own embrace. I never wanted to let go.

"Promise me you will change. Promise me you'll be good."

I nod my head, tears streaming down my face.

"I swear on Mama's grave." He smiled through his tears.

"I love you, JJ."

My eyes were closed tightly as I heard the infamous nickname. His first words were JJ and since then, became a name that only he can call me. Our parents weren't even allowed to say it because it was ours and only ours. It wasn't until I was ripped out of his arms. I screamed and kicked the nurses and ran towards him but more nurses piled on and piled on. My whole life was being pulled away from me. Sounds around became unheard, Cooper trying to chase after me but he was pinned to the ground.

I gasped.

I knocked the nurse off me and quickly raced to my brother's side. I just hugged him. No amount of nurses could possibly pull two thirty-nine year old men off each other. His trembling arms hanged on me for dear life.

Everything moved slow. My vision a blur, doctors running from down the hall in slow motion with needles and a stretcher behind them. Other patients were watching near by. I looked down at Cooper who looked up at me with bloodshot eyes. He had that same terrified look whenever he was going to die. The same look whenever we got in trouble with our parents. That look, it was special to me. He would turn to his big brother to save the day.

I smiled.

I place my lips on his forehead and hugged him tighter.

"I love you, little brother. Take care of yourself."

I lifted my hands up, my eyes never leaving him, and immediately, I was roughly attacked by white coats. I did not resist. Cooper watched in horror as they ripped me apart and shoved me to the wall. I grunted feeling my hands being handcuffed hard and tight. Regardless if you are a mental patient, they still treat you like a criminal. I saw the needle. The needle would make me weak and knock me out. I screamed.

"Tell Charmion-"

Then the needle stabbed me in the arm, I moaned. My knees slightly buckled. My body slid down the wall and my eyes rolled in the back of my head. I looked up and saw Cooper being dragged out by security.

"I love her."

Darkness.

CHAPTER 25

Lucky and I haven't spoken since we got back from the house. Of course Gabriel being the tattle tale that he is, told Cooper and now he isn't happy with me either, though he has been showing mix signals lately about the whole thing. Sonya was disappointed but I could tell she was mad at me too. She and I haven't talked either. I watched Lucky forcefully eat his lunch, his fork jamming into the chicken. I barely touch my food.

"You honestly think I wouldn't find out?"

He finally spoke, his angry eyes piercing me.

"That was kind of the idea." I muttered.

"But just help me understand, Charmion." He pushed his seat back and walked over to my side. My hands intwined with his.

"After everything that happened, all the pain you and Mrs. K and Sonya and Cooper suffered, why are you so willing to make amends with this man?"

I wish I knew the answer. I do question myself why I am doing this. Truth is, I don't know. Maybe the baby growing inside of me is turning me into a better person. Maybe, just maybe, he or she wants me to live my life in peace instead of living my life in hatred. It probably wants me to forgive and forget.

"I can't give you that answer right now."

He sighed.

"I'm not mad anymore, by the way."

"If you were you wouldn't be talking to me right now." I snickered. Lucky did the same. Least we aren't screaming at each other. It's progress.

"Have you figured out what to call him?"

I scrunched up my face.

"What makes you think we're having a son? It could be a girl."

Our laughter filled the room till the ringing of the phone was all you heard. We've been getting awfully anxious whenever the phone rings. Can you blame us?

"It was one of those robots."

I didn't realize I was holding in my breath for so long.

"So, what does the princess want for dinner?" Lucky sang obnoxiously loud as he walked into the kitchen.

"I'm thinking baked catfish maybe?"

"I was talking about the baby but I'm good with baked catfish."

I scoffed throwing a pillow at his head but he dodged and laughed pointing his finger at me. I heard my cellphone ringing and without looking at the screen, I answered it still laughing.

"Hello?" I said in-between laughs.

"Charmion?" Jason said.

The laughing stopped. My heart stopped, I had a lump in my throat. Lucky saw this and carefully came over with concern on his face. It was like I was paralyzed or something. It reminded me the same night when I got that terrifying phone call at 2AM. I have PTSD from just hearing him say my name like that.

"Hi, Jason," Lucky's eye widened, his head shaking rapidly. I put the phone on speaker.

"I have some great news."

The line was silent for a second.

"I'm getting out."

"You actually did it?"

Lucky said with a shaky breath.

Cooper nod his head with a grin on his face. We all stared at him with mixed emotions. Jason is being released a bit early, by five years. Cooper went out of his way and begged the court on getting him released into his custody, with parole of course. I don't think giving the court 10 grand is something to be proud of. Even if it's for family. My question is, where in god names did he even get 10 grand?

"So you went to the court, paid 10 grand just to have Jason live with you?"

"You make it seem like what I did was a crime." Cooper said with a scoff.

"Is it?"

I chimed in.

"If you have a really good reason why they should be released into your custody and the money, the court will listen."

Gabriel said with his arms folded across his chest.

"You're taking this surprising well right now. Did you forget to take your meds?"

Lucky said.

"Or did you lie about that too?" I said rolling my eyes.

He gave me a bitch face and rolled his eyes.

"Okay yes I did it. I persuaded the court to let him out with three years on parole."

"Three years? How'd you swing that?"

Lucky exclaimed. Cooper chuckled rubbing the back of his neck.

"I went to see him and I saw something in him that I have not seen in years. He wants to change, he looked me in eyes and said it to my face. He wants it for himself. Since he's been in there, they say he is doing good so I have a chance to get him to come home. But in order for everything to be squared, you all have to testify saying it's okay for him to live with me."

"I am not testifying."

Gabriel said quickly shaking his head.

"Gabriel." Cooper sighed.

"No! I am not going sit on the stand and say he should live with you knowing that he killed my wife and raped yours!"

"When are you going to let go of the past?"

I mumbled.

"Need I remind you that this, is still recent. It hasn't been a month since he was put in the nut house! Why the hell would they let him out when he's been in there for three weeks!"

"It's really been three weeks?" Probably a bad choice of words on my end.

"A person who committed murder and rape shouldn't be in a nut house for three weeks! It should be for life without parole! Do you not remember what he did? Oh wait you probably forgot but he killed my wife and raped your mother!"

"God enough with the fighting!"

Lucky groaned rubbing his temples.

"Okay look it doesn't matter how long he's been in there, what really matters is him allowing to come live with me and with your guys approval."

"I'll do it." I said. Cooper smiled.

"You got to be kidding me." Gabriel muttered.

"Fucking suck it up and do it for Cooper."

I barked.

"No! I don't care if God himself wants me to testify. The answer is still no!"

Our noses would've touched if I was the same height as Gabriel. He has the height advantage on this one. Gabriel and I have been budding heads for weeks now and no matter what comes out of our mouths, there's always an argument.

"So if Mrs. K came back from the dead and begged you to testify would you?"

"Don't you dare bring my dead wife into this! The man committed horrific crimes known to mankind! He should not be allowed to walk free with the intension that he did nothing wrong!"

"You committed a crime. Remember that?" I raised my eyebrows with a cocky smile.

"But I didn't rape and kill a human being! What I did was stole a car in Miami. How do you think Sonya feel about this? The poor woman is probably stressing out because the man that raped her for years and abused her might be getting out! You are being so selfish right now! Think of her for god sakes!"

"I'll testify!"

Lucky cried out just to shut all of us up. He never liked conflict. Gabriel was beside himself.

"Thank you guys so much." Cooper smiled.

"Doesn't mean I forgive him for putting a bullet in my leg." Lucky growled.

"I'll take it."

Cooper laughed then pulled us into a group hug, making Gabriel and Lucky groan.

"Just tell us when the hearing is before we change our minds."

Jason's hearing came faster than we expected. A day after Cooper announced that Jason could be living with him. A hearing isn't anything big. It's just the defendant and the people testifying against the defendant along with their lawyer, and of course the judge present. Gabriel and Sonya didn't show up. Something wasn't sitting right in me as I sat in my seat. My heart ached as I thought about how much they both went through in last couple weeks. We've all been insensitive. I was being insensitive. I can't get over how I was acting yesterday. No matter what I said it was only making Gabriel more angry. It was like I had no control over my words. I had this horrible gut feeling. My heart started racing, my palms were getting sweaty and I couldn't breathe correctly. Samson saw this held my hand but that only made me worse. I couldn't breathe, like actually couldn't breathe. I needed to get out of here.

"L-L," I tried to talk but I couldn't make out any words. Then I fell to the ground shaking uncontrollably.

"Charmion!" I heard screams but all I hear is a loud ringing in my ears. The ringing wouldn't stop, my body would not stop shaking, my eyes started to roll in the back of my head. I began to whimper and hyperventilate.

"Oh my god, what's happening?" Cooper said panicked.

"She's having a panic attack, get her some water! Hey, hey I'm right here. It's okay." Lucky cooed.

"Do something!" Cooper exclaimed.

"You have to wait it out! If you touch her she could hurt herself or you!"

I started to feel again. I can feel the carpet underneath me, my clothes, I can hear voices. My vision was coming back to me. I was starting to come back to reality. I could breathe again. Lucky sighed giving me a warm hug and a soft kiss on my cheek. He turned to Cooper with a glare.

"You are not putting her the stand."

"The hell you talking about?" Cooper said.

"She just had a panic attack! No way in hell you are putting her on the stand! I won't let you."

Just when Samson could cut in, Jason came in with a suit and tie along with his attorney. Is it a little creepy that they wore the exact same suit with the exact pair socks and shoes? I gripped the side of my chair and counted to 10 in my head to slow down my breathing.

"Mr. Mitchell, would you please come to the stand?"

I was lost in my thoughts and my feelings. I knew something wasn't right when Lucky sat on the stand. Samson saw this and pulled me aside. I couldn't speak. I thought I was going to have another panic attack. I needed to go home and be in my bed. Lucky saw this and tried run for me but the judge spoke.

151

"What do you think of Mr. Bennett living with Cooper Bennett? Would you feel safe?"

Lucky's face went pale. His eyes met Jason who stared right back at him and had a pleading look. He couldn't stop staring at Jason, he was in a trance of some sort. Lucky let out a shaky breath. He placed a hand on his leg, the same leg Jason shot. It was almost as if something snapped in Lucky's brain and knocked some sense into him.

"No, I would not feel safe. I would be absolute terrified to see this man walk free and into the arms of Cooper Bennett, my girlfriends *father*."

Lucky's head snapped to Jason when he added more force on the word father. Jason and Lucky glared at each other but his lawyer nudged his elbow to knock it off. Jason fake pouted then gave a little wink and bit his lower lip. Lucky scoffed in disgust and stood from his seat. Neither men look very please with Lucky as he stormed out of the room.

Now we're in trouble.

"What the hell, Lucky?"

Cooper exclaimed as he slammed the conference door shut. It hasn't been an hour of the hearing and it's already become a conflict of interest and it's not even my turn on the stand. My legs were so shaky that I didn't even dare try to stand up because I would fall over. Samson held me as we walked into the conference room.

"I'm sorry, Cooper but I agree with Gabriel. I cannot sit there and say I'm okay with him living with you, the chance of him walking free."

152

The strong feeling in my gut from earlier came back. Everything started to fade. I felt dehydrated and I need water desperately. All you could hear is yelling. I moaned and I fell to the ground. I was in and out of consciousness. I looked towards the door and I saw Jason. He smiled as he came by my side. Why wasn't anyone tackling him? He shouldn't be this close to me. I pushed myself to the wall.

"Look at you." Jason gasped. He placed his hand on my stomach and I tried to scream but nothing came out. We were the only ones in the room but it didn't feel like we were.

"You are glowing, Charmion. I can't wait to see my grandchild."

I was trying to find Lucky and Cooper but they were no where to be found. I panicked quickly standing back up. Jason shoved me back down on the floor. He chuckled.

"Where are you going? We aren't done talking."

His eyes turned dark and soulless. I held onto my stomach the whole time. Jason kept staring at me. His hand went to my face, pushing my hair behind my ear. It gave me the chills and I tried to shove him away but his hand gripped the back of my head. I whimpered in pain. No matter how hard I tried to say words, nothing came out. I was screaming on the inside, it wasn't any use for me. I screamed for help but no one came.

"That baby is going to grow up to be just like me. He or she has Bennett blood coursing through their veins and soon enough, they'll see the light. Charmion? Charmion?"

I suddenly woke up in the arms of Lucky. My eyes went straight to the door and all I saw was Samson looking frantic. I was hyperventilating. I touched my arm and I felt my skin. I was able to feel again and move my arms and legs.

"Where's Jason?" I gasped getting back up on my feet.

"What do you mean where is Jason? He's in the holding cell." Cooper said.

Whatever happened, it felt real. I felt him touch me, I can still feel his hand still gripping the back of my hair. I knew this was my brain playing tricks on me. I will not be afraid anymore. I speed walked down the hallway with determination. I reached the cell and I saw the poor excuse of a man. He looked happy to see me.

"My kid will never be like you. And I'll be damned if you try and reach out to them."

Jason smirked the entire time. My body jolted up when he started clapping his hands together. I forced myself to stay still as he approached the cell door.

"I hope you have a boy," his hand touched my stomach, I quickly yanked it off of me which made him snicker. There is no way in hell I will let this man live with Cooper. Not like this, he was staring at my belly like he was the father. He got onto one knee and he was eye level with my stomach.

"It's going to be a boy. I can feel it. And when I meet him for first time, he's going to love me. I'll make him love me just like I made you love me."

He whispers as he rubs my stomach. There was something about this that terrified me to the core. He had some sick plan clicking through his brain and it has something to do with my baby. It was clear to me that Jason shouldn't be anywhere near citizens. I can see right through Jason. I always trust my gut feelings and my gut is telling me that he and my child will meet under terrible circumstances. I was wrong, I can't let myself say that he should be free. I would be lying to myself if I said I was comfortable with it. I have to protect my child.

"Charmion?"

I was snapped out of my thoughts and turned over to the judge.

"Do you feel safe having Mr. Bennett live with your biological father?"

I looked at Jason, he was giving me a sinister grin. Regardless on what I know about this man and my family, this isn't what it best for society or the wellbeing of my unborn baby for Jason be out and about. The way he was talking about my baby, it wasn't right. Whatever happened in the conference room was all in my head but it sure as hell was a sign. It is clear to me that I have to put an end to all of this. I had a plan. Regardless on what I say, the court has to make the decision, I'm just simply saying my opinion. So it really doesn't what I say in the end. I want this man to burn in hell for this. I want to look at this man and watch his life fall apart, just like I did. Have fun in the prison, buddy. I smirked.

"Yes."

Jason's face dropped.

I walked through the white fence and saw Gabriel doing the same old thing, doing the exact same job for the last nine years. Changing the flower beds by the back fence. I smiled to myself. Mrs. K would always do that. She'd add a little more soil than usual even though you aren't supposed to but she did it anyway. Gabriel looked up to wipe the sweat off his forehead and saw me. I waved and he chuckled and jogged over to me.

"Well, this is a pleasant surprised." He said.

"I thought I check up on you."

He scoffed looking away from me.

"You didn't show up to court today."

"Yeah well, I didn't want to sit and defend a man who killed and raped my wife." Gabriel gave me a fake smile as he cleaned the dirty on his hands.

"I went to see Jason in his holding cell. He kept talking about how my baby will turn out to be like him and that one day he's going to meet them. He touched my stomach. It scared me."

"This was today?" Gabriel said holding my shoulders. I nod my head looking down at my stomach. I placed my hand on it and took a deep breath. It was all I could think about; I couldn't get it out of my head.

"It wasn't sitting right with me. Being there, again, I had a panic attack in the middle of the court room."

"Are you all right? Where was Cooper and Lucky?" Gabriel said with concern in his eyes.

"Lucky was there, Cooper didn't really know what to do. I'm still shaken up about it but I'll live."

"Lucky told me you said yes to having Jason live with Cooper." Gabriel said changing subjects.

"I did but that was just to throw them off so it was up to the court to decide."

"And?" He said.

I smiled.

"He's getting 25 to life without parole."

The look on Gabriel's face was complete relief. His hands went to his mouth, tears came down his face. Warm arms wrapped around my body.

"Thank god."

He sobbed. We stayed like this. I started crying too.

"So everything you said about him, all the; 'he deserves to live with his brother' and 'he's changed,' that was all bullshit?"

"Truth is, I was hurt that I saw the only man that raised me was locked up. When I walked into that courtroom, that's when I knew what an ass I've been. That I shouldn't even dare question or try to rationalize what that man has done, what I've seen what he can do. Regardless of his crimes, I thought he was still family. I was wrong. You raised me, you will always be my father."

I was pulled into another hug and broke down in his shoulder.

"I'm sorry. I'm so sorry." My voice cracked.

"It's okay honey. That is okay." My face was held in his hands. I shook my head and sobbed.

"Lucky asked me, after everything that happened, all the pain me and Mrs. K and Sonya and Cooper suffered, why I'm so willing to make amends with this man and I said I don't know. Now I do know. He killed my mom."

I feel like such a fake. I fooled myself thinking that what I was doing was okay with all of this. Okay with the fact that what Jason did was simply a my bad. I deserve you are a dumbass award for my actions. One thing that I was sure of, Gabriel lied to me and I thought this was a way to get back at him. Though, it made him lose a daughter as well as a wife. I couldn't stop crying. My body wouldn't let me. We sat at the table, didn't say a word to each other. Gabriel and I haven't had that talk about happened. Hell, I didn't have that talk with Lucky, well not everything.

"I forgive you." I said breaking the silence. I saw the tears starting to form in his eyes as he looked up at me.

"I can see why you did what you did. You thought you were doing what was best. I forgive you, Gabriel."

He smiled pulling me into another hug.

"I've been wanting to hear those words for a long time." He whispered in my shoulder. We can finally move on and stop this controversy. I'm tired of this fighting. I just want things to go back to normal. I want us to be a family again and put this behind us. All of a sudden, a white Jeep Wrangler pulled up in front of the house. It had to be a 2013 Jeep wrangler. Lucky came out of the sun roof with open arms and a smile.

"Check out the new ride!" He laughed.

"What the hell, son?" Gabriel said with a laugh.

The passenger window rolled down and saw Cooper grinning from ear to ear. I scrunched my face up.

"You bought this?"

I chuckled.

"I got my bonus check and thought I should get a few things for the family. You like it?"

"I love it." I gasped.

"Sonya picked it out. Think fast."

The keys were tossed to me and I looked at Cooper confused like.

"You're gonna need a car when the baby comes." Is this actually happening right now? Here I thought I get the silent treatment not a brand new car. I don't even have my license yet.

"You can't be serious? I thought you be mad at me for what happened at the hearing. You wanted nothing but Jason to come live with you."

"I hate myself that you had panic attack in the court room. Knowing I was responsible for that, I knew that it was a mistake that hearing. My daughter comes first."

Cooper said with a sincere smile. There is a lot of hugging today. I didn't dare bring up the confrontation between Jason and I. That pretty much stayed between me and Gabriel.

The dark clouds are going away and the sun is starting to shine, it's pure happiness. Just like this. We were all in the middle of a terrible storm that went on for years and years. We all thought it was never going to be sunny and warm ever again. From hiding in the small cold house, to being out and free in the suns warm embrace. Some were lost during the storm and some left, but we kept ourselves together and deep down we all knew it was going to get better and it did. 15 years later, that is.

CHAPTER 26

❖

March 2020

Celebrating my birthday isn't as important to me like it should. It's just a regular day for me. Though, it is a big deal to your five year old. It made me laugh to hear him say happy birthday. He's trying to get some big words out. I smiled giving him a kiss on the cheek and watched him play with his toys. Turns out Lucky was right. The day we found out we were having a son, he was ecstatic. I wanted to wait on the day of the birth to give him a name and when I saw his beautiful face, it came to me. I fell in love with the name Zachariah. The name is Hebrew and the meaning behind the name is Remembered by God and I loved that. The screen door opened and Cooper entered the backyard with a huge smile on his face.

"Grandpa Cooper!" Zach screamed.

"Zachy!"

Cooper laughed picking him up and started spinning him around. He gave him kisses on his cheek which made Zach squeal. I chuckled. Zach loves Cooper. More than Gabriel and that says a lot. They spoil him way too much.

"How's my favorite grandson doing?"

"I'm good." He blushed.

"I wasn't expecting to see you till tonight." I said putting Zach's toys on the chair.

"I thought I'd come see my daughter before the party. Is that a crime?"

"I don't know. Is it?"

I smirked.

"I actually didn't come alone."

I saw a girl with ombre hair and brown eyes enter the backyard. She was wearing classic jeans and a flannel. She was around my height and I noticed a small child hiding behind her. She looked very familiar. I got a closer look at her and I gasped. I haven't see this person in five years. I thought she was dead. Is this really her? Was this the red haired girl I met at the mall that one Friday morning? I use to think about her everyday, wondering how she was doing and I tried to reach out to her but I heard nothing back from her. How did Cooper find her? She looked completely different from the last time I saw her.

"Hey, stranger, long time no see." She said measly.

I laughed embracing her in a hug.

"It's so good to see you!"

The small child behind Kendall gave a small whimper.

"So who is this cutie?"

I crouched down to her size with a smile. She hugged her mother's leg scared like.

"This is Riley, my daughter. Say hi, Riley."

Riley shook her head and ran back in the house.

"She's very shy. She gets that from her dad."

I chuckled.

"Mommy."

Zach pulled my pant leg.

161

"Can I go play with Riley?"

I turn to Kendall who was smiling, then nodded her head. Zach smiled and ran back into the house with Cooper behind him.

"I see you and Lucky are still going strong, so I've been told. Last time I saw you guys weren't on the best of terms."

I chuckled running my fingers through my hair. It was so good to see Kendall. Especially today on my birthday, it couldn't be a better gift.

"So, tell me what's been going on with you in the last five years."

Parties were never my thing either. But I was okay with it. It was Cooper, Gabriel, Sonya, Kendall and Riley, and Lucky and Zach and I. We all shared stories of each other, mostly me, but it was nice.

"Where are the kids?" Cooper said with a mouth full of mashed potatoes. Sonya looked out the window to the backyard and it was empty. She shot up from her seat and opened the screen door and popped her head out.

"They're not in the backyard."

I stood up quickly and entered the backyard and their toys were in the same place as before. I ran upstairs to the Zach's bedroom and the room was empty too. My heart started race. Lucky and everyone else scoured every inch of the house. I tried to think that they are playing hide and seek but Zach can never stay hiding for this long because he is scared that they forget about him. I started to hyperventilate.

"Hey, it's okay. We will find them."

Sonya said trying to calm my nerves but it wasn't working. This house isn't big so there wasn't much to look and Kendall and I were on the verge of having a heart attack.

"Mommy?"

We all turned our heads and saw Riley holding her stuffed animal. She looked like she seen a demon or a ghost. Kendall and everyone else ran over and hugged her tightly. I secretly checked with my eye for any bruises on her.

"Are you okay? Where is Zach?"

Riley looked at her mother in complete fear. She was clenching onto her stuffed bunny for dear life and couldn't make out a word. It made me think of the worse. What if she witnessed Zach getting hit by a car? Or drowned in the pool and didn't know what to do? All of these what ifs were making me go insane.

"We were playing tag and a man came and took him."

My eyes got big.

"Riley, sweetheart," I pushed Kendall aside and held Riley's hands in mine.

"What did the man look like?"

Riley took a while to answer. I have a very strong feeling who this man could be but I wanted to believe that it isn't the man I'm thinking of. Riley pointed at Cooper and mine and Lucky's heart sank. No, it can't be. There is no way he could've done this. Jason is in prison. My mind couldn't process anything. I put Jason and the past behind me when Zach was born and got my life back on track. I made sure to never look back and move forward. But somehow I can't move forward, the past is not letting me. The thought of Jason hurting my son physically makes me sick. My heart once filled with sadness is now filled with rage.

Kendall knew I was going to scream and took Riley upstairs and the minute door shut, I screamed. All the rage in my heart is set free and all I could think about why my son was taken by a man who caused me and my family so much suffering. Lucky was more distraught that he knocked over a lamp.

"Cooper, I don't care if he is family, I want him dead."

Lucky gritted getting close to Cooper's face. Cooper stammered shaking his head. He was in total disbelief.

"Okay we need to call the police."

I was already on the phone with them and from what they told me, Jason escaped from prison after some kind of riot he organized. It was a five year plan and he wanted it to be exactly on my birthday. Suddenly, I remembered the last time I saw Jason. The way he touched my stomach. His face was glowing. The day Zach was born, that horrible image appeared. I feared that the door burst open and Jason was dressed as a doctor or a nurse. I was so paranoid and didn't let Zach out of my sight for the first few months. I didn't even bring him outside. I always knew he would break out of the prison, the man is criminally insane but also smart when it comes with breaking the laws of physics. I predicted this would happen.

That man is an evil genius.

"Why would Jason do this?"

I almost wanted to slap Cooper in the face for saying that. Why would Jason do this? The answer is right there in front of you.

"You're seriously asking why? I'll tell you why, revenge! He wants revenge because I sent him away! Now he's going to take out all his anger on my son! I should've known he pull something like this, it was all over his face."

"Charmion."

Gabriel said quickly shaking his head. Lucky's eyebrows furrowed and looked at the both of us. Gabriel and I agreed to never mention the last encounter I had with Jason before he got sent away. It would have created more problems. I carried that secret for five years and surprisingly, it feels good to get it off my chest.

"You would've done something that would've cost you your life."

Lucky scoffed shaking his head.

"So you lie to me instead?"

Lucky had disappointment written all over his face. Somehow that was worse than him being angry. My chest was hurting.

"Well, I thought it be best if you didn't know." I said.

"The fact that you knew this would happen and did absolutely nothing, scares me. You didn't tell me, and you, you didn't even tell me and you were supposed to be the parent." Lucky lashed out at Gabriel. Gabriel looked down shamefully.

"How can I trust you with anything at this point?"

"You don't." I whispered.

His stare was burning a hole on the side of my face. Everyone was witnessing this and I couldn't help but cry. I thought I was doing what was best for everyone in the long run. The last five years were amazing and if I said something we'd live our lives in fear and I didn't want that for Zach. Now there's a strain between me and Lucky. I don't know what to think. I thought my son would never go through what

I went through. He is only five years old. He shouldn't be scared and be traumatized. I was zoning out and didn't even realize my name was called and a hand waving in my face. This is every mother's worst nightmare.

I felt vibration on my hip.

"Hello, Charmion."

Motherfucker.

CHAPTER 27

❖

Rage. The only emotion I feel right now, when I heard his voice. Just full on pissed off and ready to pounce. Everything from five years ago is all coming back from one phone call. No mother should ever have to go through this.

"Zach is such a cute kid. Honestly, he looks just like you. I'm so happy I got to meet him. I told you I would."

He slowed down his words and I know damn well he has that grin he did five years ago when he was eyeing my stomach behind the cell door.

"I will kill you." I blurted out. Everyone's head turned.

Jason chuckled.

"You shouldn't use those words when you are on speaker with your son in the room."

"Put him on the phone." I quickly said.

"You think I would lay a hand on him?"

He gasped.

"Fucking hell, Jason! Put my son on the phone!"

The line got silent. I exhaled deeply tapping my foot rapidly. Lucky walked over quickly and raised their eyebrows. The line was still silent.

"The fuck is going on?"

Lucky whispered.

I heard rustling in the background and I hushed him and turned away. I heard Lucky scoff.

"Mommy?"

I broke down when I heard the fear and panic in his voice. All I wanted was jump through the phone and give a hug and kiss.

"I want to go home."

All of a sudden, the phone was snatched out of my hands.

"Zach, hey, buddy, everything is going to be okay. Mommy and I will bring you home. Remember what I told you what to do when you see a stranger?"

"Never look them in the eye and kick them in leg and run away."

With every word he said, he stuttered. My poor baby is terrified and he can't do anything about it.

"Don't think he should kick a stranger with a loaded weapon." Jason said in the background.

I heard loaded weapon and lost control of my legs. There's a lot of that today. My son is in the same room with a criminal that has a loaded gun. How can this be happening? My entire body is shaking and I couldn't breathe.

"We love to stay in chat but we have to get back to our playdate."

The line went dead. The whole time my body was in shock, I was paralyzed from the head down. I cried hysterically on the ground. Lucky held me as I sobbed. He cried with me. What possessed this man to take my child? What was going through that criminals mind? You would think he would have some sanity and give up after all these years but the sad truth, he will never stop until he gets what he wants. Regardless of the fact that he raised me, he still did not have a heart. Even though he was a total sweetheart when I was a baby. I was trying to move on with my life after Jason was sent away. I never thought I'd hear that name ever again.

My past is back to haunt me.

I paced back and forth in the police station, my mind jumping from one thought to another. Lucky and Gabriel were practically screaming at the officers.

"Both of you need to calm down. We are doing the best we can to find your son."

"You are not doing a good job!"

Lucky exclaimed.

"We are trying our best." The officer kept repeating that line that only made us more upset.

As I bit my nails in the corner, I got a text from an unknown number. My heart sped up when I saw a picture of Zach in the corner being held at gun point, he was holding his teddy bear. Tears stained his face. My knees almost buckled. Why is this happening right now? Am I dreaming? Is this a nightmare? Why can't it be a nightmare? I entered the hallway. My eyes constantly watching the door.

Where are you?

I typed.

The wait was killing me. My legs were shaky and my mind was racing. What if it's too late? What if he already did the worst? What if he raped a poor innocent person in front of him? All these goddamn scenarios I am thinking about all end the same, someone gets hurt and my son witnessed it all. I'm still stuck on why he took my sweet boy, what was the motive? What are you trying to achieve? Five minutes later I got an address. An address that I swore to never go back to.

Fuck.

"You're not thinking about going. Please tell me you're not."

Kendall exclaimed as she watched me pace the room.

"What about Lucky? Are you going to tell him or will I have to lie for you?"

Took me awhile to answer that. I can't tell Lucky or Gabriel or Cooper or Sonya. It's bad enough Lucky doesn't trust me, me telling him will only put more strain in our relationship. I feel like it should be me to face Jason. He is only targeting me. None of them should know because I want to be the one to get my son back.

"You know, that's a slap in the face to him."

I looked at her in confusion.

"I feel like you're being selfish. Zach is his kid too. And the fact that you are willing to go and not tell the father, only makes things worse, Charmion. You can't keep things from him, he's your husband."

My heart sped up. That word scares me for some reason. I sighed deeply with a hand going through my hair. Jason gave me the address of where he is. I have to go. If we get the cops involved he'll run again and we'll never know where he is going to go. I can't take that chance. I have strike now before it is too late.

"Look, just hold down the fort until I get back." I said holding her hands.

"Well, what if you don't come back?"

170

Her voice cracked, she turned away from me. I get her frustration. It's hard on both of us. We just saw each other after five years and now it's like we're saying goodbye again. As cheesy as that sounds. I gave her a tight hug, she cried in my shoulder.

"If anything happens, just know I'll help take care of Zach."

"Nothing will happen. I am going to bring my son back home and everything will be right again."

My eyes roamed the stairs. I knew if I was going to confront Jason I need to fight fire with fire. And that fire is locked up in a closet.

CHAPTER 28

❖

I stared at the pistol sitting there. It wasn't the first time I loaded a gun, I seen Gabriel do it. He use to go hunting. Though a hunter rifle doesn't seem the right object to bring. It's tempting, but no. I knew exactly where Jason was heading next. It was the place where it started. I wasn't prepared for what was in store for me last time I confronted Jason here.

Now I am.

One half of the house had a gaping hole and the other half was slowly turning older and moldier. It wasn't as bad like it was five years ago. Least it still looked like a house then. Knowing Jason is erratic and does things without thinking first, I couldn't step foot in that house empty handed. I took no hesitation barging through that door. Or what's left of it. It fell over before I got the chance to kick it down. Some house. I don't even want to begin to explain how this house looks.

Shit.

I'll just say that. It looked the same as when I was taken and when I came back. Of course he'd want to bring my son to the house where I technically grew up in. I cautiously walked down the dimmed hallway. Why does it look like I'm in one of those Saw movies? All we need is the doll riding in and a recorder taped on it that says play me. My heart began to race as I entered every room trying to find Zach and Jason.

They weren't here.

How can they not be here?

I sighed deeply sliding down the wall. I was startled to hear a landline. The scary part, there was never a house phone in this house to begin with. Checked the kitchen and saw nothing. I entered the living room and the phone sat on the floor. I hovered over the phone till I had the balls to quickly grab it and speak.

"Hello?"

"You're stupid if you think I ever go back there."

Jason laughed on the other end.

The phone should've broke due to my hand squeezing it so tight. He was mocking me with his laugh. Son of a bitch tricked me.

"You still haven't figured it out?"

"What haven't I figured out, Jason?" I mumbled with my hand running through my hair.

"I'm going to rot in a cell for the rest of my life! Know whose fault that is?"

Do I even need to ask?

"All I wanted was to be with my daughter and grandson! You left me out to dry!"

After all this time, he still thinks I'm his daughter?

"Even if the court changed their minds and let you live with Cooper, Lucky and I wouldn't be okay with you being near our kid."

He laughed.

"None of us were gonna let you walk free, Jason! You raped and killed my mom!"

I was screaming at this point. I haven't thought of Mrs. K in years and this isn't the way I want to be thinking about her, being on the phone with her killer. This conversation isn't making any sense. Then again, Jason never made sense. He always talks in rhymes and riddles like an actual psychopath.

"Just tell me where you are. My son shouldn't be paying for your mistakes."

"My mistakes?"

He exclaimed. I heard Zach whimper. My heart sped up when I heard a gun cocked.

"My fucking mistakes, huh? I'm sure shooting Zach won't be a mistake."

The clicking and the loud shrieks were louder than my heart beat.

"Jason no! Please!" I begged.

"We'll be at a place that you know very much. It's the same place where Sonya and I made love. You have one hour or Zach will have one good working arm."

Then the line went dead.

I screamed chucking the phone to the wall and I sobbed. Why are you targeting a little boy? What has my son done to deserve this? For gods sake he is only five! He shouldn't be terrified and have PSTD at such a young age. My baby shouldn't be punished for my past. I can't even begin to think about how he is feeling right now. Everything hurts. In the mist of my crying, my sadness quickly turned into anger. Not only Jason took my son but he also took apart of me, apart of Lucky. And for that, I am determined to put a bullet through his chest.

Charmion is no where to be found and we haven't gotten news on where Jason is. I couldn't take the wait anymore. I

174

want my son back. Why haven't they sent a search party yet? Or a freaking Amber Alert? I needed to get some fresh air. I noticed that Charmion was not in the station with us. We didn't even hear or see her leave. I asked everyone where she could've gone and one of the officers said she practically ran out of the station. Why did she leave without saying anything? We returned to the house but Charmion wasn't there either. I started to get really worried.

"Any luck?" Cooper asked me. I shook my head with a sigh. Charmion was no where to be found.

"Is anyone not seeing the pattern here or is just me?" Gabriel said sarcastically. I rolled my eyes.

"Lose the damn attitude. I am more pissed off and more worried as you."

I barked.

"And I'm not? She's my daughter."

Cooper shot up with a glare.

"In Jason's eyes, you're not. And you couldn't do the simplest task and watch our grandson!"

The two men lunged at each other. I used all my strengths to pull them off each other but their weight was too much for me. I managed to squeeze myself in between their chest separate them by an inch.

"Enough!"

Sonya and Kendall yelled.

"None of this fighting is going to solve anything."

"Then what can?" Gabriel and Cooper said simultaneously Silent.

"Wherever Charmion is, I am sure she is okay."

Sonya said.

I noticed Kendall was looking away from the rest of us. I walked over to her, studying her face carefully. I can tell when someone is hiding a secret. Kendall looked up at me nervously.

"Do you know where Charmion is?"

She was going to speak until Gabriel came down with panic written all over his face, sweating like an animal. I didn't even notice he left the room.

"My gun, it's gone." He said out of breath.

"What do you mean gone?"

Cooper nervously said.

"It was locked up in a safe in the closet. I just checked and it wasn't there."

"Charmion took it."

Kendall finally spoke. We all turned our heads to her. She was crossing her arms with a panic expression.

"What do you mean Charmion took it?"

Sonya stuttered.

"Charmion got a text at the police station. It was from Jason. It was a picture of Zach in a corner being held at gunpoint."

My knees buckled, my body was going into shock. Cooper and Sonya ran to my aid and held me back up. I felt like I was going to spontaneously combust. I kept mumbling my son, why my son under my breath. I wanted to cry but my body wouldn't allow it.

"How did she figure the code to the safe?" Sonya said calmly rubbing my back but I couldn't feel it. That's when Gabriel got quiet. He was looking down at his feet shamefully. He sighed.

"When you were younger, I showed you kids the safe."

176

"I don't remember that." I finally spoke, trying to get back my balance.

"No, you don't. You were too scared to be in a room with a gun so you left. But Charmion stayed. She watched me put in the combination and I showed her how to load it. I didn't think she'd remember let alone steal it."

"So she's going to kill Jason."

Cooper gasped.

"We don't know that."

Sonya said.

"She knew we would've gone to the police. She's going to do what she should've done five years ago. And that is, put a bullet in him."

Kendall's voice cracked.

"She's going to risk everything." I whispered.

I'm still trying wrap my head around this whole thing. A criminal kidnapped my pride and joy, my girlfriend goes on a rampage, and I am out raged. Why didn't she say anything to me? I thought we were supposed to be a team? God, I am so angry with her. She kept a secret from me for five years and Gabriel knew and didn't bother to tell me. Would things be different if she told me? Would we live our lives in fear? Would we be safe?

It should have been me who stole Gabriels gun from the safe and trying to find Jason. I want to be the one to be a bullet in him; make him suffer. He is willing to be put on the death row but he will not face the death row because I will put him on my own version of the death row.

But I'm not that kind of man.

CHAPTER 29

❖

Everything is falling into this moment right now. I have a chance to get back what I lost. My life was ripped away from me at the age of 2, I got it back at 18. Now, at the age of 23, it was taken away again along with my child. I won't sit there and wait for someone to do something. I need to do this on my own and I don't care what happens along the way. I'm willing to risk everything to get back what's mine, everything.

I was holding the gun firmly in my hands as I approached the building. It still looked the same five years ago. It gave me this pitiful, bitter feeling in the pit of my stomach. My gut was screaming run away but my legs said no. My only thought is Zach. Bringing him home is my sweet victory, my prize. I don't ever want my son to be afraid and alone for as long as he lives after this. That is a promise. I can't think about the bad stuff. I need to keep hope alive that he will be okay and unharmed.

"Jason?"

The smell of dead animals and mold burnt my eyes. The smell was so bad that it made stop walking and I started puking in the corner. My own vomit made the smell less gross. All I want is to grab Zach and get the hell out of here and maybe blow up this building with Jason still inside. My eyes landed to the room beside the fire escape. I remember that day like it was yesterday. I can hear the echos of the screams. I still have nightmares of that night, it will forever haunt me. I feel the tightness in my chest, heart racing like my heart was going to explode, my mind a blur as well as my vision. I'm so overwhelmed, I feel myself about to faint, till I was caught. I immediately picked myself up and went for the gun but I was shoved to the wall, hard.

"Wouldn't do that, if I were you." Jason said in my ear.

His voice sent shivers down my spine and heart rate increased ten times. Age has been kind to him. He had dark circles on his eyes, grey hair on his face and head, pale skin. Dear god he's wearing the same clothes from that night too.

"He's sleeping."

My eyes practically popped out of my skull and tried to move my legs but his weight was dropping on me and made it impossible to breathe.

"Where is my son?"

It amazed me that I was able to make out words with this huge bolder on me.

"I told you, he's sleeping." He said.

"Where?"

I screamed and my head was banged on the wall and my body fell. I gasped for air. My lungs hurt as well as my bleeding head. I seriously couldn't breathe.

"Took me a long time to get him to bed and now that you yelled," suddenly I was kicked in my ribcage. I groaned in agony.

"He's gonna get grumpy. You know how babies gets when they are woken up from their nap."

"Where is he? Where is my son, Jason?"

I panted deeply, I manage to get back on my feet. Jason laughed.

"Kid cries every minute." Jason chuckled.

"That's because some stranger decided to take him and torture him all because he didn't get his way and cried like a little bitch."

I don't know what happened after that, I got a very large blow to the head and everything just went black.

My eyes slowly fluttered open and all I feel is the cold. There was no light, I couldn't see a damn thing. I heard nothing but a leaky pipe. I yelp when there was a loud crash and big, bright lights turned on that burned my eyes. Jesus, I thought. As my eyes were adjusting, I saw not one, but two figures hanging from the ceiling. My first thought was he killed two innocent people, but as I looked closer, I screamed in terror. What hanged was the corps of Mrs. K, the woman who raised me, was hanging by the neck and the person next to her was my pride and joy. Zach was dangling from his little hands. I've never been this terrified in my life. Two people I care deeply about are being stung up like piñata's. I began to sob hysterically running towards them as if I could save them. The chance of possibly breaking my arm from pulling on the chains is high.

"What did you do to my son!"

He wasn't moving. I tired to run towards to him but I was chained to the ground. I pulled and pulled on the chain. The more I pulled, the louder I screamed. I don't care if I have to break my hand or my arm to get free, I need to get my son down. I went to stand up but a bullet went past my face, cutting my cheek in the process.

I gasped.

"Maybe you should think about to say next."

Jason casually leaned against the wall, spinning the pistol by hooking his finger in the trigger. The metal chair scraping the floor was more satisfying than the sound of a gun shot still ringing in my ears.

"I have the upper hand, Charmion. What are you going to do? I didn't want to do that but you forced my hand. I hate to see my daughter in so much pain."

Half my face was dripping in blood and it wouldn't stop bleeding, it hurt like a bitch. Jason's eyes landed on the gash on the side of my face and pouted.

"I am not your daughter."

I huff and puff in-between my words. I was still winded from the kick to my ribs. The pout slowly turned into rage. A chair was thrown across the room, he screamed and the next thing I heard, a crack on my ankle. I screamed a blood curling scream. My foot was completely shattered and I can feel the pieces getting out of place. My heart rate was through the roof as well as my anxiety. I was hyperventilating.

"I could kill your son right here, right now!"

That one sentence gave me hope, hope that his little heart is still beating and is being quiet and not moving because he's scared and wants to go home. As wrong as that sentence was, it gave me just a little bit of strength to hop on my other good foot. I gotta keep that strength, for the both of us.

"Although," he bent down as he looked up at Zach.

"Maybe he is dead."

Jason is trying to get inside my head and make me believe Zach is dead when really he's perfectly fine. That was his plan. I will not fall for his games. But how can I not? This is my son. The only person who matters most to me aside from his father and my family. He's the greatest thing that's ever happened to me. If I lost him, I'd never be the same ever again. He is toying with my mother instincts and I can't stand it.

Jason laughed.

"He really was sleeping. While his back was turned from the door, I had the knife in my hands. I slowly but quietly, jammed it in his back. You know, the one place where a knife shouldn't go in. The spinal cord? Yeah, you know that. So, after that, he screamed but I grabbed a cloth to shut him up and whispered,"

Jason was the master of manipulation. He can easily get you to believe into something that you know it isn't true. The fact that he described it in very gruesome detail, I was stunned, my body shut down. Everything after that, I didn't pay attention to anything else other than hearing my whole world crash in front of my very eyes. Tears just wouldn't stop coming. I don't think there's a feeling that I could use to express how much emotion I have in me. The pain in my cheek and foot seemed to vanish and the only pain I really feel is my heart physically shattering. He could be lying. He's probably saying that to just torture me and toy with me but I looked at him and saw blood on his shoes and it got me. I didn't even listen to him after that.

That one bit of strength I had, suddenly became a lot. I head butt him right in the face regardless of the huge cut on my face and the amount pain my body is in. Jason screamed pulling out his gun and placed it on my forehead. At that moment, I wasn't afraid of death. In fact, I was ready. I didn't care what would happen if I did die right now. Cooper and Sonya were the least of my worries, as well as Lucky and Gabriel and Kendall. Call me selfish but they don't matter to me right now. It isn't the first time a gun was pointed at my face. It's been a long time but I'm not afraid nor flinching. Jason looked at me confused.

"I have never begged for my life and I am not going to start now. You took everything from me, so why don't you do what you always wanted to and shoot me."

It's like what more can happen? What more can you do to hurt me? You already done the most brutal, most revolting thing by stringing up my dead mother and killed my son. I could careless if I live or die. Jason saw that and lowered his gun.

"I didn't take anything from you, Charmion."

"Bullshit!"

I shouted. Jason was startled.

"You took my mother's life and now my son's life! What did my son do to deserve this? Nothing! He did absolutely nothing!"

My heart was so heavy and full of grief that I couldn't control what was coming out of my mouth. I'm hurt. I lost my son. There is sadness but there is also anger. I can't look at this man without wanting to put a bullet in him. This is how my son died, in the hands of a rapist and murderer and he didn't even live to start middle school or high school. He didn't live to have his first girlfriend, get married or have children of his own, that was all taken away from him and that tears me apart. I don't care if I get sent prison, I want this man dead. He does not deserve to rot in a cell, he doesn't even deserves to be buried 6 feet underground. How low of a human being do you have to be to kidnap a person's kid and dig up a corps? The look Jason had in his eyes were pure fear. I showed no remorse, all I see is red and I'm out for revenge. I have nothing left to lose at this point.

"I'm going to kill you."

He scoffed shaking his head.

Then the unthinkable happened. He removed the chains. My arms were free and he stood on his two feet and kicked over his pistol. It's like he wants to die. He doesn't feel the need to be alive because if he did stay alive, he'd be sent back to jail or get the death penalty(doubtful).

"I'd like to see you try."

Fine.

As fast as I could with my good foot, I grabbed the pistol and right as I was about to pull the trigger, a bullet went pass Zach's feet, just barely touching him, he screamed in fear. I fell to my knees.

He's alive.

Dear god he is alive!

A wash of relief and happiness took over me. I was ready to die, I didn't care if it be gruesome. The man described in grave detail about the idea of killing Zach and my emotions were flying over the place. I'm a mother, I'd do anything to protect him but at that moment, I thought I failed him.

"You'd really think I'd kill a kid?" Jason laughing hysterically made me growl. I tried moving my damaged body but my broken foot stopped me. I cursed under my breath. Jason laughed and kicked me. I feel so helpless with only one working foot. If I even dare put pressure on it, I'm on the ground.

"Mommy!"

Zach cried.

I was grabbed by the throat and my breathing suddenly came to a halt. I gasped trying to push him off but his grip was getting tighter. I was fading fast. I had to do something. My legs were dangling and I had just enough strength to kick him between his legs. His hand loosened and my body went down as well his. He held his groin and groaned in pain. I crawled to the wall where the rope was and grabbed it. I whimpered pulling myself up with the rope. I turned to Jason who was starting to get back up and I quickened my pace. Suddenly I was tackled to the ground and the rope flew out of my hands. Large hands went to my neck again and I couldn't breathe again.

"It doesn't have to be this way. We can still be together. I kill you, I get the death penalty and we'll see each other again. Don't you worry." His sinister grin would be the last thing I see before I die right here.

My vision was starting to fade. My lungs were slowly losing strength. When it was about to be lights out, I heard a gunshot. My neck was free and finally felt air getting back into my system. I looked up and saw Zach holding the pistol with his eyes wide and his little hands trembling. I groaned trying to get up. Zach ran to me and hugged me. Sobbing in my chest, I managed to hug him back with my broken body.

"I'm sorry, mommy!" He sobbed.

I gently pressed my lips on his head.

"It's okay baby."

Then there was coughing. He was still alive. I took the pistol from Zach and stood on my good foot with every fiber in my body and limped my way towards him. I used the wall to help me. Zach somehow knew what I was going to do and turned around covering his ears. I stared blankly as Jason laid in his own blood. He was shot in the shoulder, barely missed his heart.

"Kid has good aim."

He snickered then groaned.

"They say that when you're about die, you have 7 minutes of brain activity left and you experience your entire life all over. I see myself getting my first car, first arrest at 15, holding you the day you were born."

Blood stained his teeth as he spoke.

"I love you, Charmion. Even through all this, I still love you."

He was on his knees holding his injured shoulder.

"Please. I know what I did was wrong. If I'm gonna die, I rather die in prison."

"What makes you think they'll send you back to jail?"

I said coldly.

He stuttered searching my eyes with panic and fear. I'm not going to show this man sympathy. He doesn't deserve it. This man doesn't deserve to live. People like him need to be put to death. When a baby pup is taken from its mother, the mother wolf goes after whoever took them with vengeances. She will kill whoever is in her way to get her baby back. But this is a little different. Yes, I'm the wolf and Zach is my pup, but Jason is the sheep. I am the wolf. And wolfs eat sheep.

"You tried to kill my child, and then tried to kill me. It's one thing to go after me but to go after my kid?"

"I needed you to see that I wasn't going to take no for answer."

"So you take my son and dig up my mother and hang her like a goddamn Christmas ornament?"

I screamed which made Jason stumble back.

"You targeted a little boy who had no idea who the hell you were and what my past was. He was minding his own business and you come out of no where and take him. And for what? Because we said no?"

I have a choice here. I can end all of this, right now. I could pull this trigger and not lose one bit of sleep. But I stopped and thought of Zach. I carefully made my way to him and held his hands. I smiled at him and even though he just saw his mother almost die, he smiled back.

"I don't want you to see this."

He nod his head and gave me a hug. I cried as he wrapped his arms around me. I really am grateful to have my son alive. Just hearing him cry out was enough for me to keep going. He is a strong boy.

"Call 911 then call daddy. Do you know daddy's number?"

He nod his head again and took the phone that was on the ground and ran out of the room enough for me to see him but not enough for him to see in the room. I turned my attention to Jason who was still in the same spot but on his feet this time.

"You don't have to do this."

Jason said eyeing the gun in my hand.

"You kidnapped my son, Jason. And proceeded to kill me in the process."

He sighed.

"I remember when you said your first word. It was on a Sunday and Cooper just left for work, Sonya too, and we were watching Elmo and then you said cookie. It was the cutest thing I've ever seen."

Jason laughed. I wasn't laughing or smiling, he saw that and sighed.

"How about we go for a walk?"

I can barely walk as it is because he shattered my foot. The only way I'm even standing right now is the support from the wall. He saw my foot and nearly laughed. That made me more angry. I cocked the pistol and placed it on his chest and he wasn't even surprised by it. He only stared at me with the same loving look he gave me when I went to visit him at the mental hospital five years ago.

"I'm so proud of you." Was all he said.

"I knew you'd turn out to be me. You are nothing like Cooper or Sonya. I knew the day you were born you were going to be just like me and now look at you, you're a spitting image of me!"

I allowed my body to stay still as he hugged me. My body was about give out, I feel it. My only working leg is going numb and if I pass out now, Jason will do god knows what to Zach. I have to keep myself up. Jason was laughing as I struggled to keep myself up with the wall.

"Soon enough, Zach will be just like me. I'll be his favorite grandfather."

Wrong.

"My son," I groggily slurred,

"Will never be like you."

The bullet went through his skull, his body fell onto me and I gasped loudly. His blood was sinking into my clothes and I was stunned. I laid there with a dead body on top of me. I started to think about where Zach was. I turned my head and saw him in the corner covering his ears, his back was turned which made me sigh in relief. He didn't see any of this. I couldn't get past the gaping hole on the side of his head. I kept staring at his face, my eyes were completely wide eyed, his eyes were looking right at me and his mouth was slightly open. I couldn't look away.

The one person who mainly caused so much agony on my family is laying on me dead and all I have to say is I need to take a long shower. I pulled myself together, I couldn't let my kid see me cry after what I did. I rolled the pile of trash off me and quickly pushed myself into a corner. I should be embracing my son right now, I should be telling him everything is going to be okay but I am frozen in fear and guilt. I looked at my trembling hands, that were covered in blood, his blood. My entire body was trembling. I started to cry in the corner. I can still hear the gunshot. How did we end up here? What did I just do? I heard tiny footsteps and my motherly instinct kicked in.

"Zach, stay out there! Don't come in here!"

I stuttered my words but he didn't listen. He took one look at me and nearly ran for his life. I put my hand out, signally him to stay away but he only walked closer towards me. I didn't want him to see me like this. It amazed me that the amount of blood on me, was not scaring him. It probably was but he was brave enough to get past it. What he did next blew me away; he hugged me. Then he tells me everything is going to be okay with his eyes and that was all I need. I heard the sirens. I got up as quickly and carefully as I can, Zach dashed

189

out the door but I didn't follow him. I turned around and saw Jason laying there. Leaving him here wouldn't feel right.

I grabbed his hand and my mind played a trick on me. I shook it off and proceed to drag him and myself out of the building. I left Mrs. K behind, they'll soon realize who it is once they enter. For all I know Gabriel could be outside and if he sees me dragging out his dead wife, it will crush him. I couldn't add pressure to my left foot. I searched for something I can use as a cane. I found a metal pole by the door.

As I got outside, everyone turned to me and they were almost too scared to even walk towards me. A whole bunch of snipers that were once pointing at me, were lowered. My eyes were filled with sorrow. What surprised me was that I was actually crying. Was it because I killed a person? Or that my child was taken and will be traumatized? No, I was crying because after all the shit this man put me through, I still have love for him. And it kills me. Jason put me and everyone I love through hell and I still feel something for him, it makes me sick just thinking about it. Zach was already in the arms of his father and I was content.

I grunted dragging Jason's body as I took my first steps with a broken foot. As I walked, well, limped, with the support of this metal pole, everything went slow, everyone is blurry. All I see is the flashing blue and red lights and red figures. I panted getting closer and I dropped his body at the detective's feet, my foot gave out and I stumbled back on the ground. I looked like I came out of a horror movie. I was drenched in blood, and it wasn't mine. Half of my shirt was pure red and the other half was spotless. My blue jeans that were once blue aren't even the same the color anymore.

Chuck Taylors that were once grey now had holes and blood leaking in. No one didn't move or even bother to say anything.

Cooper was on his knees with his eyes widened, Gabriel was hugging him. Lucky had the same expression, Zach in his chest crying. Lucky's eyes met mine and I broke down. I felt this huge weight of regret at this very moment. I started to regret doing all this now. We were at the police station when I got that picture and I should've told them. I thought doing this by myself would be the best but it wasn't. If anything, I lost most of everyone's trust here as well as the police. My whole body gave out. I reached for Lucky. One of the officers saw this and looked at Lucky, he was in disbelief. I needed him to come to me. Lucky handed Zach to Gabriel and pushed through the swarm of officers.

"Hold your fire!"

I'm sorry, I repeated it over and over again as he made his way towards me. It is all I can say after what I done. I can see on his face he didn't want to come anywhere near me. Lucky wanted to gag at the sight of me. I sobbed wrapping my arms around his legs. He exclaimed which made everyone jump. I was trembling under his touch. I wanted him to yell at me, tell me I'm a horrible mother, insult me. It's what I wanted him to do, but I also wanted him to just hug me. Even if I was covered in someone else's blood. After a few seconds, we were at eye level. His large hands clasped my broken, bleeding face with tears streaming down his face. Carefully, I was pulled into his arms and I heard him slightly gag. My eyes immediately landed on Cooper, he was staring at me in complete disbelief. I looked at Jason who was being putting in a body bag and sobbed. Lucky pulled away, looking very relieved. His shirt had blood on it.

Then he kissed me.

"Are you fucking insane?"

Gabriel screamed.

I was transported to the hospital to get my foot checked out and I assumed get questioned. As I was getting screamed at, I was zoning out. I stayed in Lucky's arms. He finally got past the blood and didn't let me go. I can still see Jason's face being deformed by the bullet. I close my eyes and I see him. Is this a dream? Did this really happen? I don't know where I am or how I got into this mess. I know how, the day I was born.

"Charmion!"

"What?"

I snapped.

Gabriel swallowed a lump in his throat as I got closer to him. Everyone seemed to be doing that in the past few hours. This hospital room isn't the big enough for the six of us. It certainly isn't big enough for this argument. Cooper hasn't said a word since we got to the hospital. The man was staring blankly out the window thinking god knows what.

"Charmion, why don't you get some rest."

Sonya stuttered from across the room. I forgot to mention no one hasn't even dared to get close to me because I was covered in human blood and was not allowed to get into a shower just yet. Though, I could shower but my body won't let me.

"Don't you think I would if I could!"

192

It wasn't fair to Sonya that I was lashing out at her but I am so angry that I am no longer the same sweet, caring Charmion. That girl was long gone the day she found out the truth.

"Charmion, stop, we need to be more sincere to Cooper."

Something with that sentence just made my blood boil. More sincere? Who would feel sorry for what happened tonight? No one, so why should I be more sincere to Cooper? Better yet, why the hell is it Cooper? Shouldn't it be me? I looked at Gabriel in complete disgust.

"Are you fucking insane?"

I mocked.

Gabriel sighed. My face has not changed since the police came. It's still blank and lifeless.

"You want me to be more sincere? Are you joking? None of you had the balls to do what I just did tonight! I'll be more sincere when pigs fly!"

Veins popped out of my neck as I yelled. Nothing was holding me back. What I saw tonight will forever be glued to my brain until the day I die. When I sleep at night, this will pop up.

"You should be more sincere to me. I saw things tonight that will traumatize me for the rest of my life."

Mrs. K came into my mind. The way she was being hanged. I thought I seen scarier things but that by far made it to the top of the list.

"You want to know what was the most scariest thing I saw tonight? Seeing my mother being hanged by the throat in the ceiling."

The look on Gabriel's face made me burst into tears. Everyone's jaw drop. I close my eyes and I still see her. She

193

looked the exactly the same as she did five years in that hospital bed. I can never unsee that. I started trembling again.

"He tried to hurt my son. He intentionally tried to hurt my son." I mumbled.

"But he didn't. You got your son back. Look, he's fine. You need to be there for him after what happened."

Sonya said with a nervous smile.

"All right, they won't say it so I will." Cooper said with that same blanket stare.

"Oh he speaks." I faked a smile then rolled my eyes.

Cooper scoffed.

"You're scaring everyone. Quit being a little bitch and do us all a favor, get your ass in the shower and wash off my brothers blood."

"See, you don't get to do that. You don't get to come into my life and tell me what to do. You lost that privilege years ago. You weren't there for me. Jason was."

"And yet you killed him!" Cooper got into my face, his veins were popping out of his neck. Made me want to laugh.

"Because he kidnapped my son and tried to kill me in the process. He was a danger to society. I did what I had to do to protect my son and myself and everyone else. Don't I get a Thank you at least? You want to call me a bitch, you want to be angry at me, so be it, but you can't seriously be *that* angry."

"Jason was the only family I had left! Sure, he was locked up but he still was alive and breathing! My mother and father died when I was younger and now I have no one!"

Why did this feel so familiar? My chest was getting so heavy and I could feel tears form yet again. It made me remember that fight Lucky and I had when he came to see me after so long. It always starts with I have no one or somewhere around those lines. No one seems realize that I'm right here. No one seems to appreciate me or what I did. If I didn't do what I did, me and Zach be in body bags.

"You could've just shot him in the leg and he still go back to prison and be alive!"

"That would not matter! They could lock him in maximum security and he'd still find a way to escape. The man deserved to die."

"For god sakes he is my brother!" He screamed in my face. I can smells the cigarettes.

"The minute he raped and killed Mrs. K, he was no longer your brother!"

Cooper groaned in frustration putting a hand on his face. His eyes landed to Zach who managed to sleep after what happened. The amount of screaming couldn't wake him up. Thankfully he is a heavy sleeper.

"Look at your son," he pointed at him.

"You did this to him. Because of you, he is going to have PTSD. Because of you, he's going to be in therapy for the rest of his life. You let this happened and for that, that makes you a terrible mother!"

It was almost comical to me hearing Cooper speak complete bullshit. Have I lost my mind? I have not yet. Gabriel couldn't take any of this anymore. He carefully picked up sleeping Zach and left the room. I'm out here looking like the bad guy. What could I have done? Play possum? I wasn't going to let that man hurt anyone else. Dead or alive, I did what I had to do.

"You are supposed to set an example for him not scar him for life! You don't get to call yourself a mother when you pull a stunt like that! Zach is better off in foster care!"

"Okay, enough! Zach is my son too!"

Lucky glared at Cooper.

"Don't you think this hard on me as well? Surely you understand the feeling of having your child get taken away? Can't you just give her the benefit of the doubt?"

"No, he doesn't."

I barked.

"You don't know the feeling, you never once did. Even when child services took me. Maybe you did but at least someone fought to get me back. Hell, your brother hunted me down and found me a day later. You wanna blame for being a bad mother? Fine I blame you. You were there but you never really were. You weren't the one I walked to, he was. He spent more time with me than you. You didn't say anything because you thought you weren't capable of raising a child and yet a fucking ex convict provided more for me than you ever did in your entire life."

"Instead of stepping up and being a fucking man, you ran away and looked for happiness over and over again. You walked out on the best thing that could've happened to you!"

I've been called a lot things. I've been called a bitch, asshole, worthless, garbage, a whore, and amongst other things. I can take an insult to the face without crying. But I will not, I repeat not, take being called a bad mother. There's so much I can take but I will not take that. Especially from a man who is my fleshing blood.

"Not only you left your child but you also left your wife too. You let her to get raped and tortured for years courtesy of your own brother. And you did nothing about it. That means, you're a piece of shit."

I spat. I wanted to actually spit in his face because that's how pissed off I am.

"That is enough, Charmion. Don't talk to your father like that." Sonya said with a glare. I started laughing.

"He's not my dad! And you're not my mother. Gabriel will always be my father and Mrs. K will always be my mother. They may not be my blood but they raised me to this day. Hell, least when my boyfriend left, he came back for me."

"Charmion, stop that right now." Lucky said getting in between the three of us. I really don't care about what is coming out of my mouth. I am being honest. And if you can't handle the truth, then there's the door. Sonya gasped and cried into Cooper's chest. Cooper shook his head at me with disappointed written all over his face.

"You could've done something about it, you did this to yourselves. The point is your beloved husband, is a deadbeat father and a worthless piece of-"

Then a hand collided with my face. I hissed in pain at the cut on my face that was patched up. My cheek started bleeding again.

"You son of a bitch!"

Lucky shoved Cooper to the wall about to punch him but I beat him to it. This whole time, I've been experiencing anger, sadness, regret, guilt, and every other emotion there is. The minute his hand made contact with me, something broke inside me. I don't know what happened after that. Cooper fell to the ground holding his jaw. He was in disbelief but not because I punched him. And the thing is, I refused to stop there. I was a wild animal. No one can tame me or hold me back from whatever was taking over me. I lunged at him and threw punch after punch till I was ripped off of him. I kicked and screamed and tried to break free. I wanted to go off on him. You're just adding more fuel to the fire. I had so much adrenaline, so much spunk. I have reached my breaking point, I knew it was going to happen sooner or later. I just didn't think it be now.

"Should've shot you in that car when I had the chance!"

This time I spat at his face.

I hit my own daughter. And she hit me back. Like it was nothing. I was in a total daze. I did something I promised I'd never do if I had a child. I broke that promise and now I'm disgusted with myself. I don't deserve to call myself a man after this. How can I do that? I tried not to be in that category of scums who hit their kid and now I'm at the top of the list.

I can hear Jason beyond the grave laughing and grinning at me saying; you'll never be half the father I was. It angers me that I'm thinking about Jason poking fun of me. Like I didn't do my part. I did do my part. Only, it wasn't enough. A wave of regret hit me, not saying anything about the confrontation between Jason and I, a part of me wishes that I wasn't so afraid to even hold my kid. I wish I didn't think I was going to drop her or feed her the wrong food or crush her if she was sleeping in my bed. Most importantly, I wish I never laid my hands on her.

"How's the jaw?" Gabriel said walking into the room.

I groaned in agony.

Gabriel chuckled handing me an ice pack.

"I never should've laid my hands on her. I'm a terrible person."

"Well, most people would agree. I'm sure Lucky does. I wouldn't recommend paying him a visit just yet."

Gabriel said with a chuckle.

"Jason was a psychopath and may have not known the difference between right and wrong, and doesn't care about others or society, but he'd never hit a kid. That I'm sure of."

"Yeah, one good trait that he had. I'm sure that's something to be proud of."

I wasn't having it with Gabriel's snarky remarks. It's been like that since the hospital but I don't blame him for being that way. I sighed.

"Look, I'm angry with you big time and I'd like to punch you too but I managed to control my anger pretty well since this whole thing. Well, maybe a little. Point is, you have a lot to say. That slap was just the introduction."

Gabriel is right. I do have a lot to say. It's been pepped up in me for years and years and now that Jason is dead, I can let that unleash. I won't feel one bit of shame and it'll feel so good to let it all out. But that punch said a lot too.

I couldn't get her voice out of my head. A lot of things were said today and it killed me. I forced myself not cry the entire time. My heart was in so much pain when I saw Sonya crying. She ran out of the room. I told myself that this was the anger talking, this isn't Charmion talking. Emotions were high and she didn't mean anything she said. She's seen so much tonight and I made things worse by slapping her.

He's not my dad!

It was like a ringing in my ear. That's all I heard in my head. It kept playing over and over again like a record. I'll never step up as her father. I'll always just be uncle Cooper.

I cried in my hands.

CHAPTER 30

Our minds are the most powerful tool we humans have. We have memories we think about almost everyday. Some of us want to find joy and look back on the good days, some want relive the pain of their past. We have memories that we wish we didn't look back on, if we see or hear the slightest trigger it comes up. The only memory I truly will forever love and forever look back on is the birth of my son. Seeing him for the first time, his little hands and feet. He looked identical to Lucky. He had the same brown hair, brown eyes, and that perfect smile. It was the happiest day of my life. Out of all the wonderful memories we have, there are also ones we are ashamed of and wish to never even think about for as long as we live. I have several.

It pains me that this is what it had to come to. Speaking to the police about a man who was killed and now explaining why he is dead, and how much he has done to not just me, but my family and my boyfriend. This isn't how I wanted my life to turn out. I have to live with the fact I killed a human being and don't know if I should be prosecuted or go home a free woman.

"Well, from what you told us, we looked into Jason's and your record and we found out that when you were a little a girl, he did change your name so child services wouldn't find you."

What?

"The consent form we have in file was signed by your foster father, Gabriel Klein. He changed your name twice. Before you were taken from child services and after. Your original name is Charmion Monica Andrews Mendez. We believe Jason somehow found where Mr. Klein worked and forged his signature and changed your name a day before you started living with the Klein's. We didn't think much of it because Mr. Klein's signature was on paper."

I'm beyond shocked. How can this be right? My name was changed twice and no one knew except Jason. Hell, the fucking government didn't even know. My whole life I thought my name was Charmion Smith but I was wrong, so wrong. It's just more life changing news after another. How much more can I take?

"Stop."

I muttered with both hands on my head. I can't take this anymore.

"When you were 1 years old you were living with a completely different foster home. One day, you were in the yard and you saw Jason and you ran to him. You were missing for a year until you were found in the same house you were originally living in when you were born."

My body felt like it was going to spontaneously combust. A person can take so much until they break and that's what happened to me. My entire self could not handle any more news. I completely lost control of my senses. I lost control of my emotions, my mind, my words, my legs, my arms. I screamed and screamed till I no longer can scream and my throat was on fire. Soon enough, nurses came in strapping me to the bed. I wasn't in charge of my body, I couldn't find the right words to say stop I'm fine.

There has to be an explanation on why this happened. Why did this all happen to me? Why can't I get a break? Here I thought I'd get closure with Jason dead but instead it only made things worse. I'm finding out things that I wished I never knew. If things would've just turned out normal, I wouldn't be in this mess. If Cooper would've been the father I needed, none of this would've happened. If Gabriel, minded his own business, my life could've been fucking normal. But nothing was ever normal. The minute Cooper backed out on being a father, my life already went to shit. I was fed lies about my parents, I was forced to live in an environment that was not healthy for a baby, I was drugged! And they knew that. They knew I shouldn't be living like that and they continued to let me live there. This whole thing started because of jealousy. The chaos of what my life is, began with jealousy. On and off for years, people fought for me and I just sat there staring at them while they yanked my little arms screaming; no, she is mine.

Why fight over someone? Why lie and claim to be that child's parent? Why make my life a living hell even after you're gone? This is what Jason wanted. He wanted me to live my life with that constant fear that things will never be the same. And he proved that today. Because of him, things will never be the same.

I want this to be over.

CHAPTER 31

❖

I've been thinking about Mrs. K lately. If she was here right now she would hold me and tell me everything is going to be okay. I want someone to tell me that everything is going to be okay. My family is too scared to even approach me, they think I'm glass and could break any second now. That, and I killed a man. My son is terrified of me. I haven't seen him in three days let alone his father. They're probably better off without me. Cooper was right. I am a terrible mother. I don't deserve to keep my kid. Lucky be a better parent than me. I sat in my bed and cried in my knees. I couldn't stop crying. I ruined everything for myself. If I just watched my kid then he wouldn't have been taken and no one would've gotten hurt. But someone did get hurt. And it was all because of me. I can't get what I said to Cooper and Sonya out of my head. It slipped out, I couldn't control what I was saying. But it was the truth. I did not lie. It was everything I've been holding in for years.

When I found out the truth, it tore me apart and I had a lot of resentment towards Cooper and Gabriel and Sonya. I brushed it off to the side like it was nothing but deep down, I still hated them for lying to me.

"Shit."

I muttered.

I'm sure Cooper has a lot to say with that slap. I can see it in his eyes that that slap wasn't the only thing he wanted to let out. He's just lucky it was a few weak punches, other than that I would've kept going with more power till you couldn't recognize his face. But I'm not that kind of person.

I finally had the courage to move around my room even though my left foot was in a boot. I was tired of being in bed all day and being a slug. I feel more content than I usually am. Everyone seems to finally realize to leave me the heck alone and just recover. No visitors but that doesn't bother me. For once I'm enjoying the silence. Until I heard a knock on my door. A giant bouquet of roses came into the room first then Lucky with a shy smile. I smiled in return.

"You didn't bring Zach?"

I sat down in one of the chairs by the bed.

Lucky rubbed the back of his neck with a nervous chuckle. My guess he didn't want to see his mother who scarred him for life and wants nothing to do with her.

"He hates me."

"No, he doesn't. He's just…"

"He's afraid of me."

I finished his sentence, he frowned. I sigh.

"I heard everyone's opinion on this, but not yours. Do you think I did the right thing?"

That response took longer than I thought it would take. He was opening his mouth but no words came out. Almost as if he didn't want to say his opinion because it would hurt me or piss me off.

"You want me to be honest?"

"That's all I want."

He sighed.

"No."

"No?"

I said with my eyebrows raised.

"You asked me to be honest."

He said with a shrug.

"Well, tell me why you think that."

"Charmion," he sighed.

"Lucky,"

"All right! No, I don't think what you did was right. I think you should've shot him in the leg and just hold off until the cops showed up. You left me in the dark and took off halfcocked with a gun, a gun! What you did affected all of us, not just you."

Wow, his yelling could be heard in the ICU. So much yelling in the last few days and I'm surprised I don't have a headache already. Hell, I am surprised I still have the energy to fight again.

"And what about *us*? You can barely look me in the eye right now."

As I watched Lucky speak, he was completely avoiding eye contact with me. Not only that, he's not even sitting down as he talks to me. He's standing up, talking down to me. I hate that. I absolutely hate that.

"You're talking down to me, Luke."

His eyes were filled with sadness when I said his real name. If he can't stand to look at me then I sure hell shouldn't call him Lucky. He did say he didn't like when I call him that.

"I need to ask this. When Jason kidnapped me, you and Gabriel filed a police report. Did you know that Jason changed my name?"

206

I had a hunch. After the police questioned me, I kept thinking about what happened five years ago. The police must have told them that Jason changed my name. Though, they never told me. I'm pretty sure Cooper didn't even know. Something about that question made Lucky uncomfortable. I already figured it out just by his facial expression.

"So you knew. You knew for five years and didn't say anything?"

I scoffed.

"Charmion," I cut him off and went off on him.

"How can I trust you with anything at this point?"

Tables were turned and I call them like I see them. I kept something from Lucky for five years and he kept something from me for five years. I guess I had that coming. But in this case, I can't really complain because we both did something that hurt us.

"You know what? Just go. Take your pity flowers too."

I tossed the bouquet of roses to his feet. The thing is, I don't even like roses. He knows I don't like roses and he still got them.

"Please, Charmion, don't shut me out." He begged.

"I am not shutting you out. Clearly we can't trust each other with anything. It's better if we just stay away from each other for now on. The only thing we're good at is keeping secrets and raising our son. Though, I have not been doing a good job of that."

My heart ached so much. She was right, we can't trust each other anymore. She hid something from me for years while I did just that. I assumed Gabriel told her so that

207

dropped some of the tension. But a lot happened after that and I just forgot. I was upset with myself and I feel more to blame. I came here for a reason, well, many reasons but one of them is really important. We have to squash this in order for us to move on and take care of each other. I took a deep breath sitting down on the bed.

"I'm so sorry, Charmion. Not telling you right away killed me. I just assumed Gabriel told you and you didn't want to talk about it with me. I just brushed it off. And I understand if you didn't want to tell me about what went down with Jason."

Charmion scrunched up her face at me, she looked confused and quite frankly, shocked.

"You do?" She said eyeing me suspiciously.

"You were doing it to protect Zach as well as the family."

"And you still want to give us a shot?" She said eyeing me. I chuckled rubbing the back of my neck.

"Yes, I do. I don't want to end this. Can we just agree to not keep things from each other and be completely honest?"

Charmion half smiled nodding her head. I returned one back and leaned in to kiss her. The spark was still there when we kissed and the butterflies never left. She's the only woman to give me butterflies. I let my lips linger longer before pulling away and gazing into her eyes. It amazes me how pure her blue eyes are, I could lost in them for days.

I kissed her again longer this time. I didn't want to stop kissing her. I gently leaned her back the chair, my hands on her hips and waist. Her arms snaked around my neck deepening the kiss. I traced my tongue on her bottom lip, asking for entrance and she gladly accepted. A small moan escaped her lips just before I carefully placed her on my lap. She stumbled a little which made us both laugh. I wanted to do this for a while now. Aside from the events that occurred, the last five years of my life with Charmion were amazing. We have a child together and soon I hope to have more children with her but as my wife. I pulled away looking into her eyes, I knew this was the perfect moment. My heart was pounding so hard, I feel the beads of sweat on my forehead and my hands. I haven't been this nervous since I came to see her after I left the house. Every man gets nervous when they are about to propose to their girlfriend. I don't know a man who wouldn't be. I don't want us to just be a couple, I don't us to be a boyfriend and girlfriend when we have a five year old. I want us to be husband and wife. Quickly, I slipped the ring into her hand. I watched her eyes lit up as she stared at the 7 carat diamond ring.

"Yes."

CHAPTER 32

"Grandpa Cooper!" Zach laughed dropping his school bag on the ground and leaped into my arms. I love picking up Zach from school. The look on his face when he sees his favorite grandfather. Okay, second favorite.

"Where's daddy?" He asked.

"He's at work, he'll be out soon."

I notice Zach kept looking down and playing his hands with a sad look on his face, I knew something was wrong.

"What is it, buddy?" I placed him on the ground and crouched down to his height. He looked up at me with those big brown eyes and pouted.

"Is mommy going to jail?"

My heart stopped. How do I respond to that? Frankly, I don't know if Charmion is going to prison. It was self defense but a judge and jury might not believe that. That is, if we take this to trial which I surely doubt that. I shouldn't lie to my five year old grandson. I sighed deeply.

"Am I bad?"

"Of course not, why would you say that?"

He started kicking the dirt around, his hands were behind his back now. His head hanging low. I was getting really concerned at this point. I know Zach wouldn't hurt anyone, he's a total sweetheart and would never hurt a fly, literally.

"Mommy was on the ground, the bad man was choking her. I saw the gun and I grabbed it. I hurt the bad man."

I did notice Jason was shot in the shoulder but I never thought Zach was the one who gave him that. A child would be terrified to even think about picking up a loaded weapon in that situation. My heart was heavy just thinking about what was going through this little boys head. He shouldn't have to carry this weight on his shoulder. No child should. He must've picked up how Jason held it and pointed at it at Charmion.

"Hey, you're good. You saved your mom and you guys made it out of there alive."

Poor choice of words, in my part.

"Can we go see her?"

I smiled.

"Of course we can. How about we go get her a little something."

"Yeah!"

He laughed running to the car.

He's excited to see Charmion, but I'm the opposite.

I took a deep breath before opening the door and seeing Charmion on the chair reading a book. I carefully entered the room without her noticing until Zach ran in screaming. Damnit, I forget he gets overly excited.

"Mommy!"

Shit.

She put her book on the table and held Zach with a big smile. It was a beautiful sight seeing those two together. Every boy needs their mother. Sometimes I wish my mother

211

was still here. I think about her everyday. Charmion's eyes met mine and her face dropped. She looked back at Zach and smiled.

"Why don't you watch cartoons while I talk to grandpa?"

I wouldn't want Zach to hear what we have to say to each other. Kid seen enough in last 72 hours. He sat peacefully with my phone and wore headphones. I swallowed hard. She stared at me with this blank expression.

"Can we talk?"

"Depends. Am I going to get slapped again if we do?"

I guess I deserve that.

"I'm sorry, Charmion."

"No, you're not." She said.

"I'm trying to apologize, Charmion."

I said slightly getting irritated.

"You're not doing a good job. How's the jaw by the way?"

I exclaimed. I don't need her being a wiseass right now. I don't have patience when it comes to stubbornness. I just need to get my breath back and relax. I sighed leaning back against the chair but it slid back and I fell to the floor. Charmion and Zach started laughing. I shot back up grinning.

"I am sorry, Charmion. I was overwhelmed with what happened and I took it out on you. I shouldn't have done that, it was wrong."

She folded her arms across her chest giving me an uneasy look. There was a silence. I stood there rocking my feet back and forth.

"Have the police spoken to you?" I awkwardly shifted. I already know they spoke to her. It just feels weird right now and I feel the tension between us.

She nodded.

"Jason was more mental than we thought. The son of a bitch changed my name twice. But I assume you already knew that."

"No, I didn't." I scoffed.

At this point, nothing can surprise me about Jason. I'm finding out more things that I never knew Jason was capable of. It's like he was a completely different person aside from his family and friends. God, it makes me so angry that Jason would go to great lengths to ruin my life as well as Charmion's life. And for what? So he can have a family of his own? He would go this far? For once I'm glad he's not able to do more harm on us anymore. I sighed before thinking about what I was going to say next.

"I know there's nothing I can say that will make this better. But…"

Goddamnit, Cooper spit out!

The little girl in front of me was staring back at me with her big blue eyes, how can I bring myself to say words? My throat is so dry, its begging for moisture of my words. Breathe, Cooper. You got this. I took a calm, soothing breath with my eyes closed and then slowly opened them. This time, a little girl wasn't staring back at me. I was in control.

"I'm truly, truly, sorry, Charmion. I didn't want this to happen. I wished none of this ever happened and Jason to never bothered us. But things went bad, I couldn't do anything about it. What I can do, right now, is try to make things right. It's over now, we can move on with our lives."

Charmion smiled nodding her head. Pretty sure that's a good thing. That, or she is being passive aggressive and still wants to punch me in the face. I swallowed a lump in my throat.

"What took you so long, old man?" She laughed.

We had a full house. Same people who were here the night of Jason was killed, minus Zach. We were expecting two more visitors in suits with badges. Charmion sat on the bed bouncing her knee rapidly. She was nervous. We all were. What if she gets arrested? I can't think about the negative. I need to keep positive and hope we all can home.

"Relax, Charmion."

Lucky kissed her head.

"How can I relax when I'm going to get arrested?" She exclaimed.

"You are not getting arrested, Charms."

Gabriel said.

"Jason was psychopath, they won't charge you with anything." I said.

Just when someone was going to speak again, the door opened and in came in an officer I've never seen before. He had jet black hair that was slicked back and these green eyes that can touch your soul and leave you feeling unsatisfied. Him and I were the same height. I figured it be the officer that already spoke to me, Charmion, and Gabriel, that's what I've been told. He had this cold expression as he looked at Charmion. Why does he look familiar to me? He looks at me and grinned. That's when it hit me. I knew who this man was and I feared that everyone's lives are in danger. I haven't seen this man in years. To be honest, I thought he was dead.

"What are you doing here?"

There was a stutter in between my words. It's like I'm seeing a ghost. What the hell is he doing here? How the hell did he end up being a cop?

"Charmion Smith, you are under arrest for the murder of Jason Bennett."

"What?"

Charmion exclaimed looking back at us. I shook my head stepping in between them.

"Derek, you can't arrest her!"

"We have proof. Oh and Cooper," he smirked and scooted closer to me, I swallowed a lump in my throat.

"Whole crew can't wait to see ya."

My eyes widened and stumbled back. Dear god this can't be happening right now.

"You can't do this! Charmion!"

Lucky yelled.

Charmion was handcuffed and pushed against the wall, she grunted as he yanked her out of the room and shoved her into the squad car. She hissed in pain and the officer grinned.

"So, you're the girl Jason kept talking about."

Derek grinned. Charmion's eyes got big.

"You knew Jason."

Her voice was shaky as she made out every word. She was terrified.

"I didn't just know Jason, we were brothers."

CHAPTER 33

❖

"Who was that guy, Cooper?" I exclaimed. Cooper sighed putting his hands on his head. We all stood their staring at Cooper who looked like was having mental breakdown. Gabriel was on the verge breaking the window, Sonya and Kendall stepped out because Sonya was about to pass out. I'm this close to losing my shit with this family.

"Cooper, you better tell us who that guy is or so help me." I gritted.

"Okay! Okay. He's Jason's half brother, which makes him my half brother too."

"What?" Gabriel and I exclaimed.

It's one bump after another, it won't stop coming. What's next? His sister shows up?

"How fucked up is your family?"

Gabriel snarled.

I keep asking myself that since the day I met Jason in that shitty house. I shouldn't be so quick to judge but how can I not? Sure, every family has it's crazy but this specific family is fucking full of psychopaths. This family is at the top of the most insane family in the goddamn planet. I pray to god a sister doesn't show up

"Jason and I have the same dad but Derek doesn't. Our mother hooked up with some random guy and it turns out he got her pregnant. At the time, it was just me, Jason, and my mother. When he found she was pregnant, he took off too and Derek ended up in foster care and I never saw him after that. That is, until today."

"Why did he end up in foster care?" I said weirdly.

"Because he is more twisted than Jason! As a kid, he was violent, very violent. When he was living with us, he tried to choke me in my sleep and he put itching power in mine and my mother's underwear. He was so violent that me and my mother had to lock the bedroom door so he wouldn't hurt us. He even chased me around the house with a knife. But he never did any of those things to Jason. Somehow he got along great with Jason just not with me."

"So we're dealing with another psychopath."

I groaned with a hand on my forehead.

"I did not, I swear I did not know he'd end up a cop. I thought he was dead."

"Well, he's not!"

Gabriel screamed then punched the wall, making a gaping hole in the wall. I sighed. Guess we're paying for that.

"What did he mean by, the crew?"

Cooper's face went pale again. I can tell this crew was a sensitive subject for him. From what I can tell, these people could be ten times worse than Jason and Derek combine. Jason could be in a gang of some sort, that's what I'm thinking. It wasn't hard to figure that out. Gabriel was having a fit in the corner of the room, I'm right there with him.

"I can't go to another trial. I can't stand another minute in that courtroom."

Gabriel said. His hands were up in the air like he was surrendering. Of course there's going to be trial. Not unless if

Charmion admits she is guilty but we all know she's not. It's all fuzzy in my head right now. All this yelling, this hospital might as well lock me in the psych ward because I'm losing so much brain cells and I'm going insane by the minute.

"Just shut up and let's go to see Samson!"

I didn't wait up for them.

"I'm sorry, but there's going to be a trial."

Samson said with a deep sigh.

"But you know it was self defense, Samson. Look at Jason's record. He kidnapped her and Zach. He shot her in the shoulder and leg, broke her foot, and nearly killed my son!"

This is outrageous. The amount grey hairs I have right now, all this stress is killing, literally killing me. When can we catch a break? When can we finally settle? When damnit?

"Okay, I can offer a plea deal."

"She's innocent! You know Charmion is, it was self defense."

I said.

"I believe you but I don't think the jury will."

"What made them decide to bring this to court?"

Samson sighed and pulled out a piece of paper. Gabriel and I scanned the paper till our eyes widened and our heads shot up.

"They can't charge her with this. That was five years ago. Isn't there a statute of limitations here?"

"There isn't in the state of Delaware, which is why it was brought up."

"How? She was being held against her will along with Cooper. Not to mention beaten too. No way they can say she kidnapped them."

"I tried to dismiss this, believe me I tried, but they have enough strong evidence and a witness."

"Charmion, Cooper, and Jason were the only ones there. The only witness was a lady jogging and found blood mixed in with the dirt and that was after they left. Who's this damn witness that saw all this happen?"

Samson took a slow sip from his coffee. The longer he sat there sipping his coffee, the longer I wanted to yank his tie and scream in his face. There was only three people that day, not four. Charmion would've said there was a fourth person. The look on his face made our stomach's drop. What's the bullshit excuse now?

"The man who arrested Charmion, Officer Derek Davis."

I waited outside of Zach's school. Cooper and Gabriel were with Samson discussing the case. I don't know how to tell Zach that his mother's been arrested. He's already been through so much and I don't want to add more trauma to him. And he is only five. I cannot stress that enough. The bell rang and kids came sprinting out the building. I saw Zach walk out with two other boys laughing. I smiled as I watched them do a little handshake.

"Hi, daddy!"

I laughed picking him and giving a kiss on the cheek.

"I made this for mommy."

He pulled out a medium sized card from his backpack that said get well soon with a bunch of hearts and her and Zach holding hands. He even drew the cast on her foot. It was the cutest thing. My smile slowly turned into a frown. Zach looked at me confused.

"What's wrong, daddy?"

I sighed getting down to his level and held his hands. How can I begin to tell my son? I can barely look him in the eye. Fight back the tears, Luke. Fight them.

"Zach, I don't know how to say this but,"

"Is mommy okay?"

My heart is slowly breaking as his happy face turned into a sad face. My boy shouldn't be in more pain.

"Mommy is,"

How can I look him in the eye and tell him that his mother's been arrested and is going to trial? I can't just say it. But I can't leave him in the dark. Even if he is only five years old and won't understand any of this, he needs to know the truth.

"Mommy has been arrested."

"Why?" He was on the verge of tears, so was I.

"We're gonna bring her home, I promise."

I pray we do.

CHAPTER 34

❖

I hate lawyers. Always have and always will. I miss my normal clothes. I was forced to wear a prison jumpsuit. That's what happens when you spent overnight in a jail cell. My heart sank when I saw Zach in Lucky's lap. I looked down and walked towards my table. The sound of the shackles weren't helping my anxiety. It was good to see Samson's face. He gave me a nod and pulled me closer and whispered in my ear.

"I will do everything in my power to make sure you walk out of here a free woman."

I smiled nodding back at him.

"All rise."

Just when I knew things couldn't possibly get any worse, the same lawyer who I saw five years ago walked through those doors in the flesh, Mr. Gallows. My heart sank. He didn't look any different other than his suit and maybe a little on the hair. I look behind me and see a bunch men staring down at me. That's when Derek came in wearing the exact same suit Jason did at his hearing. It made me sick to my stomach seeing him wear that suit. If I wasn't scared before, I am now.

"Charmion Smith, please stand in the middle of the courtroom."

I gulped.

The sounds of the shackles echoed in the courtroom, my eyes set on the judge who wasn't as pleased with how slow I was walking.

"Turn and face everyone."

My eyes landed to Lucky and Zach. I wanted to cry. My son is seeing his mother in an orange jumpsuit and chains. He's already traumatized.

"You will be standing for the rest of the trial."

The room filled with murmurs. That's an odd thing to do during a trial. Samson was staring at the judge in confusion and started looking through his papers. I looked down as I heard the scraping of a chair. I don't doubt that Mr. Gallows is the family attorney.

"Nice to see you again, Miss Smith. I thought five years ago be our last encounter."

Mr. Gallows still has that smug look that I absolutely hate with a burning passion. He was overly confident in his role as a lawyer and I'm not surprised it hasn't caught up with him yet. I stared at him.

"Speaking of five years ago, you were with my former client, Jason Bennett and his brother Cooper Bennett in a car. Is that correct?"

"Yes, because he kidnapped me."

"At some point, you held a gun to him, didn't you?"

"Yes but-"

He completely cut me off mid sentence.

"Did you know Jason had another brother?"

"No."

I said.

"Did you ever think about who would be affected about Jason's death?"

I hated myself for taking too long to answer the question because I was screaming the answer in my head but my mouth went dry.

"Miss Smith?"

I couldn't even move my mouth, everything was blank and blurry. It was too loud and yet no one was saying anything, it won't stop. I started hyperventilating, my head hung low and I was shaking.

"Miss Smith, answer the question." Mr. Gallows clenched his jaw.

Why can't I move? Why was this question hard for me to answer? I opened my mouth but only fearful shriek came out which made Samson stood up.

"Your Honor, my client is having a panic attack. She is traumatized with everything that Jason and officer Davis has done to her. I demand a 15 minutes recess."

"Motion for a recess is denied. Miss Smith, answer the question!"

The judge was not having it. He yelled at me, Mr. Gallows is yelling, voices in my head are yelling at me and I can't stop it. Cooper was on edge and yanked Samson aside and practically yelled in his face. At this point, I was sweating buckets. I see blank faces and dark souls piercing mine, my knees went numb from the shaking and my body feels frozen in place. All for one simple question that I could've easily answered like any other question. If anyone was in this position, god forbid someone is on trial for murder, I'm sure they'd be better than me right now.

"Miss Smith!"

I lost it.

"Fuck you!" Zach quickly covered his ears. Lucky hugged me whispering in his ear to calm him down. I never swore with Zach being in the room but in this case, it was acceptable.

"Your Honor, permission to treat the defendant hostile?"

The judge gave me a glare and gave Mr. Gallows the big thumbs up.

"That night, you shot Jason in the head and he begged you for mercy. You didn't give him the benefit of the doubt and instead you killed him cold blood. I mean, I'm no judge but that's murder."

"Objection!"

Samson yelled.

"He nearly killed my son! The bastard deserved to die."

The swarm of men sitting behind Derek all stood up shouting and instead of the judge screaming order in the court, he sat in his chair staring at me. What kind of judge is he? I'm looking around this courtroom and can feel the animosity. I didn't look at the jury because they were giving me the same glare as the judge and the large group of men. Then it hit me. This judge is working with Derek. And I bet the people in the jury are too. It's no wonder I saw a wink from the judge, he was looking at the Derek the whole time. This is whole case is rigged. This entire case is in Derek's hands and no one knows it. I couldn't believe it. It's the People v. Charmion Smith, I'm at odds with everyone in this room and I barely know half of them and yet, they know everything about me.

"All he wanted is for you to be his daughter, be the father he was."

"He was not my father! A mental case and drug abuser is not my father!"

I exclaimed with a stare.

"And yet you managed to steal a phone for him when he was in treatment. In your mind, you thought he was your father."

"At the time, yes but I was delusional-" Mr. Gallows threw another question at me. Didn't even let me answer the last few questions he asked.

"If you thought that, then why on earth kill the only father figure you had?"

"He kidnapped my son and made my family's life a living hell!"

Gallows chuckled.

"Nothing further."

Samson quickly stood up and adjusted his suit.

"When did you realize your sons life was in danger?"

Samson said with his hands by his side.

"When Jason took Zach and later calling me that he has a gun."

"Were you aware of what Jason was capable of?"

Samson said.

"Yes, he was a master at manipulating people. I knew he was going to try and hurt him in some way, even if he was lying I wasn't going to risk it."

"Nothing further."

I got nervous when it was Gallows turn to ask the questions. I gulped which made me think everyone heard it.

"You told the police that it was self defense, correct?"

I nod my head quickly then looked down.

"Was it really?"

225

"Objection, Your Honor," Samson had a finger on his temple. He is most likely getting a headache.

"Sustained."

Samson sighed in defeat and sat back down in his seat.

"What were the last words Jason said to you?"

My mind goes back to him saying we were so much alike. How I turned out to be just like him. I started to get really nervous at this point. For a moment there, I was okay with Jason. He freaking hugged me. But then I remembered why I'm there and that he took my son and nearly killed the both of us. And that made me angry.

"He told me the story when I said my first word." But I didn't mention the other part.

"Was your life in danger at that moment?"

"No."

I said.

The courtroom filled with murmurs and looks of concern and disbelief. Wearing this orange jumpsuit was making me hot, you could see the sweat forming under my arms and back. I already know the next question he was going to ask.

"So you and your son were no longer in danger and he was only telling you a story about you as a baby, is that correct?"

The entire time I was looking at Cooper, he was staring back at me begging me to say no it was self defense. I can't stand here and say it was when I know in my heart it wasn't.

"So, Miss Smith," he stepped closer to me so he was looking down at me. I hate that.

"Was it really self defense?"

My eyes glared up at him.

"No."

I whispered so only he can hear.

"Please speak up for the court, Miss Smith. Tell the court what you did."

Cooper was now standing up with his hands clenched. Samson was tapping his foot rapidly shaking his head. Lucky was practically bitting his nails, Gabriel is trying not to explode, and Zach is staring at me with his big brown eyes. They were screaming for a hug. I forced myself to not cry in the middle of this courtroom. I shouldn't cry, I don't deserve to cry.

"Say it damnit!"

Cooper finally exploded, the judge banged the gavel and shot daggers at Cooper. You want me to tell everyone in this room what I did? So be it. I have no fight left in me anymore.

"It was not self defense, I shot Jason Bennett."

CHAPTER 35

I sat in the cell feeling completely hopeless. I thought there be hope for me to be a free woman but at this point, they have ever right to throw me in jail. This is my third trial and somehow it always starts out not like we planned it to be. But somehow we always turn it around. Now, I don't know if we can turn this around. I heard loud doors close and rapid footsteps and Cooper stood there shaking his head, an angry look. I stood up and walked towards him.

"If you get any closer, I will grab you by the shirt collar."

He gritted. I slowly backed up with a nervous expression. All of a sudden he kicked the cell and it raddled hard.

"Why would you lie?"

I never liked when he raised his voice. I especially didn't like how it echoed down the hall and was louder. Cooper exhaled sharply with his hands tangled in his hair. I feel awful. We just patched everything up between us and now there's this. Yes, we're in the middle of a trial but we were still cool, until earlier. He can barely look me in the eye right now. I don't blame him.

"You lied to the police, you lied to Samson, and you lied to me."

"Okay yes I did lie but you have to listen to me. This case is rigged. The judge and half the jury are working with Derek, they are in his pockets."

Cooper scoffed shaking his head.

"I'm not lying! Why do think the judge made me stand in the middle of the court room? When all those men started shouting he didn't even say order in the court or anything."

He just stared at me, still pissed off as ever.

"Cooper, please. You have to believe me, Samson needs to know before the jury reaches a verdict. Please."

I was dangling a carrot to his face. I am practically throwing myself at him, I'm basically throwing a bone to him to help me out. He knows every man out there watching this whole thing. This "crew" thinks they have the case in the bag. I have to find some way to get a new judge and new jury because for all I know they'll just dismiss this case and send me to jail without a fair trial.

"Cooper, I'm begging you. If you were really my father you'd make sure I wouldn't end up in jail."

Cooper's face didn't change. It's like nothing I say is getting through to him. My eyes pleading with him to believe me, tears were already streaming down my face. I'm running out of things to say. Just like that, Cooper walked off.

"No, Cooper, no!"

I cried.

"Please don't do this!"

But he was already gone. The large doors slammed and I was alone again. I sobbed falling to my knees. This can't be happening. I am living in a nightmare where I can't wake up from. I want to wake up! I've lost all hope at this point. Derek, the judge, and jury will eat me alive and no one knows that Derek is controlling this entire case. Not even Samson knows. Cooper officially disowned me as his daughter. Everyone else I know thinks different of me now. It's over for me. The minute I go back into that courtroom my life is over and I'm going to rot in a cell for the rest of my life. I'm going to miss out Zach growing up, birthdays, Christmas, Thanksgiving, even New Years. Lucky and I will never make contact ever again. I won't be able to hug him, or kiss him. The only way to see him is through a glass and it kills me. It kills me that in a matter of few minutes I will no longer have freedom, I won't be a free woman.

I'm done for.

CHAPTER 36

❖

I love you. I will always love you. No matter where I go or where we'll end up, just know, I'll always love you. You are my whole world and we have a child together and we're engaged to be married. The amount of love I have for you is indescribable. You're the best thing that ever happened to me and I'll miss being in your arms.

My sweet boy, you are a blessing and I thank god everyday you were born. With all that you've seen, you still managed to be the happiest out of everyone around you. You are far more braver than me and far more stronger than me. Maybe even more braver and stronger than your father. I know I will miss seeing you start the first grade, see you learn how to ride a bike, first crush, birthdays, holidays, and the first day of high school, but no matter what you will always be my son and I will love you always.

You have been my huge support ever since you and Mrs. K took me in and raised me as your own. I'm eternally grateful for everything you and Mrs. K have done for me. We had our ups and downs and crazy, intense fights, but you always stuck by me and stepped up on being the father I needed. I don't say it as much but you mean the world to me.

I don't even want to begin how upset you could be. You are the woman who brought me into this world, you took care of me before things went bad. We've built a stable mother and daughter relationship that was years in the making. I'm sorry for what I said to you. I wish I can tell you how sorry I am in person but this letter will have to do.

I wrote letters to my family, it'll be the last time I'll ever talk to them. It hurts that I'm thinking about this and makes me break down in tears. Not only Zach's seeing all of this but he's seeing his mother being ripped away from him. I was ripped away from the only family I knew and now I'm watching my son go through the same thing. One thing I never want my son to ever face and that is losing a person he loves. How is he going to handle it? How will he manage to live his life without his mother? I stood by the front two doors waiting for Samson and he came up next to me with a not so great look. He couldn't look at me.

"Samson, you gotta believe me. This trial is rigged. Derek has the judge and the jury in his pocket."

He still didn't look at me.

"When will the lies end?"

He muttered, thinking I didn't hear him but I did.

It was that moment, I officially lost hope. My own lawyer doesn't believe me nor have faith in me. If anything he will throw me under the bus, so far everyone has done that. I didn't say anything after that. What's the point? I'm going to jail.

"Has the jury reached a verdict?"

"We have, Your Honor." One of the female jurors said. Could've sworn she gave me a dirty look.

"What's say you?"

I closed my eyes.

I've accepted my fate. It is painful for someone to accept they will spend the rest of their life in a cell but what can I do? There's no way to make this right, no one is going to come barging into this courtroom with a ton officers behind them and arrest everyone including the judge and the jury. That's the only thing that can save me at this point. Will it happen? I seriously doubt that, my friend.

"On the counts of murder in the first degree, we find the defendant, guilty."

I collapsed.

CHAPTER 37

❖

Everyone changed in that courtroom. We just lost someone who was the heart of the family. To no longer wake up next to them, not being able to pour them a cup of coffee anymore. Or just go for a walk because the only outside they got is the prison yard. How can we live like this? How will we proceed to live our lives without that special someone? Do we just forget that person? Do we move on?

It's been five months since Charmion was sent to prison and everyone still is having a hard time dealing with it, including Zach. The poor boy prays that he will see her in the kitchen making lunch but all he sees is an empty dark kitchen with nothing but her soul. I tried everything to reopen the case, I tried calling Samson but he hasn't gotten back to me. Last time we talked was the trial. Something happened in that courtroom that shouldn't have happened. There has to be some kind of legal clause or a fine print or law to bring this case back up. It can't be like this.

I went to visit Charmion everyday since she was sent to prison and day by day, she's starting to lose the life in her eyes. Her hair was now black and pink, dark circles under eyes due to the lack of sleep she has gotten, bruises from getting beat up for being the fresh meat. I haven't brought

Zach to visit her. I don't think he's ready. I don't want him to see her like that.

"You would think a cup of coffee would make my day a little better."

Gabriel said with a sigh.

"We pretty much just lost interest in everything since Charmion went to prison."

Gabriel sighed again, this time with a hand on his face.

"How she doing?" He said with sad a look.

"Horrible, she looked liked a completely different person, I hardly recognized her."

"I can't visit her. I want to believe me. I can't, I just can't."

No one really has the guts to see Charmion, except me but even at this point I can't bare to see her. Whenever I visit her, she doesn't say a word to me. She doesn't even look at me. All she does is stare at the corner of the window with no expression. I saw her two months ago.

"Has Cooper gone to see her?"

"For all we know Cooper probably skipped town because he couldn't take it anymore, Sonya too."

Cooper hasn't contacted any of us since the trial, same for Sonya. They both completely went AWOL. He was the last person to talk to Charmion and then after he took off. That was five months ago.

"Should we call him?"

I said uneasy.

"And say what?"

Gabriel shrugged then entered the kitchen. I heard a knock as I was going to open the door, Gabriel speed past me with a glock. I exclaimed and I grabbed his arm because it could anyone knocking at our door. Hell, could be the neighbors. We don't want to scare them. But when I saw who it was, I said have at it. I can't control a 48 year old man.

"Hi!"

Derek smiled and waved. Gabriel pointed the gun at him with a glare.

"Whoa, hey now," he grinned.

"You have exactly 5 seconds to get off my property or I will put a bullet in your leg."

"Is that a threat?" He raised an eyebrow.

"Yes."

We both said simultaneously.

Derek shrugged.

"Fair enough, what lovely home you have. May I come in?"

He waltzed in as if this was his house. Gabriel and I just stared at him as he sat at the table and poured himself a cup of coffee. The man took off his jacket and literally is drinking coffee on our table. I wanted to put a bullet in his leg but I bet Gabriel will beat me to it.

"Aren't you going to sit?" He says with a smile. God that smile, makes my skin crawl. What I would love more to do is punch it right off his stupid face.

"Get the hell out of my house!"

Now Gabriel was shouting and practically shoved the gun his throat.

"Listen, I just want to see how y'all doing. I'm sure this is a big adjustment." Derek's feet were on top of the table, had this smug look on his face.

"You put my daughter in jail for something she clearly did not do!"

Gabriel was screaming at the top of his lungs and what blew me away, Derek was smiling the whole time. I did not see any fear or intimidation.

"No, that's not true, she killed Jason, and it wasn't self defense."

Derek shrugged.

"Regardless if it was or wasn't, Jason was still a threat to society. He broke out of prison and kidnaped my grandson, Luke's son."

Gabriel's face was bright red. I stepped away from him because I can't be close to him when he is angry. No one can. He's like a fire cracker. He can go off at any moment.

"You're probably right, but she didn't have to kill him."

Am I really hearing this man speak? He has a lot of nerve coming here and ask us how we are doing since the trial. God I want to punch him on how arrogant this bastard is. He has to be carrying. No way a cop wouldn't be carrying their weapon while being on the job. Derek then stood up and opened his jacket. He wasn't carry anything, not even a taser.

"You expect us to believe you're not carrying?" I scoffed.

Gabriel nudges at me to check him, I patted his body down and felt nothing but the belt around his waist. I even checked under his pant leg if he had a knife but he didn't. I nod at Gabriel. He lowered the gun a little.

"Why are you here?"

Gabriel said nudging me to stand behind him.

"I'm willing to make a deal."

Derek said with arms behind his back like some school boy. As arrogant and egotistical that he is, the man has manners which is very frightening to me.

"What kind of deal?"

I said eyeing him.

"You want to see Charmion?"

Our hearts stopped. Gabriel dropped the gun but still held it tightly in his hands.

"Charmion can do her time at home. I'm sure she misses you and her son along with everyone else."

"Bullshit. You have no control of the courts."

Gabriel scoffed.

"Oh, but I do. I'm sure Charmion would love to come home and be with all of you." He winked.

It's been driving me crazy for months now, no years. Why is this family so fixated on Charmion so much? It is mind boggling. So many men are after her and yet when they finally get her, it is not enough. What does Charmion have that has everyone hooked? Why would they go out of their way to hurt her? It hurts me to see people hurt her. I can't stand it anymore. I just, can't.

"The judge and I are very close friends and it just so happens he was very, very good friends of Jason. We all went to school together. Some members of the jury were also good friends of ours too. They found out that Charmion killed Jason and well, the rest is history."

It got me thinking; why is he admitting to this and not think that either of us could be recording his every word? Maybe it's because he thought we wouldn't have any luck with trying to prove him wrong, thus reopening Charmion's case. Or, that even though he is saying this, we can't do anything about it and no one would believe us because he has the court system literally eating out of the palm of his hand. So he pulls out that cocky charm and thinks he's untouchable

238

regardless if he is admitting it because he has so much power for being a cop. I had this sick feeling he's done this before. Some poor person was tangled up with his crew and got an unfair trial and is probably behind bars for a crime he never committed. Derek tells his court buddies to jump and they'll say, how high? Regardless of those, even though Derek is annoyingly cocky and arrogant, that's going to get him in trouble. This feels too easy.

"Okay! Let's eat! I know a great place that does margaritas in the afternoon."

Derek smiled with open arms.

"You need to leave."

Gabriel muttered. He wasn't himself. I can see he was starting to lose his balance a little but he got it back and shot Derek a glare and cocked the gun to his face. Derek's face didn't change, it was almost lifeless, almost as if he didn't care if he died nor cared about his humanity. That seems to run in the family. The man wasn't scared.

"All right, message received. I'll keep this between us."

The door slammed and Gabriel was furious than ever. So was I. But then I remembered, I recorded the bastard. I got every single word. We got the son of a bitch.

CHAPTER 38

I asked Kendall to watch over Zach while Gabriel and I head to Samson's office. We have to show him the recording. It could give us a nudge to consider reopening the case. I prayed and prayed that this will be our chance. It has to be. Samson never returned any of our calls and his assistant said he just stepped into a meeting but we know he only has meetings on Thursdays. It's Tuesday. So we knew something wasn't right. The door to his office was unlocked. A smart lawyer would always keep his office locked even if you are going down the hall for a cup of coffee.

We patiently waited for Samson's return, the door opened and the lights came up and Samson gasped dropping the cup of coffee in his hands. His eyes widened as he saw us sitting at the table, we were not impressed. His tie was slightly undone, hair was messy as if he was up all night, I assumed with the bags under his eyes. And just by looking around his office, with the lights on, they were empty cups and beer bottles on the floor. His dinner from last night was still untouched on his desk. It barely looked like an office anymore.

"What are you doing in my office?"

He said still baffled.

"Thought you stepped into a meeting." I said with a sarcastic tone then gave a sassy eye roll.

"I've been busy."

He muttered.

"Too busy to get back to us?" Gabriel arched an eyebrow with his arms folded across his chest. Of course we didn't get a response after that. I mean he's *really* been busy judging from the mess in the room. Please. Busy with what? Getting drunk?

"We have something that we can use to reopen Charmion's case."

Samson scoffed walking through the pile of rubble to what looked like his desk, and let out a huff.

"You know she doesn't deserve to be in jail."

Gabriel scowled.

"She lied about saying it was self defense. Doesn't matter what I think. She said it herself. There was no doubt in my mind that she was going to lose this case. The minute she lied under oath, her chances of winning were gone."

"Jason was a dangerous man. He would've done something way worse and escape from prison again if he was alive. Forget the fact that Charmion killed him, look at how much damage this man caused on one little girl. He kidnapped her, he raped and tortured Sonya in front of her. He shot her five times within the five years, shot me in the leg twice! And admitted to killing Gabriel's wife in open court. You honestly think we'd be safe if he was alive? The man would've put a target on our backs and I'm well certain he'd put a target on your back too."

I refuse to give up on this. There is a little girl locked up because of a false trial and false crime. The whole thing is absolute bullshit and we have proof from the horses mouth. Though, it seems too easy. Something in me is telling me that this is a trap, like if we were to get this to the higher ups, we'll get shut down.

"Do you have the recording?"

I didn't realize I was spacing out and I felt my phone pulled out of my pocket. I instantly grabbed his hand. Gabriel was in disbelief.

"What are you doing, son?"

Gabriel exclaimed snatching the phone out of my hands.

"This is what can get Charmion out of jail! Don't screw this up now."

"I have a bad feeling about this. He knew we were going to record it and go to the authorities. He did that on purpose. He's playing us I just know it."

"Wow, you're smart."

I didn't even have to turn around and see who it was, Gabriel pulled out the gun that was in under his shirt. Derek followed us. With everything that has happened, I'd be guarded every moment of every day. Our family constantly has to sleep with one eye open, we have this fear that we can never be happy only for someone to come along and ruin us piece by piece.

"You brought a gun to my office?"

Samson stammered.

"It's licensed."

Gabriel rolled his eyes.

"Is it now? That looks police issued."

Derek said with a curious look, then took a step forward.

"I was in the academy but I drop out due to my wife getting breast cancer."

"Really? Officer Klein?"

Instant reaction I had, shield Gabriel. Yet he had a gun to defend himself. He was shielding me and Samson. I still didn't see a holster on Derek's hip, he wasn't carrying anything again. What surprised me was that Mrs. K had breast cancer. That woman handled it all on her own without telling us. She was a strong woman, Katherine Klein.

"You always carry a gun?"

The gun clicked and then pointed it to Derek's face. He had this overly joyed grinned on his face, he was almost aroused by it. It made my body shiver.

"I like it. Has a nice ring to it, Officer Klein, wow, I would not want to get pulled over by you,"

My inner self was pleading with Gabriel to shoot him in the leg like Jason did to me but what good will that do? It will surely make me feel better, that's for sure. But we all have to play nice if we have an ounce to get Charmion out of prison. If I have to spread a red carpet below Derek's feet with a smile then so be it. Time will tell eventually.

"You need to leave now."

Samson finally spoke while he adjusted his tie, all doing that with a nasty glare.

"You going to make me?"

Gabriel shoved him to the wall, Derek gasped, completely off guard, looked disbelief. Derek kept staring at Gabriel with that same shocked look on his face. His glance was so focus and almost with determination, like he was trying to solve a puzzle. I grinned. We got him now.

"You're going to pay for putting Charmion in jail. And we will make sure to expose you as the criminal you truly are."

243

CHAPTER 39

❖

Zach was getting more and more handsy with Charmion in prison. It hurts because I can never give him a straight answer. I just smile and hug him, it's all I can do for the time being. Typically on a Friday afternoon Charmion is home, probably doing laundry. I would be at work while Zach is at school. Today school was closed due to teachers and staff meetings that will run all day. I've taken a few days off from work. I have been overwhelmed with all this legal stuff and Zach and actually, keeping the entire family alive and standing. It's hard when you're the only person trying to keep everyone in line and just behave for once. By everyone I mean Gabriel. Guy's been way out of line. Everywhere we go he always has a gun. Like when we went to Samson's office, I didn't know he brought it and same goes for Samson. We were both terrified. In my mind I know Gabriel wouldn't do anything that could possibly land himself in jail. He's too smart for that. Derek on the other hand, I don't doubt for a second.

It was killing me to not see Charmion. I feel the urge to go to see her but I don't think I can face her alone. I sighed in my hands. I barely spent time with Zach as it is. After this whole thing spiraled out of control, Kendall moved across the street from us. She felt like she couldn't be too far from us, that and she was having issues with Riley's father but that's none of my business.

"Are you sure you don't want to take Zach with you?"

Kendall tried to reason with me, I just think he shouldn't see her when she's a total mess right now. I don't think I'm ready to see her. I'm still deciding.

"I don't want his image of his mother to ruin him. Kendall, when I mean I barely recognize her I meant it. It's like she's not the same person anymore."

"Prison can do that."

"Yeah."

I sighed.

"Okay, I'll watch Zach."

I thanked Kendall and swiftly exited her house. I was mentally and physically preparing myself when I see Charmion. Will she say something? Will she smile when she sees me? Will she cry? Or will I get a lifeless person staring back at me? My heart was pounding as I reached the gate. It was pounding even more when they stripped searched me. They escorted me to the visitation room. I was a little confused at first because usually I would sit in a box but I sat in front of a table. That's when I got really nervous. I waited for about 15 minutes until I heard the door open and heard chains being dragged on the floor.

I couldn't hold back the smile when I saw her. I ran and hugged her tightly in my arms till I heard the officer yell, no touching! A little smile creeped on her face as we sat down. She looked so much better the last time I saw her. Her hair was no longer pink, it was her naturally hair color, brown, the bags that were once there are now gone, her eyes are filled with that same full of life and passion. I have my Charms back. I just kept staring at her. And she stared back at me with the loving look. I want to kiss her so bad right now. I'm thinking that we're going home after this but the reality is, this is her new home. Behind those doors she's stepping into her living room, her kitchen, her bathroom, her bedroom, all in one open space. She doesn't have her privacy anymore. And there's one person to blame.

"We believe Derek set you up, look," I pulled out my phone and played the recording. Charmion placed her ear to the speaker that way the officer couldn't see the phone. She looked up at me. Not looking as excited as I hoped.

"You know why he confessed? Because I'm in here. He thinks he is untouchable because he is a cop and he has friends in the court system. I knew since the trial he set me up."

"Why didn't you say anything, Charmion?" I sighed.

"I tried. I was up for murder. You really think anyone was going to believe me? No one was on my side that day."

"I was." I held her hand, she smiled reach over the table. Thankfully I can still make her smile.

"How's Zach and everyone else?"

"The same, they're taking it hard."

I shrugged with a sad look. She sighed shaking her head. I noticed one of the officers giving us looks. I saw another officer approach him and whisper something in his ear. He started to smirk. Charmion saw this and started panicking. She started mumbling under breath, shaking her head rapidly. I quickly held her hands in mine and she instantly relaxed at my touch. I heard her unfolding something under the table. She was trying to be very discreet but it's hard to do that when we are in a small room and very thin walls.

"This morning, when I went back to my cell, I found a note on my pillow. It was from Derek."

She slid the note under the table, keeping eye contact with me. I gripped the paper firmly in my hands before reading it. My heart stopped.

I'm always watching.

"Samson, I'm begging you. You need to pull Charmion out of that prison."

Gabriel pleaded.

I've been shaking since I read that ransom note. I couldn't sleep or eat or do anything. I'm on edge right now. I don't feel comfortable with her there. I fear for her safety and my worst fear is that I'm going to get a call that she's been killed in a prison fight or one of the officers raped and killed her, courtesy of Derek.

"At least let her come home until the trial. We are still going through with the trial right? Can we let her come home until then? Can't you swing that?"

Samson sighed. I was barely paying attention to the conversation at hand. I can still see the fear in her eyes, her voice was shaking. I didn't want to leave her, I wanted to yank her out of there. There has to be a way to pull Charmion out of that hell hole. I screamed.

"Get her the hell out of there!" Samson froze in his seat.

"I don't care if I have to pay 10 grand! She is being tortured! So do your fucking job and get her out of there!"

I was livid. I had all this pepped up emotions and it was oozing out of me. All my rage was coming out and I couldn't control it. I couldn't think straight. Every officer in that prison is all buddy, buddy with Derek. It's insane! The guy is a dirty cop and he needs to be prosecuted. I growled seeing his parked car outside behind the building.

"What, you stalking our every move now?"

He chuckled.

"Don't flatter yourself."

It's like he's mocking me. He thinks he's untouchable. I wanted to punch that little grin off his face. I tried to lunge at him but two people from behind grabbed me. I grunted trying to break free.

"Look at you. You really think you can outsmart a cop? Face it boy, I have every single person working for me. You really think people are going to take your word over mine? Charmion is better off rotting in that cell."

That's it, that was the last straw. I kicked the two jerkoffs off me and punched him square in the face and he went down hard. I didn't stop there. My fist did the talking. A wave of anger took over my body, my mind, every thing. From the moment I heard Mrs. K was raped and killed, Charmion being kidnapped and shot, Zach being taken and Charmion in jail, I was boiling it up inside and just now it exploded out of me.

I suddenly became Jason. I was so violent and I feel every thing float away. I was like a firecracker, popping off every second. I didn't care if I got arrested, that was the least of my worries. My main purpose at this very moment is to inflict pain on the man who ruined my life. The two goons tried to yank me off but I was too strong.

"Shoot him!" Derek yelled. I looked at him confused and that's when I screamed and fell to the ground. I gasped when I saw the gash on my shoulder and blood on the ground. I was hoping to see one of Derek's henchmen but I was more surprised to see who it really was.

CHAPTER 40

❖

I was in awe, petrified even. I wasn't expecting to see Cooper holding the other end of that gun. He was the last person who would shoot me. Son of a bitch actually shot me. A sharp pain traveling up my body and all I did was scream at the top of my lungs. Derek immediately fled the scene. Cooper pulled out a rag from his pocket and wrapped it around my shoulder which only made me scream in pain louder. Cooper covered my mouth and dragged farther into the alley.

"Just be quiet for a second." He whispered looking back every few minutes.

"Take me to a fucking hospital!" I shouted.

"I will. When the coast is clear." I was still taken back at what just happened. Where the hell has Cooper been? I haven't heard from him in months. I tried to move my arm but the pain in my shoulder was so bad. I couldn't move without wanting to scream. I was fading in and out of consciousness. The last thing I saw before I blacked out, Charmion running towards me.

I woke up to the sound beeping and yelling. I couldn't make out the voices, everything was still fuzzy. I looked over and saw my shoulder was wrapped up. I was able to move my arm and not feel a thing. Pain killers.

"The hell is wrong with you?" Then that's when I heard Charmion.

"I had to do it. It was just part of the plan." Cooper loud whispered. Charmion scoffed rolling her eyes.

"What plan? Shoot first, think later? Is that what they taught you?"

"If I wasn't there, he would've gotten arrested and got thrown into the slammer with you and would've ruined the plan! So how about a, Thank you, Cooper!"

Yup, I figured that was Cooper yelling. He wasn't doing a good job on being quiet. Now I'm starting to awake up and feel again.

"Thank you? You want me to thank you? For what? Running away again? You can't seem to get away from that, can you?"

"Um, guys?"

I chimed in, fully awake and conscious.

They both glared at each other. I noticed something here. Charmion was wearing the same clothes she wore when she was arrested, only difference they aren't covered in blood anymore. They both looked at me. Cooper nudged Charmion without looking at me, she scoffed then punched him in the arm. Cooper whined in pain.

"The DA dropped the charges."

My eyebrows raised and I couldn't hold back the tears. I hugged her as tight as I could. I brushed it off the pain in my shoulder. I was so happy and relived to have the love of my life home. I can't describe this feeling right now; I'm content. And so will Zach. Cooper looked down, bitting his lower lip.

"I did what I had to do to get Charmion out of there. I'll just leave at that." I stared at Cooper in confusion.

"The day of the trial, Charmion told me that everyone in the courtroom was eating of Derek's hand."

"You knew?" I snapped.

"Yes, I did. That's why I left. I had to get more legal help. By doing that, I pretended to be on Derek's side and convince them that I don't trust Charmion, that I'm an asset. It took months but it worked. Everyone trusted me. My next plan was somehow get Derek to admit that he staged the whole trial and framed Charmion."

"And did you?"

Cooper grinned with a chuckle.

"He's in custody as we speak."

Charmion wrapped her arms around me. I sighed and melted into the warm embrace. I forgot why I was sitting in this hospital bed. And I don't care. I'm just glad Charmion is home. I'm in the arms of my true love again and now I am certain, no one will take her away from me and Zach. We can finally be normal again.

CHAPTER 41

❖

I never thought I'd ever come back home; I was so anxious as we got to the door. I felt a hand touch mine and warm lips on my cheek. Lucky's forehead touched mine, we stayed like this for a while. For once I enjoyed the silence. There was something about it. I was in the arms of the love of my life instead of the scratchy sheets. I feel warmth instead of cold, love and passion. I moaned in delight. I soaked it all in. My hand touched the cold counter and I smiled. I missed seeing actual furniture, an actual kitchen, living room, a bedroom with a real door. It's like I'm seeing it for the first time. I was amazed in everything. I never thought I'd see any of this again. I'm so excited to taste real coffee. I just had to pour myself a cup. I sighed. This is home. I was spacing out, really enjoying the scenery, Lucky walked into the room.

"I thought I was never going to see you again." His voice cracked, I saw the tears forming in his eyes. I smiled placing a hand on his cheek. He sighed letting his eyes shut at my touch.

"I really missed you." He mumbled on my lips. I never thought I'd ever feel his lips again and when I did, the spark never left. My mind went blank and I fell into this moment; I didn't want this to be taken from me. We moved to the bedroom and I was already getting excited, our clothes leaving a trail behind us. I moaned in pleasure as his lips went to my neck, I bit my lip as he lifted me up and dropped me on the bed. All of a sudden, Lucky stopped and stared at my scars. He never got real close and personal for a while. He didn't want to touch it. I carefully placed his hand on them and smiled softly. I gently pulled him back down and kissed him. He was very gentle, it was nice and slow. My eyes never left his as our hips moved together. I gasped. Lucky moaned softly as he pressed his forehead on mine. I can tell he was getting close because his breath hitched and his pace was much quicker.

"Look at me."

His eyebrows furrowed, still at a fast pace, I then felt myself getting there too. Lucky gasped. His intense gaze never broke, suddenly he came to a stop and he and I had our orgasm.

I just held him, our chests heaving in sync. We laid in the bed in silence. Lucky started to get up and he pulled me up with him. My head rested on his chest. I smiled when I heard his heartbeat. It was starting to slow down. I saw him reach for the night stand and he pulled out a ring, the same ring he gave me 7 months ago. I imagined I wore it even if I was going to spend the rest of my life in jail. I still call myself his wife if I was never going to have physical contact with him. I looked up at him with a loving look, he was giving the same look. There's no question in my mind. This is the man I want to spend the rest of my life with; forever and always.

We stayed in bed for what seemed hours. I needed this. I needed to just be with Lucky at this moment. It feels right again. Then it hit me. I shot up from bed with eyes popping out of my skull.

"Where's Zach?"

"It's okay, Gabriel is watching him, he wasn't feeling well so he stayed there. Him and I spent the night."

I sighed in relief. After this whole thing I'm considering putting a chip in Zach. Can you blame me? He was taken from us once I can't have him taken away from me twice. But I won't have to worry about that. I feel confident that nothing will ever to happen to us for the rest of our lives.

I swallowed hard as I stood in front the white fence surrounding the house. My hand was grabbed but I didn't even notice. I didn't have to knock. The door burst opened and Gabriel yanked me into his arms. He cried into my shoulder. His hand was brushing my hair. I look behind him and see Kendall and Sonya running. I shoved Gabriel to the side and ran to them. I sobbed in their shoulders. I never thought I'd see my mother again. Seeing her beautiful face everyday, hearing her voice, hugging her. I turned to my best friend, she was a sobbing mess. So was I. God I missed her like crazy. I then heard tiny footsteps coming down the hallway. My feet started picking up speed and what I heard made me cry even more.

"Mommy!"

Zach leaped in my arms and we fell to the ground. I was finally reunited with my sweet boy. My heart felt like it was going to exploded with love and excitement. I am so overwhelmed with love I feel like I'm dreaming. But I know I'm not because if I was, I would be seeing Mrs. K.

"Oh, my sweet boy, I missed you so much."

What I'm feeling right now, I can't put it in words. I didn't think I'd ever be able to hold my son again, I made peace with that in my cell and I was fine. But a huge part of me wished for this moment. Even if I got visits and was able to hold him for a second, it wouldn't be enough. I'd be devastated seeing him walk out. Now I don't need to worry about that anymore. I can hold my son for as long as I want, no officer will scream at me for touching my visitors, no one can take me away from my son ever again, not even Derek. The difference between me and Derek now, I have freedom. As I was hugging Zach, I saw Cooper standing by the doorway with a shameful expression. I let go of Zach and Cooper stormed out of the house and slammed the back door, startling everyone. I followed him and found him pacing by the pool.

"I know what I did was wrong and I take full responsibility, but I'm sick and tired of you beating me down because of the mistake I made 20 years ago."

I stared at him puzzled. I haven't been out for nearly seven hours and I'm already being blamed for something I didn't do. I'm just watching Cooper walk back and forth, wondering what is going through his head.

"Cooper, I haven't said anything." He swallowed hard. Where did that come from? Wait, I think I know. I approached him but he stepped away from me. Why is he being like this? He was fighting back tears, I can see it. Once I touched his hand he lost it. Something about a 44 year old man crying made my heart hurt. He's been carrying this much weight on himself for 20 years. Cooper had demons in his mind playing dirty tricks on him, like I was still blaming him for leaving again.

"Don't you hate me? I shot your boyfriend, left you when you needed me, god, I'm the worst father. Gabriel is more a father than me. I'm good at running away." He says in between sobs and hearing that killed me. God what this man feels right now. I can't imagine. And I made him feel worse by saying he always runs away at the hospital.

"You're not the worst father. I'm sorry for what I said at the hospital. I would never hate you. And who says I can't have two fathers?" He nod his head with a smile and tears.

"I know it's hard living with your mistakes, trust me, I know. It can hurt when you are being reminded of it and I am sorry that I did for you. But part of living with your mistakes is forgiving yourself for making those mistakes. You need to forgive yourself, Cooper. We can't change the past but that doesn't mean our past defines us. I learned that the hard way. My point is, you are doing a great job."

I won't get tired of the hugging. I'm going to be doing a lot of that in the next few days. Cooper and I haven't had a talk in years, and I mean *that* talk. About everything that has happened within the last five years. It was going to happen anyway and I'm glad it is we're doing it now. I sighed looking up at him. I saw him staring off into space. I got an idea. I pushed him in the pool, he gasped. I broke out in the fit of laughter. I kicked my shoes off and did a cannon ball. We laughed together. His hand went to my face, with a smile and a few tears in his eyes.

"I will never let anything happen to you ever again. That is a promise."

"I know. Hey, what's that?"

"What?" He said turning around like a lost puppy.

I grabbed one of Zach's pool noodles and whacked him over the head. As he turned around, I sprayed him with water. I knew I was screwed from the look he was giving me. Uh oh, think I started a war.

"Oh you are so going to get it, missy." I shrieked and quickly got out of the pool and ran back into the house. I laughed running into the kitchen and see Gabriel grabbing a beer from the fridge.

"Should I ask?" He said with a grin.

"Hey, Gabriel how about we do a cookout," Lucky came into the kitchen with Zach sleeping in his arms and stared at me.

"Why are you soaking wet?"

I was going to speak but I heard Cooper coming back inside. I shook my head with a chuckle and ran out of the kitchen. I screamed when I saw Cooper around the corner with a water gun.

"Charmion Monica get back here!" Cooper yelled.

Ah, it's good to be home.

CHAPTER 42

❖

Comfort. That's the only feeling I have right now. The comfort of being in my own bed, comfort of seeing my boyfriend and son. I feel comfort when I go over my best friends house and Gabriels house, conversations with Sonya. I don't think I can use any emotion to describe this. I feel strong. Nothing can break me anymore; I will not let the darkness consume.

"You're engaged?" Sonya gasped. I saw Cooper spit his beer out. I never seen him run so fast. He grabbed my hand to take look at the ring and his eyes popped out his skull.

"That's a big rock." I laughed.

"When is the wedding?" Sonya had the biggest smile on her face as she clapped her hands together.

"We don't know. It happened really fast and I don't know if I want a wedding."

"No, you have to! It's every girls dream to wear a big beautiful dress. When you were younger you use to sneak into my closet and yank my dresses off the rack and you crawled around the house with them covering your entire body."

"I remember that."

Cooper smiled.

"Did I really do that?" I asked.

"Yeah, you did. That's why you should have a wedding. It can be a small ceremony at Gabriels house, friends and family only."

I never really thought about it. I didn't think I would get married. I mean I did just not with Lucky. I had a crush on him, of course, but a little part of me thought about marrying him. I didn't care that we were foster siblings which ideally, be wrong. I knew him and I wouldn't become a thing with him living with us. But when he got adopted, it was fair game.

"Can I be the best man?" Cooper's eyes lit up.

"I think you'd have to ask Lucky." I laughed.

"Not his, I mean yours." I scrunched up my face. "I don't think the bride can have a best man and a maid of honor."

"Says who? It's your wedding." Sonya winked before entering the kitchen. Cooper laughed and spun me around till I got dizzy.

"I'm so happy I get to walk my daughter down the aisle. I always wanted you to get married. I knew you would one day."

"You'd still walk me down the aisle?" I chuckled nervously.

"Of course I would. Who is else is going to do?"

"I'm thinking Gabriel would." I laughed. He playfully shot a glare at me. I would love to have Gabriel walk me down the aisle but it is only fair to have Cooper do the honors.

"You're still my daughter, After all the shit we gone through, you are and will always be my daughter."

I am.

CHAPTER 43

❖

Watching my son sleep in his own bed, in a safe environment, no one can hurt him anymore, puts me at ease. I gently kissed Zach's forehead and quietly stepped out of the room. I turned off all the lights and went to my bedroom. Lucky was already in bed watching TV. He looked so serious watching Family Guy. He broke out in a fit of laughter at the one scene where Peter dressed up as Spider-Man to seduce Lois and worked.

"Maybe I should do that." He smirked.

"Please, you don't need to dress as Spider-Man to get me to sleep with you." He laughed again as I climbed into bed. I laid my head on his chest.

"So, when do you wanna get married?"

I have been thinking a lot about when I think we should get married. Maybe in the spring? Or maybe December, winter? A beach themed wedding has been on my mind for a while now. Though, I wouldn't be able to wear big puffy dress if we were gonna be on sand and I'm gonna want to dance. I still have to get a dress. Who would I bring with me? Maybe I'll bring Kendall, or Sonya. I didn't realize I was saying this out loud till Lucky chimed in.

"How about, we do November the 5th, and you could bring Kendall and Sonya when you pick the dress." I blushed from embarrassment. I haven't thought out loud since I was 6 years old. But something about November the 5th, has me thinking. Why did he choose that date?

"Why November the 5th? That's 3 months from now, we're in August."

"Because, it's the day I met you." I sat up and stared at him. He remembers the day we met? All I know is that we ate lucky charms that one warm day. I didn't think he'd know the month and day. I'm actually a little shocked.

"You were 8 years old, wearing a pink shirt and khakis with your light up Dora the explorer shoes. And your hair were in pigtails. I thought you were the most adorable thing in the house. As we got older, I saw how beautiful you were getting and I started to have feelings for you but I knew it wasn't allowed since we foster siblings. When we kissed that one Sunday afternoon, making brownies, I knew my feelings for you were right."

I had the biggest smile on my face. I don't deserve this man. I didn't know any of that. This man continues to amaze me everyday. I was flattered that he thought I was adorable as a kid. I chuckled.

"Did you ever think about me when you left?"

I asked.

"Of course, I did, everyday. Did you think about me?"

"Nope," He gave me a blank stare which made me laugh.

"I'm kidding. Yes, I did. I'm glad you came back." I laughed planting a kiss on his lips. Our lips lingered a bit longer.

"I told you I would."

CHAPTER 44

I never felt so nervous entering a dress shop. It was so intimidated seeing all the brides to be, dresses everywhere, people running all over the place, fiancé's smiling and nearly crying of happiness. Wow, that feels good to say, *fiancé.* I swallowed hard as we got closer to the front desk. I didn't even have to say my name to the clerk, she knew my name and why I was here. I nod my head nervously as she led us to the sitting area. My leg was bouncing up and down. I felt a hand on my knee. Sonya gave me a reassuring smile. I nod my head and turned away still feeling anxious. Why do I feel this nervous to try on dresses? Maybe it's because how I'll look in them. I wouldn't say I'm fat, more like chubby in some places. The girls aren't that big, if you know what I mean so strapless is out of the question. My only option is long sleeve. Though, what if I look weird in long sleeve? I don't think a short dress would even be appropriate. I just don't know. In the mists of my thinking, a lady came by with this huge smile.

"Hi! You must be Charmion!" I shook her hand smiling, completely not saying a word because I am still a little anti social. That, and I was in jail for six months and completely forgot how to be around good people.

"So tell us what kind of dress you are looking for."

She said with a bright smile. You can tell she really loves her job. I mean I guess I would be too being surrounded by happy people and a positive environment. I said I guess, not the place for me.

"I have no idea. Never have I been wedding dress shopping nor know what type of dress I'd look nice in."

"That's fine, I have tons of dresses, tons of different styles that will probably be the right fit. When's the wedding?"

"It's in November, three months from now and it's autumn themed wedding."

"Oh perfect, so that means you don't want a big puffy dress weighting you down as you walk down the aisle."

"That's one way of putting it, I guess." She looked very happy with that response.

"I'm going to bring you to a dressing room and I'll browse for some dresses for your liking."

This feels so bizarre for me. I'm in a silk robe and yet I feel uncomfortable sitting here. I was having anxiety. This seriously is making me a nervous wreck. Maybe I should go home. I can't even begin to describe how many dresses came through the door. All I saw was feet. She hanged up the dresses on the rack with a beaming smile. I forgot to mention her name is Cindy.

The first dress didn't fill all the right places. It was a little too big and it fell whenever I took a few steps. I didn't want to come out and show Sonya and Kendall. I tried on at least four dresses and didn't come out because it just didn't look right for me. Some sucked the oxygen out of me. I scanned the rack till my eyes landed on one dress that I didn't think I'd like. It was a strapless, lace, I think it was a mermaid dress. The bottom had ruffles but not too dramatic. Not my usually type of dress I was going for but it really caught my eye. It fit like a glove. I was in awe. It was perfect; I couldn't stop smiling from ear to ear.

"Are you ready to show them?" I didn't even have to answer. The smile on my face said it all. As I walked, all eyes were on me. Not just Sonya and Kendall, but everyone in the whole store. I think one girl looked angry because I took the dress she wanted. I just smiled. I couldn't stop smiling. I turned to Kendall and Sonya and they were already in tears.

"You look beautiful, Charms."

Kendall nodded her head in agreement with a smile. I zoned out on most of the talking, I couldn't stop staring at this amazing, gorgeous dress. The minute they put the veil on my head, I started to cry. I never thought I'd see myself in one of these ever. The veil matched the dress amazingly, it was so long and elegant. I was speechless. This is happening right now.

"What do you think?"

Again, I was speechless. I laughed covering my mouth. This was the dress. I knew it in my heart this was the perfect dress. Can you be in love with a dress?

"It's perfect."

And it was.

CHAPTER 45

I've been having dreams, bad dreams. Dreams about Derek coming for me and doing god knows what to me and Zach and my family. Yeah we put him away but the guy is more mental than Jason and he's a cop so he can get his cop buddies to help him out. Not to mention he is part of a gang. I started to get really bad anxiety. What if he's secretly watching the house from a far? Or what if he's taking pictures of me or Zach or Lucky and sending them to strangers? All these what ifs was not helping with my anxiety. I tried splashing cold water on my face to calm myself down but it didn't work. He was still in my head. It's like the time where I found out I was pregnant with Zach during Jason's trial. I had that same anxious feeling; the man is a freak show. I should not be thinking about a man who threw me in jail and tried to hurt my family. Derek is the last person I wanna be thinking about.

Just thinking about Derek gives me this awful taste in my mouth. I'll never forget the face he gave me when I was dragged out of that courtroom. He had this grin on his face, along with the rest of the peanut gallery, and he winked at me. I heard them chanting. I didn't realize someone was trying to get attention till a hand was slammed on the table in front of me.

"Charmion, you with us or not?" I shook out of my deep thoughts and saw Samson staring at me worriedly. I nod my head.

"Yeah, I'm good."

He didn't seem convinced.

"So good news, Derek took a plea on abusing his power as an officer. But,"

Uh oh.

If I have to go through another trial I won't. I already gone through four so far and I'm not going for a fifth. Samson sighed staring at me. Great, another trial, can't seem to run away from those.

"The court is asking for your testimony. Frankly, I don't know why we have go through this again but you don't have to worry. This trial is about Derek and not about you."

He said with a reassuring smile. I nod my head fiddling my thumbs on the table. I still feel weird that after all that's happened, Samson still agrees to be my lawyer. I thought he'd just dump me after the trial. Samson saw this and looked concerned.

"I'm sorry. I'm just surprised that you still agreed to be my lawyer after everything."

Samson grabbed a hold of my hand and smiled.

"I've been the family's attorney for many years. We talking since Gabriel was a teenager. I've seen worse and been through tougher trials. I remember meeting you in the house when you were 9 years old. You asked me if I wanted draw."

I chuckled, so did he. I can barely remember that. Honestly I can't even remember anything from my childhood.

It's comforting hearing stories about me from other people. It puts a smile on my face.

"I can understand why you lied. But I can assure you, you are not the one on trial this time. That I promise you."

Finally.

CHAPTER 46

I didn't like having to sit on the stand and explain myself once again. It's ridiculous at this point. I've been through so many trials that I don't know what was the worse one. Every single one of them were stressful, even Jason's hearing and there was no jury. At this point, I don't bother dressing nice. I just want to get this over with and pick up my son from school at 3pm. And of course it is the same lawyer from every single trial I have ever attended to. Mr. Gallows, you ever take a vacation?

"Charmion?" I shook my head and brought back my attention to Samson. He was looking at me uneasy. I cleared my throat.

"I never met Derek. Jason never brought him up."

"Why do you think that?"

Samson asked. I shrugged.

"Jason was good at keeping secrets. Not to mention led a double life."

"Thank you, Charmion."

Okay, let's get this over with. Mr. Gallows stood, adjusting his suit, never leaving his eyes off me, as well as Derek. I sat still in my seat with his intense stare. I'm not intimidated by this man. I'm not the one on trial.

"Miss Smith," I growled at that name. Why hasn't the courts or the government been told that Smith isn't my last name? Jason has changed my name twice that I don't even know what my name is at this point. For all I know my real name could be Jennifer.

"What were your first impressions of my client?"

I snorted at the question,

"I thought he was a regular cop."

"My client was your average human being. He had a good paying job, pays his taxes on time, never got in trouble with the law, hell, not even a parking ticket."

I laughed at that statement. Seeing Mr. Gallows angry just made me laugh even more.

"Is something funny, Miss. Smith?" Even Samson was trying hold back his laughter.

"You said your client has never gotten trouble with the law. Look where we are."

I said with a chuckle at the end. Mr. Gallows did the same and walked back over to his table, he was going through papers and the judge was not having it. I sensed anxiousness from that side of the courtroom. Am I done? Can I go now?

"Is there a question, counselor?" The judge said with an annoyed expression.

"There is, Your Honor. On the day you were arrested,"

"Objection, the witness is not on trial. Mr Gallows is turning this trial." Samson growled. Gallows chuckled.

"I can't ask a question?"

"Mr. Samson is right. The witness did her time and is not on trial. Rephrase or cut her loose counselor."

Oh, I like that. Finally someone was able to shut him up. Rephrase or cut her loose. For once I'm not sweating and shaking in my boots. The judge adjusted her seat and sighed. Gallows stood there for a second before asking another question. How long have I been sitting here? Mr. Gallows

270

couldn't give me a question without stuttering. You can see the sweat starting to form on his forehead.

"Tell me, Miss. Smith, what do you think went on that day? The day you met my client?"

That took me a while to think, believe it or not.

"It was a blur. I was in the hospital waiting for Officer Torres. And then Derek walked in and I had no idea who he was. He wanted to-" I was cut off.

"How can you be sure on what he was thinking or what he wanted?"

His voice was getting louder and Samson stood up.

"Objection, badgering."

"Witness will answer." The judge nod her head. "It was pretty clear on what he wanted."

I glared.

"My client just wanted justice for what happened to his brother."

Mr. Gallows leaned against the table with his arms folded across his chest.

"The man deliberately attacked me and my family. He was abusing his power as an officer and used the trial to get his way. He had everyone in his pocket and now, the law has caught up with him."

I exclaimed.

"And what does that say about you, Charmion?"

I shifted in my seat as he got closer to the stand, I swallowed a lump in my throat.

"A man is dead and yet, you claim it was self defense. Maybe it was, will we ever know? But my client has to live with the fact that his brother was killed and whether you chose to believe it or not, that blood will always be on your hands."

I told myself I wouldn't shed any tears today but I broke that promise. I wasn't crying because of Mr. Gallows jumping down my throat, but the fact that I do have to live with the fact I have taken a life. I understand that Jason was a twisted, vindictive person and would use anyone to get what he wants, but at that moment my life was not in danger. When he hugged me, I was not in danger, yes. If I hadn't done what I did, he would be back in jail but he would find a way to break out again and do god knows what to my family. I would still be a target. It's been almost 8 months since Jason died and I'm still being reminded of it everyday. When will I stop being tortured with this? When can I let go?

It's like everywhere I go, I'm reminded of it. By everywhere, I mean the law and the system. I wanted to bash my head against a wall. I needed to keep myself calm and collective. I cannot lose my temper on the stand, I'm 23 years old, I am not a little girl anymore. As Mr. Gallows walked back to his seat, I asked the judge if I can address my final statement. She gladly said yes and gave me the floor. I stared at Derek, he was staring right back at me.

"I lost my foster mother in 2015, she's been dead for five years now. She was a beautiful, intelligent woman. She had a loving husband, beautiful children who weren't hers but raised them like they were. Katherine Klein was a happy, young sprit until her life was taken. I'm finally at peace with her not being here but when I saw her being hung from the ceiling, it killed me. Your brother did that and that will always haunt me for the rest of my life,"

I stopped mid sentence and really gave him a long look. Derek shifted in his seat clearing this throat. If only I can read his mind and know what he was thinking. I can tell by his facial expression, he was scared. The law has finally caught up with you and I don't doubt he has done this before. I have a hunch. I chuckled shaking my head. Samson was nodding his head, asking me to proceed. I took a deep breath.

"This is about him, not Jason, that man sitting right there. So how about you stop asking me about him and move on. Your former client and his death won't haunt me for the rest of my life. Hugging him the very last time will."

I win.

CHAPTER 47

I refuse to be an adult. I refuse to be in a position where I have to defend my intentions and stand in open court yet again. It's not right. After yesterday, that will be the last trial I will ever go to. I was in the backyard at Gabriel's house playing with Zach, we were having a water gun fight. I laughed when I hit him right in the forehead and he screamed. I didn't even realize someone was behind me till I heard them clear their voice. I turn and saw Samson. What's he doing here?

"Is this a surprise inspection?" I playfully mocked. He looked serious. I sighed deeply. I turn to Zach and he looked worried.

"Sweetie, how about you go inside and see what daddy is doing." I kissed his head and he ran back into the house. I turned back to Samson.

"Was it something I said?"

"No, he confessed that what he did was wrong and that he only did it because he thought he needed closure for himself." Samson said.

"That's bullshit, the judge actually bought that?"

"She did. And this was a new judge, fresh out of law school. There was a whole new jury so they did not know anything about Derek or his history. They took away his shield."

I scoffed.

"So he's not doing any jail time?" Samson nod his head with a defeated look. I look at him and say how? Actually, I can already figure out how. His buddies got him off.

"I wish I can give you the answer you want. I'm more upset and angry as you are. The only punishment they gave him was five years probation. The one thing I did get is that all this be put on record so wherever he goes this will follow him."

One good thing Samson said in this entire conversation.

"Can I file a restraining order? I don't him anywhere near me or my family. The man is a complete freak show."

"You most certainly can."

"Great, get the paper work ready." I patted his shoulder.

Right as I was going to walk away, he said something that I wished my ears didn't hear it. Out of anything he could've said.

"You can't be serious." I groaned.

"I don't want to be anywhere near that guy! Can't he get one of his buddies to get him?"

"He specifically asked for you to get him. He won't let anyone get him." Samson said.

I can never get a break, can I?

My guard is very up as I wait in this empty hallway. Wished I brought a gun in case anything happens but I know I'm in good hands. Guards were put on each end of the hallway. I refused to sit down. The alarm blared loudly as the door opened and in came the douchbag and Derek. He had this huge smile on his face. Mr. Gallows, hope you burn in hell.

"You look great!" Derek said way too cheerful. I stared at him. He sighed.

"Guess I'm getting the silent treatment."

I didn't say a word. I only want to punch him in the face. I'm starting to regret picking him up but he refused to leave until I came to pick him up. Why would he want me to pick him up? He threw me in jail and stalked me while I was in there. What the hell is clicking through his brain?

"So, where we off to?" Cheerfully he said, again.

"I rather eat broken glass than hang out with you." I growled. He sighs again. "Look, I am sorry for what I did. You may not believe me but I am truly sorry."

"You threw me in jail!" I exclaimed.

"Yes, and I do apologize for that." He said frowning.

"Don't apologize to me, apologize to my son and my fiancé. You're dead to me."

The look he had, I never seen before. He genuinely looks guilty and had regret in his eyes. It reminded me of the same look Jason gave me when I went to see him the mental hospital. It made me feel weird. The car was silent, then all of a sudden the radio was turned on and I jumped when Hated You From Hello by Downplay blared through the speakers. I turned off the radio and glared at him. He tried to hide his laughter by covering his mouth but he failed. I started to chuckle.

"I made you smile." I playfully rolled my eyes shaking my head. "Can we start over?"

I pondered for a moment. A voice in my head is saying he's a liar, don't trust him. I bit my lip trying to wrap my head around this. I need to think about my family. Do I want this man in my life? Do I need the negativity? I pulled over to the side of the road and turned to him.

"You and I will never be friends. You are nothing to me. We are not related so you have no obligation to get to know me and I don't want to get to know you. I know what kind of person you are. You will never be apart of my life."

I exhaled sharply, my eyes never leaving his. I'm replaying everything that this man has done to me, it's on loop. I will not let myself be weak around this man. This man has made my life and my family's life a living hell. I'll be damned if I let him come anywhere near me or Zach. I was so pissed off that I punched the steering wheel. I need to talk to my family. And that's not going to go well.

"You did what?" I figured Gabriel would scream, his face was redder than a fire truck. Lucky covered his ears. I sigh.

"Would you relax? I did not agree to this. It just made me angry that he even asked me that after everything he put us through."

"Charmion, did you not learn anything from what you've been through? The guy cannot be trusted." Gabriel whined.

"I did not agree with this! I am venting what just happened!"

I groaned.

"Charmion, he is right. He ordered Cooper to shoot me and he tortured us with you in jail and threatened us. He not only threatened us but he also threatened our son. I do not want that man near us."

I watched Lucky stormed inside the house and I sighed once the screen door slammed shut. And when it fell to the ground. Gabriel groaned loudly before grabbing the screen door and shoving it in the shed. We all know how we feel about Derek and the kind of person he is. So I feel for Gabriel and Lucky. But they didn't have to go harsh on me. I found Lucky in the kitchen leaning over the counter shaking his head.

"I shut it down, right away, Lucky. I don't want him near us anymore than you do." He sighed deeply.

"I just, all of this, what happened to you and Zach, I can't let that happen again. I don't care if he's your family, I don't want him anywhere near you two."

"We're not even related. So there is no point."

Five minutes later there was a knock on the door and I'm thinking it is Cooper being fashionably late. I opened the door and saw Derek in nicely dressed clothes with a nervous smile. Son of a bitch, can't he take a hint? I looked behind me to make sure no one was looking.

"What the hell are you doing here?"

"I came to see you." He half smiled. What in the actual fuck is going through this mans head right now? Didn't I make my point very clear in the car? I want nothing to do with him.

"Let me make myself clear, again. I want nothing to do with you. There is no reason why we have to be friends."

"Actually, I looked it up and asked a specialist. Since Cooper and I are half brothers that kinda makes you my niece."

My face dropped. I almost puked out my breakfast. No way in hell this man is my uncle. I'd rather lick the inside of a toilet bowl than get to know him. How can, what? We cannot be related. Half brothers or not, he is not my uncle. I refuse to have this man be something in my life.

"Well, congratulations. You put your niece in jail and now she wants nothing to do with you." Right as I was about to walk back inside, he grabbed my arm.

"Wait, please. I just want to talk."

"Mommy?" Shit. Zach stood there with his head turned to the side in confusion. Derek smiled and walked up to him. I panicked and pushed him out of the way and picked up Zach. Derek frowned.

"I wasn't going to hurt him, Charmion."

I feel my heart pounding and I'm terrified. I have to be 100% guarded, I can't trust this man or his word. Doesn't matter if we're related or whatever, I will not let him go anywhere near my son. I held Zach tightly. My hand immediately went to my hip thinking I had a gun. Derek saw that and gasped.

"You'd actually shoot me for talking to your son?" He shouted.

"You ordered Cooper to shoot my fiancé. You really think I wouldn't?"

I didn't want to Zach to hear this. I knew if he went back to the house he'll tell everyone a man is here and they'll know who. I set him back down.

"Sweetie, why don't you go out back? I'll meet you there okay?" Zach nod his head and ran away. I sighed in relief. Derek stood awkwardly. I wasn't going to deal with this anymore. I groaned walking to the door and right as I opened the door, Gabriel stood there. His face dropped when he saw Derek. My eyes got big. The wind was knocked out of me then I was shoved to the floor and the door slammed. Gabriel had his pistol pointing at him.

"Up against the wall." Derek grunted as Gabriel roughly searched him.

"Hey I didn't know what kind of beer to get so I got Bud light," Cooper stood by the door and dropped the bag he was holding. Pretty sure I heard glass break.

"What is he doing here?" Cooper snarled.

"Beats me. He should know better than to come here unannounced with someone who knows how to handle a gun." Gabriel gritted through his teeth. Derek grunted as his arm was twisted tighter.

Something fell out of his pocket and that made me and Gabriel freak out. It was two shinny objections that nearly blinded me. I got a closer look at it and gasp. I wanted to cry. I couldn't believe what I was seeing.

"Gabriel, look," He turned his attention to the little bag and his face dropped. It was Mrs. K's necklace she use to wear everyday. When she and Gabriel took me in that was the first thing I noticed about her. It still had its shine. Gabriel started to cry when he saw the ring he used to propose to her 30 years ago. I never thought I'd see it again. Derek brought it to us.

"Why?" I said with a chuckle.

"I understand if you want nothing to do with me or want me in your lives but I feel like I should clean up Jason's messes."

Then, I hugged him. I just went for it. And he actually hugged me back. I can tell he was smiling as he wrapped his arms around me. Never in a million years would I hug Derek, frankly, I wanted to punch him a few moments ago. But this was different. He brought back something that meant everything to us. I felt as if it was a natural reaction. For once, it was a nice reaction.

"Thank you." I whispered. The door opened and Lucky came in with Zach holding his hand. He growled at Derek and made Zach go upstairs. Better hide the gun, Gabriel.

"Lucky, no!" I knew he was going to attack him, I felt it in my gut. It took all my strength to hold this large man back and I was surprised at how well I am doing that. The one thing that surprised all of us, was Derek being totally scared of Lucky's outburst. I wanted to laugh because this grown man is hiding in the corner by someone who is less his age. I couldn't contain my laughter anymore. I lost it and everyone just stared at me. Lucky glaring at me just made me laugh even more.

"This is funny to you?" Lucky growled.

"Oh, my sides! I have not laughed that hard in years." I sighed smiling.

"How did you get this?" Gabriel finally spoke, never taking off his eyes the objects in his hands.

"I didn't know your wife was Charmion's foster mother until yesterday. I remember reviewing her autopsy, they took off what she was wearing which was the ring and the neckless. I went back to the evidence locker to see if it was still there and I was shocked that it was. Usually have four years we send evidence upstate but I told them to hold it for me. I figured you'd want them back. I knew they meant a lot to you."

This was huge for Gabriel. He never thought he'd ever see the neckless he gave her on their wedding anniversary nor the ring he used to propose to her. This meant everything to

Gabriel and me as well. Then the unthinkable happened, he hugged Derek. He had tears streaming down his face. For once in our lives, I think we can heal from this. We can finally put all of this to rest and move on with life. We got our closure and frankly, just having those two objects is enough closure for us. I truly see the change happening and I can honestly say, at this moment, we are going to be okay.

CHAPTER 48

❖

November, 5th 2020

I'm getting married today. Where has the time gone? It feels like just yesterday we were picking the date and here I am. I haven't seen my dress since I picked it out. I forgot how it looks like. I gasped. It was more beautiful than the last time I saw it. As I was admiring the dress, I felt sick to my stomach. I rushed into the bathroom and vomited. I sighed flushing the toilet. I brushed it off as if it was nothing, must've been something I ate. But then it came back up again. I didn't even think about getting up because it just upset my stomach even more. Damn it, I thought. I heard a knock at the door and I groaned.

"It's open!" I yelled. I heard bags and feet shuffling as the door closed.

"Charmion?" Kendall said.

"In here!"

"Okay, so I found this and I think it will go really well with your makeup and, why are you on the floor?"

Before I could speak, I felt the vomit coming back up and hurled it out. Kendall shifted awkwardly.

"You need me to run to the store?" She said. My face was buried in the toilet. I gave her a thumbs up and she quickly ran out of the apartment. Damn it.

Kendall and I paced the room. I was shaking in my boots. My eyes were glued to the test and the timer on my phone. I exclaimed banging my hand on the table which startled Kendall. The wait was killing me! Finally the timer went off and we both dashed towards the counter. Kendall laughed hugging me tightly, I still stared at the test with wide eyes. As my eyes began to softened, I started to smile and embraced Kendall back. Out of all days, I find out on my wedding day I'm pregnant. I was hoping maybe on my honeymoon. The door opened and Derek came in wearing the suit Cooper picked out for him. Cooper wanted to go with the traditional black tux and bow tie. Derek didn't look too happy.

"I hate this suit." In came Cooper, completely out of breath, probably chasing Derek from the hall.

"You look great." He says breathless.

"I look like a dork."

"You do not! You can't just wear jeans and a flannel to a wedding!" Cooper snapped.

"I mean he can if he wants to." I said with a shrug. Derek gave Cooper a smug look which annoyed Cooper.

"It's your wedding. It has to be formal attire, not bum attire."

"Who you calling a bum?" Derek glared.

I watched these two go back and forth and wonder how we got here. The day Derek returned Mrs. K's ring and neckless, he also rekindled with Cooper by going to their mothers grave. Cooper never had the guts to go alone, Derek gladly went with him because he too didn't have the courage to go alone. Derek has proven himself that he has changed. I didn't think he had it in him. It also took a while for Lucky to really trust Derek. Eventually he warmed up to him. After he surprised him with floor seats to a Lakers game for his birthday.

"So, we ready to get married today?" The nerves finally kicked in when Cooper asked me that. Holy crap I'm getting married today. In three hours! I started to really panic. I have to get my makeup done and hair. Derek and Cooper were kicked out and the room was filled with hormonal women. First we did the hair. Nothing crazy, french braid crown.

A french braid crown was the ideal look for me. I saw so much things for my make up and I was very intimidated. So much foundation just for me, my skin tone isn't that complicated. After fighting with myself about the paint going on my face, they already started. How can this be happening? As a kid, I had this fantasy I was going to marry Chris Hemsworth or Liam, I don't know which, but here I am about to marry the one person I never thought I'd get a chance with. I also didn't think I would have a child with Lucky. If you were to tell me that five years from now I would have a child with him, I'd laugh in your face and move on with my life. Finally, it was time to put on my dress. I only wanted Kendall to help me put on my dress. Sonya of course was in the room sorting the flowers.

"You look amazing, Charms." Just seeing myself in the mirror, the veil on, all of the fighting was worth it. Everything that led up to this moment, what I had to do, to just stand here in this beautiful dress, I'm glad I did it. The moment of truth has arrived. Cooper came in adjusting his tie with a bright smile.

"You look beautiful." He bit his lip to hold back the tears. I felt some welling up too.

"Don't make me cry." I laughed.

"Okay, ready?" I took a deep breath before linking arms with him and smiled. Everything happened so fast so we didn't get a fancy location or find some venue. I wanted a certain location where I would feel most at home. A house that once had a gaping hole on the side is gone, the mold was now freshly yellow paint, and the front door was brand new and opened without any issues. I chose the house where I really grew up in, my first real home. Music started playing and my heart sped up as I walked closer and closer to the tunnel. My feet stopped working. Cooper saw this and pulled me aside.

"Hey, what's wrong?" He whispered. I shook my head.

"I can't do it." My was voice shaky.

"Yes, you can. This is just the nerves talking. Look." I saw Lucky giving a kiss to Zach and smiled. Everyone was getting in their seats and I see all the excitement on their faces. It made me calm down a little.

"That man is going to be the best husband in the world. I've said it before, I'll say it again. I can see how much he loves you and Zach. The minute he came to me for my blessing I knew he was the one for you. Kid has earned my respect. And if you get nervous again, squeeze my arm. I'll be with you the whole time. Ready?" I nod my head smiling. I gave Cooper a hug. That talk made all my nerves go away. I was ready.

My two boys waited till I got there and I couldn't help but fight back the tears. Zach was wearing the suit I picked out for him, looking handsome as ever. He was holding Lucky's hand. Lucky's free hand was over his mouth, he was crying. Cooper then put Lucky in a strong head lock and laughed. "Take good care of her." He gritted then let out a hardy laugh. I playfully shook my head with a hand on my forehead. Lucky chuckled nervously and turned to Derek who was giving him the finger and stank eye but I knew it was playfully banter. I saw my mother be in completely awe the whole time. I was too focused on my soon to be husband to even listen to Gabriel reading from the bible. Is this really happening? Am I really getting married in my childhood home? This isn't weird to you? My heart quickly sped up when Lucky pulled a piece of paper from his front pocket.

"Charmion, we met on this day, it was a sunny day. I tell you this all the time but I remember exactly what you were wearing. You were the most adorable thing I saw that day. As we gotten older, I noticed you got so much beautiful and I started to fall for you. The moment we kissed on that Sunday afternoon, I knew I was in love with you. You have given me so much. You gave me your life and with that, we have a son together who I love so dearly. We did have some rocky moments but we got through it together and it made us stronger. You make me feel things I never felt before and I'm so in love with you, Charmion. I can't wait to spend the rest of my life with you with our son by our side."

I didn't have my vow written down. I figured it come to me as I stood in front of him and it did. My news will come soon but this is what I have been waiting for. I took a deep breath.

"I didn't think I'd be here. I thought I'd marry someone with far more different features and personality. But when you showed up at my apartment, I knew what was in store for

287

me. You didn't give up on me even though I gave you a million reasons to walk out the door. You saved me. I was in love with you the minute you kissed me but that goes way back on my birthday when we sat on the roof watching movies and looking up at the stars. I saw you watching the fireworks, I wanted to kiss you but I stopped myself and just stared at you. Then you looked at me with those big brown eyes and I was sold."

Everyone laughed.

"I never thought my life would change from the day I met you. I thought you were a kid passing through. You stuck around and because of that we have a family and it's only expanding."

Time for my announcement. Lucky looked at me confused. I turn to Gabriel and he was in shock but had the happiest look on his face. I placed my hands on my stomach and that made Lucky cover his mouth with his eyes popping out of his skull. He then started to cry again.

"Yes, another grandchild!" Cooper shouted with glee, Sonya and Derek pulled him back down his seat. I chuckled shaking my head. Gabriel rolled his eyes at Cooper.

"We're having another kid?" Lucky's voice cracked. I nod my head with a smile. Zach jumped and cheered for joy. Lucky nearly fell to the ground but Gabriel pulled him back up. I chuckled softly.

"Luke, you take Charmion to be your lawfully wedded wife? For richer or poor, sickness and in health, as long as you both shall live?"

I watched the smile on his face grow and our hands touching slightly.

"I do."

"Charmion, you take Luke to be your lawfully wedded husband? For richer or poor, sickness and in health, as long as you both shall live?"

It is now or never.

CHAPTER 49

❖

I stood in my wedding dress and in front of my soon to be husband. Something I never thought I'd feel; excitement about a question. I slid the ring on his finger which was the most satisfying feeling ever, my eyes never left his brown eyes.

"I do." I smiled.

"I now pronounce you, husband and wife. You may now kiss the bride."

"Wait," Lucky spoke. "I always wanted to do this." I was swept off my feet which made me squeal. "Go ahead, say it again." Our eyes were filled with love and pure happiness. I can see our future in his brown orbs.

"You may now kiss the bride." Gabriel smiled.

I held Lucky's face in my hands, planted my lips on his. I was set down, not breaking the kiss, and a hand went to my waist. Our foreheads touched and we smiled. There was love in the air as we walked down the peddled path. I kissed Lucky again when everyone piled inside the house. I just stayed in his arms, the only thing I heard was the trees moving with the breeze and the sound of his heart beating. It was so peaceful. We were both smiling the whole time. Never have I ever thought this would happen to me. The amount of love I have for this man is indescribable. I am so glad that he came back into my life and I am so blessed to have a child with him and have another one that is on the way. We both gone through rough moments and they were times where I wondered if he should leave me but he didn't.

Even when I was in jail. He didn't give up on me, neither did Zach. I thank God everyday for saving me. I truly believe I was put on this earth to be great and do great things. Zach came running out and leaped into our arms. This was perfect, everything felt right. I looked up and saw Cooper standing there with his hands in his pockets, smiling at us. We didn't have to say anything to know that all the fighting, the hell we both were put through, was worth it. Who would've thought me pulling a gun on him, not knowing who he was at the time, turned out to be a great guy and a great father. Lucky and Zach went inside so Cooper and I could talk. I didn't realize Derek joined us. Cooper grinned putting him in a headlock. I was thrown into the mix which made me laugh. I have a crazy dad and a crazy uncle, both sane and normal.

"Never thought this house have a better turn around than us." Derek scoffed.

"Not true, you turned out better than I imagined. For crying out loud you were in my wedding." I laughed as I punched his arm.

He chuckled nodding his head. Cooper patted his shoulder with a huge grin. I had to ask this.

"Were you really mad that I killed Jason?" Derek snapped his head at me. I swallowed hard. That came out of my mouth and I wasn't thinking. But I have thought about that for a while. I was too afraid to ask. Cooper and I waited for his response that took longer than we expected. Did I make a mistake?

Derek sighed, "If it were me, I would've done the same." His cold stare made me squirm inside. But I had to ask again.

"You think if Jason was alive, he'd turn his life around? Like you guys did?"

That really made the two men think. I have thought about that a lot lately. What if I let Jason live? Would he still be in jail? Would me and my family still be a target? It is not everyday I think about these, it's every now and then when I see little things that remind me of him. I could be at the store and I see someone with the same haircut as Jason. Or when I'm going for a walk and I hear the same raspy voice as him but it turns out it is only a 85 year old man. Those type thoughts I have constantly but I always keep it to myself.

Cooper sighed.

"Honestly? I think he would've had the ability to do so but he was so twisted that he wouldn't even try. Regardless of his mental state, they'd probably put him in maximum security and not allow him to have any contact with the outside." Derek nod his head in agreement.

"I agree with Cooper. I feel like he would listen to Cooper because he's the little brother and he loved him just as much as he loved you, but that is no excuse for what he did. He would still be listed as a sex offender, a murderer, and criminally neurotic." Mine and Cooper's face dropped.

"Where the hell did you find that out?" I said uneasy. Derek casually looked around whistling. Cooper smacked him on the head.

"Ow! Okay I stole a copy of his criminal record. We all can agree I wasn't the best cop."

"Yup," Cooper and I said in sync. Derek playfully scoffed then grinned.

"You fuckers, you are so lucky that you are family. If you weren't I beat the shit out of you both. Well, only Cooper." He winked at me which made me laugh. They both headed inside and it left me wondering something else.

CHAPTER 50

❖

What if I didn't do what I did? You think he'd stop being violent? Out of all days, I think about him on my wedding day. Life is for the living. I should join the living and let what has happened go. It is not worth thinking about on my wedding day. Here I thought I finally let Jason go and I am thinking about what might've been if he was alive. To be honest, I don't think I'd be left alone right now, or Zach. He would still be torturing my family. There is good out of this. I am safe, he can longer hurt or control me. I have more important people in my life now who mean the world to me. Yes, I am talking about Derek. I also wonder, if Mrs. K was alive.

I can imagine what she would've worn today. She would be wearing her favorite purple maxi dress with white daisy's all over. Those gorgeous, white sparkling heels she only wears on special days, and her hair would be in a french braid crown since it was her go to style. I chuckled as I looked down at my feet. I was wearing her white sparkly heels and my hair is in a french braid crown. I honored Mrs. K tonight and I know she is looking down at me with tears streaming down her face. I wish I was able to wrap my arms around her. I felt a presences behind me. I smiled when warm lips touched my cheek.

"Well, Mrs. Mitchell, I believe you are due for a dance." Everyone began to reenter the backyard, I chuckled when I saw Derek and Cooper fighting over the camera. Zach was holding Riley's hand with big smiles. Who I'm Meant To Be by Anthem Lights played and we took our first steps. As we swayed to the music, I reflected on every part of my life. How I got here, how I became the person I am today. I am a mother, a wife, a daughter, a sister, and a niece. I may have made poor decisions and mistakes but I am only human.

Every decision I made, every choice, was all because of Zach. I don't ever want him to live his life in fear and that kid has seen things that no five year old should ever see. But what blows me away is that he still kept smiling. He was still my happy boy even when I was locked up. It is because he had an amazing father, grandfather's, grandmother, and aunt by his side and showed him the way. And I am so proud. I turn my attention to Lucky who was giving me the same loving look in his eyes.

"You look like the most beautiful rose here." He says pecking my lips. My face turned bright red and I let out a small laugh. I remember as clear as day when he first told me I was the most beautiful rose.

"You're my best friend. I'm always going to be shy around you. You're the most beautiful rose in this house and I'm the dirt."

I think about that night everyday. I am not a rose, I never was nor liked roses, I thought they were boring to me. I see a sunflower and I see life; it stands out, it's bright and that's me. That is who I am. But maybe a rose symbolizes beauty and love, whereas a sunflower symbolizes fun, playful and life. Perhaps, I am both. I wanted to capture this moment. I ordered everyone to do one giant group family photo. Cooper was having a difficult time getting the camera on the stand. Derek got annoyed and shoved him away from there, the timer was turned on. I watched everyone huddle together and smile. Though, my eyes weren't at the camera. I was smiling at them. This is my family. This is my home.

I cried.

Made in the USA
Las Vegas, NV
19 March 2021